Understood

When she breaks free from the bondage of her past, he'll be waiting.

Jake made the ultimate mistake—falling in love with Ellie, his best friend's wife. Distance was the only solution, but it prevented him from seeing what a bastard his friend turned out to be. Now Ellie is free from the bondage of her past, and Jake waits. Needing, wanting, and ready for her when she spreads her wings.

Warning, this title contains explicit sex, graphic language.

Overheard

Gracie Evans wants a Valentines she won't forget. Luke Forsythe plans to give her exactly what she wants.

Gracie is tired of the men in her life never satisfying her in bed. None of her boyfriends have come close to fulfilling her vivid fantasies. When Luke overhears her talking about what she really wants, he's stunned—and very turned on. So Gracie thinks no man alive can satisfy her? Luke aims to prove her wrong.

Warning, this title contains explicit sex, graphic language, ménage a trois.

Undenied

Another chance to make a night gone bad very, very right.

Payton Ricci is the last person Wes Hoffman ever expected or *wanted* to see again. After the disastrous sexual experience between them twelve years ago, he was only too happy to put the whole episode behind him. After all, he's come a long way since that awkward encounter between two gawky teenagers, and his ego needs no reminder.

The night he sees Payton—a very sexy *grown up* Payton—in Zack's Bar and Grill, he's mortified by this blast from the past. Payton harbors no such reservations about seeing Wes again, and it's clear she wouldn't mind catching up on old times. However, Wes can't get over his mental block where she's concerned.

But that's nothing a blindfold and a little mad seduction scheme can't fix, and Payton is a *very* determined woman.

Warning, this title contains the following: explicit sex, graphic language, mad seduction schemes, and the hard fall of a drop dead sexy hunk.

Look for these titles by *Maya Banks*

Now Available:

Seducing Simon
Colters' Woman
Love Me, Still
Stay With Me
Amber Eyes

Brazen
Reckless *(stand-alone sequel to Brazen)*

Falcon Mercenary Group Series
Into the Mist (Book 1)
Into the Lair (Book 2)

Print Anthologies
The Perfect Gift
Caught by Cupid

Coming Soon:

The Cowboys' Mistress

Unbroken

Maya Banks

A SAMHAIN PUBLISHING, LTD. publication.

Samhain Publishing, Ltd.
577 Mulberry Street, Suite 1520
Macon, GA 31201
www.samhainpublishing.com

Unbroken
Print ISBN: 978-1-60504-161-2
Understood Copyright © 2009 by Maya Banks
Overheard Copyright © 2007 by Maya Banks
Undenied Copyright © 2009 by Maya Banks

Editing by Jennifer Miller
Cover by Anne Cain

Understood, ISBN 1-59998-302-8
First Samhain Publishing, Ltd. electronic publication: December 2006
Overheard, ISBN 1-59998-315-X
First Samhain Publishing, Ltd. electronic publication: January 2007
Undenied, ISBN 1-59998-469-5
First Samhain Publishing, Ltd. electronic publication: May 2007
First Samhain Publishing, Ltd. print publication: May 2009

Contents

Understood

Chapter One

Jake Turner glanced around at the gaudy Christmas decorations adorning the interior of Zack's Bar and Grill and suppressed a grimace.

He motioned for another beer and ignored what his buddy next to him was yammering about. Things were always lively at Zack's close to Christmas. Jake could never figure out if people were getting out to celebrate the season or if they were all just lonely and searching for another human being to connect with.

"Earth to Jake. Come on, man, you're in another world over there."

Jake blinked then scowled at his friend, Colin. "What the hell do you want?"

Colin nodded toward the door. "Isn't that Ray's ex coming in?"

Jake's pulse quickened, and he yanked his gaze toward the entrance. All his breath left his body in one hard rush. What the hell?

His gaze came to rest on Ellie Matthews as she stood just inside the doorway. Only it wasn't Ellie as he was used to seeing her.

She took a hesitant step forward then stopped and scanned the room, her eyes wide. Her bottom lip worked between her teeth, a sure sign of her nervousness.

Long soft curls spilled over her shoulders, hair that a man would itch to thrust his fingers into as he thrust into other parts of her body.

But what had his blood pressure soaring was her get-up. Despite it being the middle of December, she wore a top barely held up by the spaghetti strings over her shoulders. The neckline plunged, and the material cupped her breasts in all the right places.

Her miniskirt, if you could call the scrap of denim barely covering her ass a skirt, rode so high up on her thighs that Jake knew if she moved wrong, the entire bar would get a glimpse of her pussy.

She had a *fuck me* ensemble going on complete with *ride me hard* shoes. He'd never seen her in high heels once, and yet she teetered unsteadily toward the bar in three-inch, fire-engine red heels.

"Jesus, I had no idea she was so damn hot," Colin muttered.

Jake rounded on Colin with a ferocious glare. "Shut the hell up," he growled.

Colin raised an eyebrow in surprise but kept silent.

Jake turned his attention back to Ellie, who stood at the bar. The bartender plunked down a shot which she promptly drained before motioning for another.

There wasn't a single male eye that wasn't riveted to her. Two men sauntered up to the bar and stood close to Ellie. She smiled at them flirtatiously, and Jake was struck with a sudden realization.

She was taking the plunge.

A surge of red hot jealousy spilled into his gut. She was finally breaking free of the hold Ray had on her, only this wasn't the way it was supposed to happen. Jake had waited a long time for her. He'd thought she needed more space. He was supposed to be the one she came to when she was ready to take that leap.

He gripped his beer bottle until his knuckles went white. What the hell did she think she was doing? His eyes narrowed when she downed another shot. When she turned her attention back to the crowd of admirers at her elbow, he saw the fear in her eyes.

It was then he understood what it was costing her. This whole take-me-home-and-fuck-me attitude was all a brave act. She was scared to death, and the only way she had a hope of carrying through with it was by getting thoroughly drunk.

Over his dead body.

He was striding across the room even before he realized he'd gotten up from his table. In two seconds flat, he shoved by the group of men panting over Ellie and stood beside her at the bar.

She turned unfocused blue eyes up at him, the fear that shadowed her gaze disappearing as she realized who he was.

"What the hell do you think you're doing, Ellie?" he demanded.

Panic flitted across her face, and the fear returned.

Without waiting to hear what she had to say, he bent, pushing his shoulder into her belly. He stood back up, slinging her over his shoulder, his hand resting possessively on her ass.

He turned to glare at the men who'd surrounded Ellie. "She's mine," he said in his most menacing voice.

They backed off quickly.

He started for the door, Ellie's upper body swinging against his back.

"Jake?" she said in a small voice. "Where are we going?"

God, he hated that sound. The fear. The uncertainty. It made him want to put his fist through the wall.

"Home," he bit out.

He walked outside, the brisk air raising goose bumps on her bare legs. Legs he ached to touch, spread and get between. His hand lingered over the swell of her ass, just where it belonged. His cock was ready to burst out of his jeans at the mere idea of cupping her sweet behind as he fucked her nice and slow.

But he'd waited, and by the look of things, he'd waited too long.

He carried her out to his truck and promptly deposited her into the passenger seat. He carefully buckled her in before circling around to the driver's side.

When he glanced over at her, she was staring out the window, but he saw the tear that rolled down her cheek. He swore under his breath and started the engine. Seconds later, he roared out of the parking lot.

He clenched and unclenched his hands over the steering wheel as he headed for her house. Damn Ray. Damn himself for never seeing a man he'd counted as a friend for who he really was.

Jake carried a lot of guilt for not seeing the warning signs, for allowing Ellie's horror to go on while the rest of the world saw what Ray wanted them to see. A nice, successful guy with a gorgeous wife and a perfect life.

The night Jake had found out the truth was a night he'd spent in hell.

He pulled into the driveway of the small house she rented and turned off the ignition. Ellie reached for her door handle, and Jake put his hand out to stop her.

"Stay there and don't move."

She trembled against his fingers but obeyed.

He got out and walked around to her side. He opened the door and reached for her.

"I don't trust you not to kill yourself in those damn shoes," he muttered.

She didn't protest when he curled his arms underneath her and lifted her from the seat. He stalked to her door and fumbled with the handle. Damn woman hadn't even locked it.

He shouldered his way inside but still didn't put her down. He flipped a switch, flooding the small living room with light. His gaze focused on the coffee table and the bottle of liquor, the half *empty* bottle of liquor, sitting there, and he swore again.

"Just how much have you had to drink tonight, Ellie?"

She went still against him. "Jake?"

He sighed. "Yes, sweetheart?"

"I think I'm going to be sick."

He spit out several more curses as he ran for the bathroom. He threw open the door and managed to deposit her in front of the toilet before she started retching.

The sounds she made were god-awful as she rid her stomach of all the alcohol. He cringed and hovered as he waited for her to finish.

He busied himself wetting a washcloth then gently wiped at her forehead as some of the heaving subsided. She let out a low groan of misery.

"Bet you'll think twice before pulling a stunt like this again," he chided.

She opened her eyes and stared up at him. "Don't lecture, Jake."

He softened. He couldn't help it when she stared up at him with those baby blues. He cupped her cheek in his hand and stroked lightly over her skin with his thumb.

"What did you think you were doing?"

She looked down and a tear splashed onto the toilet seat. Then she bent her neck until her forehead touched the rim.

He reached down to pull her to her feet. Sitting here next to a commode full of mixed alcohol and only God knew what else wasn't his idea of a good time. He reached to flush the toilet then swung her back into his arms.

She hiccupped softly against his chest. "Where are you taking me?"

"To bed," he replied.

He walked into her bedroom and deposited her on the bed. As her head fell back, she moaned and closed her eyes.

"Ellie, don't you pass out on me now," he warned. "Ellie?"

He ran a hand through his hair and swore for the hundredth time since she'd walked into the bar. Hell of a note. Passed out cold.

Sighing deeply, he clenched his jaw and put a tight rein on himself as he started to remove her clothing. It was remarkably easy given she didn't have much on to start with.

He swallowed the knot in his throat as her pink-tipped breasts bobbed into view. *Fuck me.* He eased the miniskirt over her hips and felt his jeans tighten all over again when he saw the tiny scrap of lace that covered her dark curls. Covered but didn't conceal.

He left the underwear on then went to her closet and rummaged for something to cover her up. He'd be damned if he was going to torture himself further by having her naked body on display.

When he returned to the bed, he gazed down at her sprawled on top of the covers. She looked so damn vulnerable. When he thought of such a tiny woman standing up to a man like Ray, it made him physically ill. He didn't know how she'd survived, but he knew one thing. She'd never have to worry about it again.

He bent over and pulled the T-shirt over her head. He lifted her slightly so he could get her hands through the armholes. Then he pulled the covers back and tucked her in. She uttered a small sigh and burrowed her face into the pillow before her easy breathing resumed.

His hand lingered over her hair. He let the curls trail over his fingertips, enjoying the satiny feel. He touched her cheek for the briefest of moments before finally turning and walking quietly out of her bedroom.

In her living room, he dug around in one of her cabinets until he found an old afghan. He dragged out a few throw pillows and tossed them onto the couch. He'd stick around tonight, make sure she was okay in the morning. Then they were going to have a heart-to-heart chat about her little escapade.

Chapter Two

Ellie opened her eyes and groaned as a shaft of light skewered her head. She rolled to her side to avoid the sun streaming through her blinds. Her tongue felt heavy and swollen, and God, what on earth was the foul taste in her mouth?

She sat up, licking her lips to try and inject some moisture. Bits and snatches of the previous night danced around in her head like a bad B movie.

Jake.

Oh, dear God. Jake had brought her home. No, he'd *carried* her home. Could her humiliation be more complete?

She struggled out of bed and stumbled toward the bathroom. She made a grab for her toothbrush and lobbed a clump of toothpaste onto it before going to town on her teeth. Anything to get rid of the taste of alcohol and vomit.

The brush still dangling from the side of her mouth, she reached in to turn on the shower and waited for the water to warm. When a curl of steam rose from the stall, she gave her teeth a final scrub and rinsed her mouth in the sink.

As she started to strip, she paused and looked down at her shirt. She hadn't worn this last night. She remembered that much. How the hell had she gotten out of her clothes and into this?

She pulled the shirt off and climbed into the shower. As the hot water sluiced over her, she leaned her forehead against the tile wall and closed her eyes.

So her plan had been a complete and utter failure. She'd taken two steps into the bar and chickened out. Oh, she'd tried to flirt and smile, prepared to pick up some guy and have sex, but as soon as they'd closed in around her, she'd panicked.

Thank *God* Jake had been there. *Damn* Jake for being there.

An uncomfortable wave of embarrassment tightened her cheeks, adding a pinch of heat to her face. Why he always managed to see her at her worst, she'd never know. Just once she'd like him to see her at her best.

She finished showering and quickly dried off. She shuffled back into her bedroom and pulled on a pair of jeans and a clean T-shirt, foregoing a bra.

Then she headed for the kitchen, wanting nothing more than a glass of cold water and a couple of Tylenols. She rounded the corner from the hallway and heard a clang. She stopped when she saw Jake moving awkwardly around the kitchen, his large frame dominating the small space.

So much for him *ever* seeing her at her best.

He looked up and saw her. "'Bout time you got up."

She faltered at the raw possession she saw in his eyes. It was always there, swirling and building just beneath the surface. Jake was a force of nature she wasn't prepared to contend with. Especially this morning.

She feared men like Jake. Oh, she wasn't afraid that Jake would hurt her. Not intentionally. But she feared the way she reacted to him when she was in the same room with him.

Already, every muscle, every nerve-ending in her body was taut, stretched almost painfully. Her nipples tightened to throbbing points, stabbing at her T-shirt, begging for him to close his lips around them.

There wasn't another man like Jake, that much was for sure. Tall, well over six feet, he wore self-assuredness like a mantle. He walked and talked like a man who knew precisely what he wanted, a man who'd do what it took to get it.

He had a stocky build, his body ripped with muscles from the years he'd spent playing professional football and honed to perfection in the three years he'd worked as a building contractor with his partner Luke Forsythe. He didn't just oversee the projects. He worked every bit as hard as his hired crews.

He wore his hair short. No fuss, just like him. It spiked on top and was clipped close at his neck and over his ears. A shadow lurked along his jaw, a testament to the fact he must have spent the night on her couch and hadn't yet gotten to shave.

"Jake, what are you doing here?" she finally asked, admiring the calm with which she said it.

"Fixing you breakfast."

He turned back to the stove and pulled out a pan of biscuits.

"You cook?"

He shot her a disgruntled look. "I can take biscuits out of a can and slap them on a cookie sheet."

She plopped down on a barstool at the alcove separating the kitchen from the small dining area. "But why are you *here* cooking me breakfast?"

He ignored her and set to work arranging the biscuits on a plate. Then he reached into the refrigerator and pulled out the butter and a jar of jelly. He moved over and plunked the items down in front of her then went back for the plate of biscuits.

A few seconds later, he took a seat across the bar from her and slid a plate to her. "Eat," he directed.

She stared at him in complete befuddlement. And to her annoyance, she followed his order and began picking at the warm biscuits in front of her.

They ate in silence until she felt the weight of Jake's stare. She looked up to see his plate cleaned, and he was giving her his famous Jake look. Great.

"Just what the hell did you think you were doing last night, Ellie?"

"What do you think I was doing?" she mumbled.

Jake's green eyes glittered in anger. He leaned forward until she had no choice but to look back at him. "I will fucking take apart any man who gets within six inches of you, Ellie. Maybe you ought to take that into consideration the next time you wag your little ass into a bar looking for cock."

She flushed, embarrassment rushing to her cheeks. Jake stood and collected the dishes before setting them down in the sink with a clank. Then he stilled and turned back to her.

"I wasn't looking for c-cock."

"The hell you weren't," Jake growled. He folded his arms over his chest. "There wasn't a man in that bar that didn't know you were on the prowl. The fuck-me clothes. And the *shoes.* Jesus, Ellie, were you trying to break a leg?"

"Don't lecture me, please, Jake. I'm already embarrassed enough."

He started to open his mouth then closed it again. He took a deep breath and leveled a hard stare at her. "I've waited a long time for you to get over the issues you had with Ray. A long damn time."

Ellie dropped her gaze. Jake never hesitated to speak frankly about her ex-husband. On one hand, she appreciated it. She didn't have to pretend with him. But it still made her cringe that Jake knew so much about her disastrous marriage.

Jake's hand closed over her shoulder, warm and comforting. How had he gotten over here without her knowing? His fingers feathered over her cheek, and he took her chin between his thumb and forefinger. With firm pressure, he tugged until she was forced to meet his eyes.

"There's not going to be any other man, Ellie. There's only me. You know it, and I know it. What you did last night was stupid and dangerous as hell. The very fact you had to get three sheets to the wind to even work up the nerve tells me you should have stayed your ass at home."

She licked her lips nervously. "I'm scared."

He snorted. "Don't give me that bullshit. You're not afraid of me. You know damn well I won't hurt you. You're afraid of yourself and you're afraid of what you know to be an unshakable truth. You are mine and I'm going to take you in every imaginable way. When you get tired of running. When you get tired of looking over your shoulder afraid of the shadows, I'm going to be there. Waiting. And when I claim you, I'm not ever letting you go."

Her eyes widened at his proclamation. He'd never come out and said it. He'd been there, always there, but he'd never said anything so forceful to her.

"That's right," he said huskily. "I'm staking my claim. But you're going to have to come to me. I'm not pushing you into something you're not ready for."

He drew away and continued to stare at her. "Think about that, Ellie. Think long and hard about what you really want. And when you decide, you let me know. But if I ever catch you doing what you did last night, I'll turn you over my knee and tan your ass."

He tossed down the dishtowel he'd picked up and headed for the door. Then he simply walked out and shut the door behind him with a bang.

Ellie wilted against the bar, burying her head in her arms. God almighty, what a bomb for Jake to drop on her.

She wasn't a complete moron. She knew he watched her. Knew he wanted her. But she'd had no idea the extent of his desire. It thrilled her and scared the shit out of her all at the same time.

After Ray, she couldn't even look at a man the same. Gone was her carefree lack of self-preservation. Replaced by a wary, cautious reserve that sheltered a frightened, vulnerable woman.

Last night...last night was supposed to be her flipping her middle finger at Ray and the insecurity that had gripped her since her divorce. Last night was supposed to have been the first step in going after she wanted. And she wanted Jake.

She raised her head and stared glumly at the door he'd walked out of. She knew she couldn't have just gone to him and offered herself up like a sacrifice. He would have shoved her away so fast her head would spin. No, somehow she had to convince him, and herself, that she was past her fear.

Yeah, last night was a mistake. Going to bed with a complete stranger wasn't going to satisfy the desire she had for

Jake. Nor would it be some miracle cure that would enable her to go to him a whole woman. And she really didn't fancy getting kicked out of his bed.

"Dumbass," she muttered. All she'd managed to do was get a very large, very brooding man pissed off at her.

Butterflies danced in her stomach as she processed his parting words. He'd made it so she'd have to come to him. She couldn't even begin to count the ways that terrified her. Making the moves was so out of her comfort zone it wasn't even funny. She hadn't even known what to say last night when she'd hatched her grand plan of picking up a guy.

She wasn't flirty or cute, and she didn't have a repertoire of clever, witty things to talk about. All she knew how to do was tell the truth. And that truth was that she wanted Jake.

"Well, girl, it's your move, and you have two choices. Let him keep on walking or go tackle his ass and make him yours."

She groaned again and flopped her head onto the bar. She was gonna need a day or two to think about this one.

Chapter Three

Three days. It had been three days since he'd dropped his bomb on Ellie, and he'd yet to see hide or hair of her. And that was hard to do considering she worked for him and Luke.

He hadn't wanted to push her this soon, but in light of her most recent antics, he'd say it was time. Well, she was getting one more day before he hauled her out of her hidey hole kicking and screaming.

Jake uncurled the rolled-up plans and splayed them out over the hood of his truck. Then he glanced back at the building site and swore under his breath. He propped his foot up on the bumper and leaned in closer to try and figure out just how his foreman had managed to fuck up the design this badly.

The weather was downright balmy. Not a cloud in the sky. No threat of rain the entire week. A miracle for the southeast region of Texas this time of year. He couldn't afford to lose any time on this project, because sure as shittin', rain would move in the next week and they'd be sitting around with their thumbs up their asses.

A truck roared up next to his, and Luke Forsythe got out, a frown on his face. He strode over to where Jake stood.

"How much is this going to set us back?" Luke asked.

"Money or time?" Jake asked dryly.

"Both."

"The money depends on whether they can salvage the awning. Time lost is at least three days. Days we can't afford to lose if we're going to finish on time. We need this done by

Christmas."

Luke bent over the plans, his lips drawn into a grim line. "Did you fire Shelton?"

"Hell, yeah. This is his second screw-up in a week. I put Colin in charge. He's over cracking the whip now."

Luke nodded his approval. He studied the schematics intently then said in a casual tone, "I hear there was a bit of excitement over at Zack's Saturday night."

"Fuck you." Jake glowered at his partner. He'd have to remember to have a word with Colin. Damned big mouth.

Luke chuckled. "Well, it's not every day Big Jake Turner is seen hauling a woman out of a bar over his shoulder. Especially when the woman in question is our secretary."

Jake made a few derogatory remarks pertaining to Luke's parentage.

Luke laughed again. "You're too uptight, man." His expression grew serious for a second. "Speaking of Ellie, I see Ray seems to be doing well. He just got a big write-up in the Beaumont paper. Contract extension. Two more years."

Jake's disposition went even further south. He hoped to hell Ellie wasn't reading the damn paper. Like she needed Ray's name splashed across her consciousness. Bastard didn't deserve squat.

"Maybe he'll take a sack and break his fool neck," Jake muttered.

Luke raised an eyebrow. "You know, I'm curious, Jake. And feel free to tell me to mind my own fucking business, but why is Ray still off in the NFL prospering and doing well? I don't get it. Why didn't Ellie go after him with both barrels?"

Familiar anger seethed within Jake. He rolled his fingers into balls and clenched them at his sides. Then he turned to Luke.

"Would you have believed Ray was capable of what he did if I hadn't told you face-to-face?"

Luke looked away then down. "Probably not, man. He's snowed a lot of people."

"Bastard laid the groundwork well in advance, making it

impossible for Ellie to be taken seriously. She actually went to the police once. They didn't do a goddamn thing other than listen to Ray's excuses and laugh it off as a marital spat. Then he made her sorry she ever tried to get someone to help.

"He made her out to be a jealous, spiteful wife. Even now, she gets her fair share of scorn for divorcing the local golden boy."

"It's been hard for you," Luke said quietly.

"What do you think?" Jake asked, rounding a bit too ferociously on him. "He was my best friend. We played football together through high school and college. Even got drafted by the same pro team. I mean, what are the odds? Never once did I imagine what a bastard he was, and I'll never forgive myself for not seeing it. For not getting Ellie the hell out of that situation before he hurt her so badly."

"It's not your fault, man."

Jake scrubbed a weary hand through his hair. "Yeah, Luke, it is. I was in love with her long before I had any idea what was going on. If I hadn't been so all-fire determined to keep my distance, I would have seen what was going on. As it was, I turned my back on her when she needed me most."

"Shit, Jake. You can't carry around that kind of blame. The only person at fault here is Ray."

Jake shook his head but refused to pursue the subject any farther. He didn't like to talk about Ellie and Ray. It was something he'd just as soon forget. Only he knew Ellie never would.

"How are Jeremy and Michelle doing? I heard she's having a boy? Did you go hunting with the gang this weekend?"

Luke nodded, accepting the topic change. "Yeah, we celebrated this past weekend. We spent Saturday and Sunday at the hunting camp, and damn it if Gracie didn't bag a fucking monster of a buck. Pisses me the hell off."

Jake laughed. "She's still running circles around you, huh?"

"Wes is getting it mounted for her, and now I'll have to see it every time I go over to her house."

Jake shook his head at Luke's mournful look. He liked Luke's circle of friends. Jeremy and Michelle had been married a little over a year. Both Jeremy and Wes were cops with the local police department, and Gracie was Michelle's best friend. Jake hung out with them every once in a while, and they were a hoot as a crowd.

"So, uh, have you seen Ellie this week?" Jake asked, changing the subject again.

Luke shook his head. "Nah, I figure she's laying low after the Saturday night deal. I know she's been in the office because all the paperwork's been done."

"I'm way too fucking easy on her," Jake mumbled.

Luke chuckled. "Fire her, then. It was your idea to hire her."

Jake glowered at Luke.

"Ah well, there's the answer to your question," Luke said. "That looks like her now."

Jake peered around, following Luke's line of vision to an older model Toyota Corolla turning onto the gravel road leading up to where he and Luke were. It was her, all right, but what the hell was she doing out on the jobsite?

"I, ah, think I'll head over to talk to Colin," Luke said with barely suppressed amusement.

Jake strode over to meet Ellie before she could even get out of the car. She wiped her palms down her slacks as she stepped out.

"Where the hell have you been?" he demanded.

She bit her bottom lip, and he cursed the fact that his eyes tracked every movement of her mouth.

"I, uh, wanted to talk to you," she said nervously.

He took a deep breath then sighed. "Ellie, why the hell are you so jumpy? You've never been nervous around me. You act like I'm going to bite you or something."

She flushed a delicate pink, her cheeks blooming as her eyes flared.

"Yes, but I've never said what I have to say before."

His pulse surged and ratcheted up about twenty beats per minute.

"What is it you want to say to me?" he asked softly.

"You said...you said that I'd have to come to you."

He arched an eyebrow. Did this mean what he thought it meant?

"That I did, sweetheart," he drawled.

"Well, I'm here," she blurted.

He closed the remaining distance between them in a split second. They stood only inches apart. She looked hesitant. Soft and unsure. Her eyes gleamed with need. She took his breath away.

"Do you know what you're saying?" he asked hoarsely.

She nodded. "I want you, Jake."

He cupped her chin in his palm. As much as he'd sworn never to touch her while she was married to Ray, he now ached to kiss her. He'd waited too damn long for her to tell him she wanted him.

He lowered his mouth to hers. She let out a small feminine gasp before touching him sweetly with her lips. Her hands feathered over his face, her fingertips touching and stroking as he deepened the kiss.

She tasted of mint and the sweet tea she always drank. He inhaled, wanting her scent deep inside him. Her tongue brushed lightly over his upper lip, and he opened his mouth to let her inside.

Finally remembering he was mauling her in public and they likely had more than a dozen interested onlookers, he pulled away, desperately sucking mouthfuls of air into his lungs.

He dug around in his pocket and retrieved his keys. With shaking hands, he unhooked his house key from the ring and held it out to her.

"Go to my house. Let yourself in and wait for me."

He swept her into his arms for one last kiss.

"I want you naked, in my bed, waiting for me to get home. I'll be there just as soon as I can."

She blinked and her fingers curled around the key he laid in her palm. "O-okay."

He trailed a finger through her hair before brushing it softly across her lips.

She backed away, looking hungrily at him. It was all he could do not to toss her over his shoulder again and take her home immediately. Damn it, he was going to be civilized about this.

"Go on, sweetheart. I'll meet you there."

She pushed her curls from her face and got into her car. Seconds later, she turned out of the drive and headed down the road.

Jake strode back to his truck. He rolled up the schematics and headed to the building site to find Luke. A few minutes later, he thumped the papers over Luke's chest.

"All yours, buddy. I'm out of here for the day."

Luke worked to keep a grin from his face. The smug bastard.

"I'll run them over to the office and let Ellie make the changes," Luke said innocently.

"I gave her the afternoon off," Jake growled. "Don't call me. I'll call you."

He turned and walked away before Luke could rag on him further.

Chapter Four

Ellie turned onto Jake's street and drove toward his house. She didn't glance over as she approached the house she used to live in. The one just two houses down from Jake's.

She registered its passing but wouldn't give in to the urge to see if it still looked as evil as she remembered. She hadn't been down this street since the night she'd run out in the middle of the night.

She hadn't known where to go, hadn't realized she was at Jake's door until he'd opened it and hauled her sobbing body inside.

Her hands shook, and she tapped on the accelerator, anxious for the house to be out of her periphery. Ahead, Jake's house loomed, and she turned into his driveway.

She used to love this neighborhood. When she and Ray had married, he'd surprised her by buying the house in the upscale development. She'd dreamed of children playing in the yard, backyard barbeques and socializing with the neighbors. Instead she'd spent her days praying she wouldn't become pregnant and avoiding the neighbors for fear they'd know all her dirty secrets.

Her legs shook as she made her way up the paved walkway to Jake's front door. The shrubbery lining the walk was all well maintained and manicured. The lawn was freshly mowed. It ought to be since she made sure a crew came out weekly to keep up Jake's yard.

She stopped at the door and inserted the key into the lock. When she pushed it open, she was assailed by memories of that night...

"Ellie, what the hell are you doing here this time of night?" Jake demanded.

She staggered forward, praying he wouldn't turn her away.

"My God, Ellie, you're bleeding! What happened? Where are you hurt?"

He wrapped his strong arms around her and pulled her inside, shutting the door behind him. She was sobbing. She could hear herself, but it seemed so far away. As if someone else was doing the crying.

"Ellie, talk to me. Where are you hurt? Do you want me to go get Ray?"

She'd panicked then, striking out, trying anything to get away.

Jake swore and held her tightly against him as she fought in vain to escape. She managed to break free for a moment. It was then he seemed to notice the torn clothing. The bruises forming on her face. The blood smeared on her thighs.

His entire body went rigid. He reached out and took her hands gently in his, holding her still when she would have fled.

"Who did this to you, Ellie?"

His voice was low. Dangerously low. It sent a chill down her spine as she registered the violence in his tone.

"Please," she whispered. "Don't make me go back to him. Please, please."

Hot tears ran down her face, and she stared up at him, knowing he was her only chance. If he didn't believe her, she was well and truly doomed.

His mouth opened and closed. Fury raged in his eyes. Then a sorrow so deep, so profound, crept over his face.

"Ray did this to you?" he asked in disbelief. "He hurt you?"

She turned away, knowing she was destroying more than just her marriage with her admission. She was destroying Jake's friendship with a man he'd grown up with. A man he considered a brother in the truest sense of the word.

"Ellie, look at me," he commanded. He gently pushed her chin up with his fingers. "Ray did this?"

She closed her eyes as sobs welled in her throat once more. It shamed her beyond words for Jake to see her like this, for him to know the dirty little secret that was her marriage.

"Ellie," he prompted once more. *"Did Ray do this?"*

"Yes," she whispered. And she knew with her admission that not only would she never be the same, but neither would Jake.

Ellie shuddered lightly then realized she was still standing in Jake's entryway, the door wide open in front of her. She quickly stepped inside and shut it.

She glanced around, taking in the sparsely furnished living room. It had all the male essentials. A big screen TV, a couch and a recliner, but it was devoid of any décor save for the large Christmas tree in the corner.

It surprised her that Jake would have gone to the trouble of putting up a tree and decorating it in such detail since he lived alone, but the tree was perfectly shaped, draped in old-fashioned wood ornaments.

She turned away, unable to bear the cheerful sight.

She set the key on the coffee table and looked toward the hallway she knew led to his bedroom. She started across the wood floor, her mind reliving the night Jake had carried her to his bed so he could care for her.

At the doorway, she paused, staring at the big bed centered in the room. Could she do this? Reach out and take what she so desperately wanted? She knew Jake wanted her. Knew he'd wanted her a while, but she'd been determined she wouldn't go to him so soon after her break-up with Ray.

She took a few steps into the bedroom and kicked out of her shoes. She reached for her zipper and let her skirt fall in a pool around her feet. Next she unbuttoned her blouse and slowly let it slip from her shoulders.

Now standing in just her bra and panties, she felt a surge of nervousness. At any moment, Jake would walk through that door, expecting to have sex with her. What if she couldn't do it?

She closed her eyes and banished all thoughts from her mind but Jake. Imagined his hard body pressed against hers. Those big arms wrapped around her, sheltering her from the rest of the world.

Her fingers slid up her body, raising goose bumps on her skin. She ran them underneath the underwire of her bra, around to the back until she fumbled with the hook. When it sprang free, she let the straps slide from her shoulders until the bra joined her other clothes on the floor. Then she reached for her underwear.

Soon she stood completely naked. She shivered slightly. Finally she opened her eyes and moved toward the bed. She pulled back the covers and eased onto the mattress, tugging the sheets over her body as she went.

As her head hit the pillow, she breathed deeply, inhaling Jake's scent. It was as if he were lying next to her. She closed her eyes and burrowed deeper into his pillow. He'd be here soon.

Jake roared to a stop in his driveway, relieved to see Ellie's car parked a few feet away. He got out and hurried for the door. He sure hoped she hadn't changed her mind in the time it had taken him to get here.

Shelton had caught him just as he was leaving the jobsite and forced a confrontation over the foreman's firing. Jake had wasted thirty minutes before Shelton had finally backed down once he figured out Jake wasn't budging.

He let himself into the house and closed the door quietly behind him. Had she done as he'd told her? Was she lying naked in his bed just a room away?

His cock surged to life.

He walked through the house on silent feet. When he reached his bedroom, he paused at the doorway and stared over at the bed. His chest shook at his sharp intake of breath.

Unable to resist, he moved closer to the bed. The sheet was tucked underneath her arms, covering her chest. Her silky, dark hair splayed out over his pillow. His fingers itched to touch the curls, to twine them around his hands.

While the sheet covered her body, it did little to conceal the dark imprint of her nipples. He swallowed as he imagined what they'd taste like, the sensation of the buds on his tongue.

As if sensing his presence, she stirred and her eyelids fluttered open. A shy, sweet smile curved her full lips.

"Jake," she whispered. "You're here."

Hell and damnation, it was all he could do to keep himself from ripping the sheets from her body, spreading her legs and diving in. Instead he eased to a sitting position beside her and trailed a finger over her cheek.

"Did you think I wouldn't be?"

She nuzzled her cheek against his hand as if seeking his touch. "I hoped you would."

He shifted to alleviate the ever-growing discomfort in his groin. Her voice, so sexy, husky, like a shot of good whiskey. It licked over him, and he began to imagine her tongue doing the same.

"Ellie, we need to talk." He didn't recognize his own voice. It sounded hoarse and needy.

She struggled to sit up, and when she slid upward, the sheet fell to her lap. He groaned aloud as the rosy tips of her breasts became visible.

She yanked the sheet back up, clutching it to her chest. Pink dusted her cheeks, and she peeked up at him.

He fought to remember what it was he wanted to say to her. His mind had gone straight to mush as soon as he'd gotten a glimpse of those perfect breasts.

"What did you want to talk about?" she prompted.

He shook his head and refocused his attention.

"I need to be sure this is what you want, Ellie. I don't want a martyr in my bed. You need to be absolutely certain you want what's about to happen here, because once I take you, you're mine."

He watched as her lips formed an O of shock. He leaned in closer until his lips were a hair's breadth from hers.

"Mine, Ellie. In my bed. All mine. I won't let you go. You need to tell me if you're prepared for that, because if you aren't, you need to hightail it home right now."

She ran her tongue over her lips, licking nervously then pulling at the bottom lip with her teeth.

"I don't want to go home."

"Then look at me, Ellie. Tell me who you see. Tell me who's going to make love to you in about two minutes."

"You are, Jake," she whispered.

He covered her mouth with his, his need to taste her nearly overwhelming. He'd waited years for this moment. He sucked gently at her tongue, grazing it with his teeth.

He stared at her in confusion when she ended the kiss. Earnestness burned in her blue eyes as she pulled away.

"There's something I want to say too, Jake. About the other night."

He put a finger over her lips to shush her, but she shook her head.

She took in a deep breath, and he wondered what the hell she could possibly have to say that was worth interrupting the moment.

"Jake, the reason I went to that bar. I didn't know you'd be there, you have to believe that."

He frowned. "That makes it better? Hell, Ellie, what if I hadn't been there? Have you thought about that?"

She colored and seemed to grow more anxious.

"The reason I went...I went because I hoped that if I could go through with it, I mean I did it because I wanted you. I had to be sure I could go through with it."

He looked incredulously at her. "Am I supposed to be flattered that you thought you had to test drive some other cock in order to work up the nerve to climb into my bed?"

She shook her head vigorously. "That's not what it was about."

"Then what *was* it about?" he demanded.

Her gaze dropped, and he reached out to nudge her chin

up. "I wanted it to be perfect," she said quietly. "I wanted you. I felt pretty positive you wanted me. I didn't want our first time together to be a disaster because I couldn't go through with it. I thought...I thought if I went to bed with another man, I could get past my demons."

Her lips trembled as the last words came tumbling out. He swore softly under his breath even as his chest tightened at her admission.

"I'm so damn tempted to turn you over my knee and spank your ass. Of all the fool-headed, cockamamie things. Do you honestly think I'd sit back and be grateful you went to bed with another man before offering yourself to me on a silver platter?"

Her blue eyes glimmered with a hint of moisture as she stared back at him.

He moved his hand from her chin and stroked it over her cheek. "Ellie," he said in a low voice. "I don't expect you to pretend. Not with me. Never with me. You don't have to put up a brave front and act like no one's ever hurt you.

"Do you understand how much I want you? Not your idea of perfection. I want *you*. Just the way you are. I want you so damn much I ache."

Her eyes widened.

"Do you want me, Ellie? Do you ache like I do?"

She leaned forward, reaching a hand to his face. The sheet fell once more, and this time she didn't try to retrieve it. Her fingers slid over his jaw, and he turned his face so he could kiss the smooth skin of her palm.

"I do want you, Jake. So very much. And you're right. I'm not afraid of you. You're the only person I feel safe with. But I'm afraid of *me*."

He looked hungrily at her. "Then trust me to make this perfect for both of us."

"I do, Jake. I do."

Chapter Five

Ellie's breath caught then released with a small hiccup. Jake stared so intently at her, his words wrapping around her and squeezing tight.

His head bobbed close to hers. Their noses dodged, and he tilted his head until he was at the perfect angle to meet her lips.

Heat sizzled and sparked between them. She felt him in every single cell. Her breasts tingled, and her nipples tightened painfully. Currents of desire fanned out, the sheer power making her weak.

His hand snaked around her neck until he palmed the back of her head. He burrowed his fingers into her mane of hair, and he pulled her closer.

"You taste so sweet," he murmured.

"Are you going to get undressed?" she asked.

He smiled. "In a hurry, sweetheart?"

Yeah, she was in a hurry. She couldn't wait to see his body. Feel his naked skin on hers.

He rose from the bed and stood just a foot away. With slow, measured movements, he pulled his flannel shirt from his waistband then began unbuttoning.

Her pulse sped up as he parted the lapels and she caught her first glimpse of his muscled chest. He shrugged out of the sleeves and let the shirt fall to the floor.

Holy moly. He had the most gorgeous chest she'd ever seen on a man, bar none. Broad shoulders, bulging arms, an abdomen with a pronounced six-pack. She nearly had to wipe the drool from her mouth. Never. Never had she imagined anything close to the reality staring her in the face.

He lowered his thumbs until they hooked into his waistband. His fingers worked at the snap. Then she heard the bite of the zipper.

She didn't realize she was holding her breath until it all came rushing out. He lowered his jeans, his underwear coming with them. The thatch of dark hair at his groin came into view and then the thick base of his cock.

The material of the jeans pulled at the straining flesh until finally he sprang free. Her eyes widened in shock. Her gaze shot up to meet Jake's.

He grinned. A cocky, self-assured grin. "I'll fit, sweetheart. You'll take all of me. And you'll love every minute of it."

Heat flooded her, rushing to her cheeks. Her clit hummed and strained. She shifted to try and alleviate the discomfort between her legs. She ached. Jake had asked if she ached. But she wasn't sure if the word did justice to the very real pain she felt.

The bed dipped as Jake crawled up beside her. His big body hovered over hers until finally he collected her in his arms and pulled her up tight against him.

"You're beautiful. I've dreamed of this moment. Longer than you'll ever know."

Her lips were temptingly close to the curve of his neck, and she gave in to the urge to sink her teeth into the corded muscles that formed the ridge between his shoulder and the base of his head.

He flinched and emitted a low moan. Emboldened by his response, she nibbled a path to his ear where she swirled her tongue around the lobe before nipping sharply at it.

"Goddamn, Ellie!"

She smiled and continued her assault.

"You've got to stop, sweetheart. I won't last a nanosecond if you keep that up."

He gently pushed her away until her head rested on the soft pillow. He positioned himself above her, his green eyes blazing with a need she knew mirrored her own.

She reached up a hand to trace the lines of his face, stopping when her fingers reached his lips. He sucked one of the digits into his mouth, nibbling lightly at the tip.

He seemed patient, something that surprised her. Jake wasn't the patient type. He was demanding, sometimes even surly. He tended to be abrupt, and he had no tolerance for procrastination. Yet, he lay there, regarding her with a lazy air.

"Why are you staring at me?" she asked.

"You're beautiful, that's why. I've never met a woman who makes me shake like you do."

She smiled. She couldn't help it. What woman wouldn't want to hear that she affected a man like Jake?

"I want you to love me, Jake."

With a harsh groan, he bent and slid hot, hungry lips over hers. Gone was the patience. He devoured her like a man starved.

She twisted restlessly underneath him. Her skin burned. She wanted. God, she wanted. It consumed her, tore into her like a jagged blade.

His mouth worked fervently down her neck to her chest until his lips closed around one pointed nipple. As he sucked the tip into his mouth, she cried out.

She felt the pinch between her legs as streaks of electricity raced from her abdomen.

"Feel good, sweetheart?"

"Oh God..."

He chuckled before sliding his hard body down hers, kicking the covers back as he went. He stopped when his mouth was even with her sensitive belly, and he ran his tongue around the indention of her navel.

Tiny goose bumps prickled over her flesh as his tongue trailed lower. And lower still.

Her breathing sped up until she was panting. His fingers trailed through the curls surrounding her pussy and gently spread the folds.

He touched his tongue to her clit, and she bolted upward, a sigh of pleasure escaping tightly compressed lips. Over and over, his mouth feathered across the quivering little bud until she was mindless in her ecstasy.

One finger circled her opening before dipping inside the slightest bit. Then with a quick movement, he sucked her clit between his teeth and nipped as he plunged the finger deeper.

She went wild, her hands curling tightly into the sheets. Her head flailed from side to side as her eyes closed tight against the burst of sensation that swept over her.

"Jaaake!"

He ignored her, easing another finger in to join the first.

She was close. She was on the brink of something truly wonderful. But before she could reach out and take it, he stopped.

He slid back up her body, his muscular thigh parting her legs. His cock, heavy and thick, nudged into her slick folds.

She stiffened for a moment, a tendril of panic squeezing her chest.

"Relax, sweetheart. We're going to take this nice and easy."

He propped himself up slightly with one knee and framed her face with his hands. He stared down at her, his expression so gentle, devoid of the hard-ass persona he exuded ninety-nine percent of the time.

He held her as he fitted his mouth to hers. This time, she sucked at his tongue, coaxing it inward. His taste was different from before, and she realized the sexy musk was her, the evidence of her pleasure.

One of his hands left her face and reached between them. He reared back and rubbed his cock over the sensitive layers of her pussy. Now coated with her moisture, the head slid easily inside as he pushed forward.

"Ahhh," she exhaled as he gained more depth.

Slowly, methodically, he worked his way deeper. She stretched to accommodate him. Ripple upon ripple of joy coursed through her system.

Finally his hips pressed tight to hers. Her eyes flashed wide

Maya Banks

in astonishment. Above her Jake smiled, his eyes gleaming predatorily.

"Told you I'd fit."

"Smug bastard," she muttered.

He laughed and worked his hips, flexing his cock against her vaginal walls. "You were made for me, Ellie. Only me."

She reached for him, wanting to hold him as he'd held her. He gave in to her need, lowering his body until he lay flush against her.

He placed his forearms on either side of her head as she raised her legs to circle his waist.

"That's it," he whispered against her cheek. "Hold on tight, sweetheart. Ride with me."

She loved the contrast of their skin—his dark brown, work-roughened skin to her softer, paler sheen. She relaxed her legs and let her ankles slip until they hooked underneath his ass. Then she slid her palms down his back and over his firm buttocks. They tightened with every powerful thrust, the muscles contracting underneath her fingertips.

The tension in her pelvis grew. His movements became more forceful, and he increased his speed. Their ragged breathing spilled into the quiet room.

She closed her eyes, holding on to him for dear life. She felt as though she were a balloon being inflated impossibly large. Every muscle strained to near bursting. Soon she'd pop, and yet the pressure continued to build.

"Jake!"

"I'm here, sweetheart," he rasped in her ear. "Come for me, Ellie. I'm so close."

Her cry was lost as he captured her mouth in a passionate brand of ownership. She convulsed wildly, bucking upward to meet his pumping thighs.

The room grew dim. Blackness edged in her vision. The slap of flesh on flesh ricocheted. Then she broke apart. She simply exploded, unable to bear the mounting frenzy any longer.

Exquisite bursts of pleasure overwhelmed her until she

truly feared passing out. She tried to catch her breath but found she couldn't force air into her lungs.

Jake crushed her against him, slipping his arms underneath her body and holding tight. He grunted next to her ear then collapsed onto her, driving her further into the bed.

He lay there for a long moment, his chest heaving as he sucked in great mouthfuls of air. Then he propped his body up with his arms and gazed down at her.

"Are you all right?"

She smiled and traced a pattern on his face with her fingers. "What do you think?"

"I think you nearly killed me, wench."

She laughed, astonished at how relaxed and joyful she sounded.

He rolled to her side and stared up at the ceiling. "We didn't use protection, Ellie."

She turned on her side so she could better look at him. "It's okay. I'm on the pill."

He cocked one eye at her. "Still, I had no business not using a condom. I didn't even think beyond getting between your legs. You make me as crazy as a horny teenager."

She smiled and placed her hand on his chest. He put his hand over hers and brought her palm to his mouth.

"I'll take care of you, Ellie. I promise."

An odd rush hit her square in the chest. "I know you will, Jake."

Silence descended between them for a few seconds. He tucked his arm around her and pulled her down until her head was pillowed on his shoulder.

"Why are you on the pill?" he asked. "I know there hasn't been anyone since Ray."

He said it with such confidence, but then Jake was nothing if not self-assured. And he knew her well. Better than anyone else ever had.

Oddly enough she didn't flinch at the mention of her ex-husband's name. Most people who knew her beyond a general acquaintance tactfully avoided mention of him or her marriage. She liked that Jake was so blunt with her. It proved he wasn't treating her like half a person. One damaged and scarred beyond repair.

"I started taking them when Ray and I were still married," she said quietly. "I was desperate not to get pregnant."

Jake's arm tightened around her then he turned until they were nearly nose to nose.

"Ellie...that night. Was it the first time he hurt you like that?"

She swallowed, unsure of whether she should admit the truth. Jake looked intently at her, so much *feeling* in his eyes, she had difficulty sorting out the various emotions she saw reflected.

"No," she finally said. "It's why I started taking birth control pills on the sly. I would never have willingly gone to bed with him, and I would have died rather than bring a baby into our marriage."

Jake's eyes closed, his face creased into an expression of pain.

"Jake, don't," she whispered. "Let's not think of him. Not right now. He's the last person I want between us when I'm in bed with you."

"I hate myself for not seeing him for what he was," Jake said bleakly.

She leaned in to kiss him, effectively halting anything else he might say. "I don't hate you. I hate him. You're not to blame. He is."

He pushed his hand into her hair, running his fingers through the strands. Then he pulled her to him again. He kissed her lightly, several times in succession. Each time he touched a different part of her mouth.

When he finally eased away, his eyes were glazed with need. She glanced down his body to see his semi-aroused cock coming back to life.

"Jake?" she asked, a little breathlessly, a little unsure.

"Yes, sweetheart?"

"I want to touch you. I want—I want to make love to you. Can I?"

Chapter Six

All the breath left Jake's body in one harsh wheeze. "Jesus, Mary and Joseph, woman. What the hell kind of question is that?"

Her lips, swollen from his kisses, spread upward into a shy smile.

"*Please* have your wicked way with me. I'm not too proud to beg."

Her gaze fell to his dick, and he felt a bolt of arousal as he imagined what she had in mind.

"Touch me, sweetheart," he said huskily. "Before I go nuts."

She sat up and shoved at him until he was flat on his back. He folded his hands behind his head, content to lie back and let her do her thing.

She had the look of a hungry woman ready to feast. There wasn't a nerve ending in his body that wasn't jumping like a frog on speed.

He flinched when she bent down and pressed her lips just two inches above the thatch of hair surrounding his cock. Her tongue swept out and swirled a trail to his navel, and every one of his muscles rippled in response.

His cock stood fully at attention now, begging for her touch. For her mouth. God, he wanted her mouth. Her tongue. Hell, right now he just wanted her to touch him.

She petted him, brushing ever so lightly over his chest. Down to his thighs. His hips. He arched, trying to guide himself toward her hand, but she moved her fingers down his legs.

"Miserable tease," he complained.

"What do you want me to do?" she asked, a devilish twinkle in her eye. Ah, hell. She knew exactly what she was doing.

He snagged her fingers and pulled them to his straining cock. He curled her palm around the base and moved it up and down.

"I want to taste you."

He groaned. "God, sweetheart, I want you to taste me, too."

She dipped her head, her silky curls falling over his thighs. He released her hand and shoved his fingers into her hair, pulling it away so he could see.

He flinched and moaned again when her pink tongue flicked out to swirl around the head. Her lips parted, and she slowly slid her mouth over the tip, down the base until he was lodged against the back of her throat.

"Mother fuck," he swore.

His fingers tightened in her hair as he arched into her. She made the sweetest sucking sounds as her mouth worked up and down. Her tongue felt like a velvet glide, slightly rough, hot. The ache began deep in his balls and swelled upward.

She eased her lips up from the base until the head popped out of her mouth with a wet sucking noise.

"Tell me you're not finished," he said, not giving a damn about the fact he was pleading.

She grinned. "Oh, I'm not finished."

She put one knee between his legs and worked her way over until she knelt between his thighs. Then she leaned, placing her hands on either side of his waist. She stared him in the eye, her mouth swollen from sucking his cock.

"Can I ride you, Jake?"

He heaved an exaggerated sigh. "I suppose so, wench. You won't be happy until you've completely ravished me."

She laughed, a beautiful sound, so open and free. She bent down closer and kissed him. He allowed her to dictate the motion, and he enjoyed the fact that she took so much pleasure in exploring him.

When she started to mount him, he put a hand to her waist. "There's a condom in the nightstand drawer."

She shook her head. "I don't want one. Unless you do?"

"Hell, Ellie, that's like asking a starving man if he wants a carrot. Of course I don't want to wear one. Men never do. But we suck it up and do it if we don't want to lose a testicle."

She grinned. "Well, I'm the boss in this seduction, and I don't want one."

He arched one eyebrow at her. "Well then, far be it for me to argue with the boss."

The words nearly strangled him as she sank down on him in one fluid motion. Holy hell in a bucket, the woman was going to kill his ass. Why did he ever think he was going to have to treat her with kid gloves when he convinced her to go to bed with him?

Her fingers rested on his abdomen. She wiggled slightly as she tried to accommodate his size. Then she let out a long sigh of pleasure. Really, was there anything in the world better than the sound a contented woman made? Especially when you were the guy satisfying her.

"Ellie, if you don't start moving, this is all going to be over before it gets really fun," he said in a strained voice.

Her hips began a sensual rotation. She rolled and undulated then pushed herself upward. Her hips rose until he nearly slipped from her pussy before she sank down again, taking him as deep as he could go.

He was looking at a goddess. She sat astride him, head thrown back in abandon. Her breasts thrust forward, the nipples tight beads. Her curls spilled over her shoulders, bouncing as she began to ride him faster.

He reached out, desperate to touch her, needing to feel her. He cupped her breasts, wanting to give back the pleasure she gave to him.

His thumbs brushed across her nipples, and she jerked in reaction. He smiled. "Like that, do you?"

"Mmmmm."

He leaned up, wrapping his arms around her back. He

caressed her bare skin, lowering until he cupped the globes of her ass. He squeezed and massaged, lifting her before letting her fall back onto his cock.

"You're magnificent, Ellie. I swear to God, you're going to kill me if we keep this up."

She opened her eyes. "Want me to stop?"

He smacked her on the ass. "Smart-mouthed wench. You stop and I'll tie you to this bed for a month."

She continued to ride him and let out breathy, desperate sounds. "Jake, that isn't exactly a threat. Will I still get paid for missing work?"

He laughed. God, he loved this woman.

Her breathing sped up. "Help me, Jake," she pleaded. "I can't hold out much longer."

He relaxed back onto the bed and gripped her hips. He could feel the storm building.

"Relax, sweetheart. Let me do the work for a while."

She braced her hands on his forearms as he ground her down onto his cock over and over. The contractions started deep in her pussy. Soon she trembled all over.

"Jake!"

Her body tensed into one long, continuous spasm. He felt a sudden burst of wetness within her as she slumped onto his chest.

He held her tightly, smoothing his hands up and down her damp back. She lay like a rag doll across him, her chest heaving.

Finally, she raised her head, regret simmering in her blue eyes. "I'm sorry."

"What the hell for?" he demanded.

She blushed. "You haven't even come yet."

He grinned and flexed his hips, driving his cock deeper within her. "Well now, sweetheart, we can fix that if you'll roll with me for a minute."

He rolled her over, taking her underneath him. He repositioned himself between her legs and thrust. She let out another contented sigh, one that nearly had him spilling right then and there.

He moved back and forth, allowing the rocketing pleasure to take over him. Sweat beaded his brow, and he closed his eyes to the unbearable tension building in his groin.

"Goddamn," he muttered.

Once, twice, then once more, he sank into her, and finally he erupted. He held himself tightly against her as he ejaculated deep into her womb.

He leaned down to kiss her then shifted to the side of her, flopping with an exhausted sigh onto the bed.

She turned, curling herself into his chest just like she belonged there. He wrapped both arms around her.

"That was incredible," he murmured as he kissed the top of her head.

She yawned and nodded, her head rubbing against his chest. She nuzzled closer, and he felt her eyelashes brush over his skin as she closed her eyes.

"Hold me?" she mumbled.

He smiled and squeezed her a little tighter. "I'm not letting go."

Chapter Seven

Ellie awoke to warm, sinful kisses. Jake's lips burned a trail over the curve of her shoulder to the sensitive skin at the nape of her neck.

"You're awake," he murmured.

"Like I could sleep when you're doing that."

She turned in his arms until she faced him.

"Let's go shopping," Jake said.

She blinked in surprise. "What?"

"Shopping."

"Jake, you hate shopping. What are we shopping for, anyway?"

He sat up in bed, his naked body, his *gorgeous* naked body, slipping from the sheets.

"A Christmas tree."

"You already have a Christmas tree," she pointed out.

He reached over and flicked her nose. "But you don't."

She frowned. "I don't want a tree."

"Ellie, you love Christmas, and you're letting that bastard ruin it for you. Now get your ass up so we can go buy you a tree. I'll buy you lots of nice colored lights to go on it."

She glared at him as he got up from the bed. "I want white lights."

"That's so boring," he said. "What you need is something that blinks."

She managed a horrified look. "I am not putting flashing

51

lights on my tree!"

He chuckled. "Come on. Let's take a shower. I'll let you talk me into white lights, but I get to pick out the ornaments."

She swung her leg over the side of the bed, marveling at how easily he'd won that argument. He could charm the scales right off a snake.

"No," Ellie said. "That one's not quite right either."

Jake shook his head in exasperation and set aside yet another tree. He dug around for a moment before pulling out another. He stood it up and slowly rotated it around for her to see.

"How's this?"

She drew her eyebrows together in thought. It wasn't bad. No large holes. And the symmetry was good. She was a freak about symmetry. It was tall without being too tall, and it was fresh and green.

"I like it."

Jake cocked an eyebrow. "You sure? Because we can keep looking."

She smiled at his patience. They'd been looking for an hour, and he'd been a good sport as she refused tree after tree.

"No, that one's perfect, I think."

He hoisted the tree up over his shoulder and headed for the cashier stationed outside the home improvement store in the lawn and garden section. He leaned it against the register and then dug around in his back pocket for his wallet. He flipped the cashier his credit card then glanced back at Ellie.

"Wait here and I'll pull the truck around."

Jake let out a grunt as he righted the tree, the stand firmly affixed to the base. Ellie stood back and stared intently.

"Is it straight?" he asked.

She nodded. They'd gotten the tree through her front door. Barely. Jake had set it up in the far corner, and she had to admit, she was glad she'd gotten it now. She couldn't wait to see it all aglow with the tiny white lights they'd bought.

"I like it when you smile."

She blinked and looked up to see Jake staring at her.

"I didn't realize I was," she said sheepishly.

He grinned. "Okay, hand me the boring-ass lights and I'll get them strung."

"They are not boring," she protested as she reached for one of the boxes.

"They're white. And white. Oh, and white," he grumbled. "No fun at all."

"You're still stuck back in your childhood," she teased.

"When it comes to Christmas, everyone should be a kid."

She couldn't argue with that. Sometimes being an adult hurt too much.

She took one end of the lights as Jake began unraveling them from the box. "Let me guess. When you were a child you had lots of colored, blinking lights."

"Damn right."

She giggled.

Thirty minutes later, her tree was aglow with over nine hundred lights. She stood back to admire their work and realized how much she'd missed the spirit of Christmas. She'd been so determined not to observe the holiday, not to remember.

"You like it?" Jake asked.

She nodded. "Yeah, I do. Thanks for going with me to get one. It makes me happy."

"I want very much to make you happy," he said softly.

She cocked her head to stare sideways at him, but he stared straight ahead at the tree. He reached up to hang one of the wooden ornaments they'd purchased as if he'd never uttered such a provocative statement.

An hour later, they were done. A glimmer of delight rushed over Ellie as she took in the brightly decorated tree. It did make her happy. She felt lighter than she had in a long time.

Jake slid an arm around her waist and pulled her against him. "I'm starved. You wore me out. When are you going to feed me?"

She gazed up into his eyes, her stomach doing a series of flip flops at what she saw there. "What would you like?"

"Now that's a loaded question," he drawled. He checked his watch. "It's too late to go out and get anything, and to be honest, what I'm most hungry for is you."

She swallowed as her nipples hardened. "I could fix us something. Or you could just..."

"Fuck it," he growled as he swung her into his arms. "We'll eat later."

He hauled her toward the bedroom and dumped her onto the bed. His hands went to his jeans, and her gaze fastened greedily on the area he was about to expose. She licked her lips.

"Goddamn, woman. Stop that or I'll never get my damn jeans off."

"Need some help?" she asked innocently.

He crooked his finger at her in answer.

She slid off the bed and sauntered over to where he stood. He let his hands fall to his sides as she reached for the zipper. His cock strained and bulged against her fingers as she worked the zipper down.

Finally she reached in and gently drew out his erection. As she palmed the rigid shaft, he yanked at the waist of his jeans until they fell the rest of the way down his legs.

Not waiting to see if he'd take over, she sank to her knees until his cock was but an inch from her lips. She placed her palms on the front of his thighs and slowly took him in her mouth.

He uttered a low groan, and his hips jerked spasmodically as he thrust forward. She loved that she gave him so much pleasure. It gave her power in a way she'd never enjoyed before.

She closed her eyes and let her lips and tongue glide over the smooth head. Fluid spilled on her tongue, and she moaned in reaction.

"You're killing me, sweetheart. I swear you make the sweetest sounds."

He tangled his fingers in her hair and pulled her closer. His hips worked back and forth, driving deeper into her mouth. Finally he pulled away, his chest heaving with exertion.

She glanced up at him in confusion.

"If you pulled on me one more time with that wicked mouth of yours I would have gone off like a rocket," he said. "I'm not ready for this to be over when we've only just begun."

She dragged the back of her hand over her swollen mouth and started to rise. Jake reached down for her, easily hoisting her into his arms. She circled her legs around his waist, locking them together in the back

He walked her backward until his legs bumped against the bed. Their lips were close. He bent his head, nudging his mouth against hers. They touched, retreated, then touched again.

Soft kisses, feather light, danced across her lips. He lowered her slowly to the bed. She clutched at him as her back pressed against the mattress.

"You've got way too many damn clothes on."

"You could always do something about that." His fingers worked at the buttons of her shirt. Soon the material fell open, baring her lacy bra.

"God, that bra looks good on you," he said hoarsely.

He worked to her jeans, easing the zipper down before peeling the denim from her legs. When he'd pulled the pants away, he bent and pressed his lips against the silky underwear covering her mound. His touch seared straight through the material, and she twisted restlessly beneath him.

"Don't tease me, Jake. I want you so much."

"That's good, sweetheart, because from now on it's only going to be me."

A shiver worked over her skin. Jake wasn't one to screw around. He was straight-talking and made it a habit of going after what he wanted with relentless determination. It scared the hell out of her that he obviously wanted her. For more than just sex.

"I don't like that look, Ellie. Whatever the fuck it is you're thinking, just stop it now. Look at me. Tell me who you see. Tell me who's about to love you like you've never been loved."

"You are," she whispered.

"Say my name, Ellie."

"Jake."

He pulled at her panties then slid her bra straps down her shoulders. Soon she was naked beneath him, breathless with the force of her desire.

He bent down and pressed his mouth to her stomach. His lips worked lower, leaving a burning trail. She parted her legs even as he inserted a hand between them.

She knew she looked like a wanton, all sprawled out before him, ready for him to take. His gaze worked up and down her body, and she delighted in the desire she saw there. He wanted her as much as she wanted him.

A wildness took over her. Like a prisoner breaking free from long-endured captivity. She wanted to feel everything. Touch, taste, experience her newfound sexuality. Jake delighted in it every bit as much as Ray had tried to squash it.

"I burn when you look at me like that, Ellie. I swear I've dreamed of you looking at me the way you are now."

"Come here," she ordered, crooking her finger at him as he had done at her.

He lowered his big body over hers, and she hugged him to her. She didn't wait for him, she meshed her lips against his, kissing him hungrily.

Her mouth worked hot over his, and their breathing became heavier as their tongues clashed and dueled. His hands slid down her waist, dug underneath to cup her buttocks.

His cock nudged impatiently between her thighs. He worked his hands down to the backs of her legs then spread her further. In one hard push, he was inside her.

She sucked in her breath. It caught in her throat then

expanded her chest as a rush of electricity surged through her veins.

"God, you're so tight," he groaned. "You feel so damn good."

She wrapped her legs around his waist, urging him deeper. Gone were her fears of accommodating him. She wanted every inch buried just as deeply as he could go. He stretched her. Stroked the insides of her pussy until she squirmed and bucked beneath him.

Before she could register the build of her orgasm, it exploded on her with earth-shattering force. She went wild. She buried her face in his neck, chanting "oh God" over and over again.

Jake held her tight, rocking into her as currents of fire streaked through her abdomen. Every muscle in her body strained against him. Finally she gasped as her orgasm eased. She relaxed in Jake's arms and melted into the bed.

Above her, Jake chuckled then kissed her. He was still rock hard, buried in her pussy.

"You sure were in a hurry," he said as he kissed her again.

"You make me crazy," she said. "I've never felt like this before."

He held himself slightly off her and reached with one hand to stroke her face. "I'm glad."

He moved his hips, retreating for a moment before sliding back into her. She let out a small sigh of pleasure as the tiny tremors of her orgasm subsided.

He thrust in a slow, sensual pattern. Back and forth, taking his time.

She shoved at his chest. "Turn over."

He raised an eyebrow in surprise.

"I want on top."

He grinned and gripped her hips. Then he rolled over in one swift motion, and suddenly she sat atop him, his cock buried in her pussy.

She wanted to make it as good for him as he had for her. Wanted to make him crazy. Make him beg for mercy.

She leaned forward, letting her hair fall over her shoulders as she kissed him. He framed her face and kissed her back. Hungry. Hot. Needy.

Her hips shook against him as she moved. Jake closed his eyes as she pressed her hands into his chest and slid up and down on his cock. He reached for her hips, helping her as she rode him.

She curled her fingertips into the hard muscles of his chest. Slid them down to caress his abdomen and fiddle in the fine line of hair that ran from his navel to the hollow in his chest.

Then she lowered her head and ran her tongue over the same muscled ridges her fingers had just traced. He flinched and let out a desperate moan. She smiled.

"Faster, sweetheart. Ride me faster."

His hands urged her on as his movements became desperate. He was close. She could feel the swell as he grew more rigid inside her.

She did as he asked, wanting to give him back the pleasure he'd given her.

He closed his eyes tight and arched into her. His fingers pressed into the flesh of her hips as he surged one last time. He cried out as he erupted, and satisfaction gripped her.

"Come here," he muttered as he gathered her in his arms.

He pulled her down to him until her cheek pressed against his chest. He kissed the top of her head and ran gentle fingers through her hair.

"You are an incredible, incredible woman, Ellie."

She smiled against his chest. Then she raised her head so she could kiss him. A yawn escaped her as she burrowed back underneath his chin.

"Are you staying over?" she asked. She hadn't considered whether or not he'd stay the night or want to. It seemed senseless for him to go home at this hour.

He continued stroking her hair. "Do you want me to?"

"Mmm hmmm."

"Then I'm staying. Can't think of anything better than to

wake up with you all curled up in my arms."

A warm, happy glow lit her cheeks. She couldn't imagine anything better either.

Chapter Eight

Ellie opened her eyes and yawned broadly. She stretched and curled deeper into the bed. Jake had gotten up early and gone in to work after issuing strict instructions for her to take the day off. Then he'd made some rather lewd remarks about what he'd like to do on his lunch break.

She grinned and glanced over at her bedside clock. It was still early, and she had plenty of time before Jake would pop back in. A long bath. And breakfast. She was starving.

Her body protested as she moved to get out of bed. She was sore from her and Jake's lovemaking, but damn had it been worth every second.

As she walked by the TV, she flipped it on then went to rummage in her closet for something to wear. She liked the noise. She didn't deal well with silence.

But when she heard Ray Hatcher's name, she froze. Slowly, she turned around and walked to the door of her closet. She shouldn't let it affect her. She should pay no attention, but hearing his name still had the power to knock her off balance.

She stood frozen, staring at the object of her nightmares on screen. He was smiling, but then he'd always been charming. He looked young and carefree, like a twenty-something instead of a thirty-something "old" NFL quarterback.

He was being interviewed. Her ears picked up that much. The host was abuzz with the news of Ray's contract extension. Several minutes passed as she stared dumbly at the screen.

Then she heard her name, and horror crawled over her,

clouding her mind in a flash of fear and hatred. The interviewer was asking about Ray's marriage and the bastard, the *bastard*, sat there and let the lies roll off his lips as easily as if he were talking about the weather.

Infidelity. Adultery. He was crushed. He loved Ellie, and it had devastated him when he discovered their marriage was in ruins.

Her hand flew to her mouth as the host donned an appropriate expression of pity as they discussed the intimate details of Ray's private life.

But things were looking up. He'd found a new love interest. His career was back on track after a shaky few years. He'd moved past his ex-wife's transgression.

Oh God, she was going to vomit.

She ran for the bathroom, tears streaming down her face. How could he? How could he destroy the only thing she had left? Her integrity. The knowledge that she had done nothing but love the wrong man.

She threw herself at the toilet and dry heaved as her stomach rolled and protested.

There had been plenty of speculation surrounding Ellie's divorce from the local golden boy. Lots of stares and whispers, but the locals never had anything to back up their idle murmurings. Until now.

She forgot about a bath. Breakfast. Jake. Nothing mattered but getting out of the house. The walls were closing around her, stifling her, smothering her.

She stumbled to the sink and threw cold water on her face. She hastily pulled her hair back into a ponytail and secured it with a rubber band. Then she went into the bedroom to yank on some clothing.

Ray still stared at her from the TV. She picked up a vase from her dresser and hurled it at the offending image. The vase and the TV screen shattered on impact, and she had the satisfaction of seeing Ray's face disappear.

She shoved her feet into a pair of loafers, grabbed her purse from the dresser and headed out to her car. The cool air rushed over her cheeks as she stepped outside. She shivered slightly. She hadn't stopped to get a jacket.

Her hands wrapped around the steering wheel. She had no memory of getting into the car or starting it. She backed from her driveway with no sense of direction or purpose. She needed to escape. And so she ran.

"He said what?" Jake all but yelled into his cell phone. "You've got to be shitting me. If this is some sort of joke, Luke, it ain't funny."

"I wouldn't fuck with you or Ellie over something like this," Luke said. "Ellie wasn't in this morning when I hit the office. I'm hoping you have something to do with that and not Ray."

Jake dragged a hand through his hair and started for his truck. "Goddamn. I hope she hasn't seen it. Not that it fucking matters. It'll be all over town by tonight."

Luke sighed over the phone. "I didn't see the show, but Gracie did. She called me awhile ago. She said he really did a number on Ellie."

"Fuck! That slimy little bastard. I'd like nothing better than to kick his ass right now."

"Calm down, Jake. I didn't call to piss you off. I was hoping you knew where Ellie was and if she was okay."

"I'm heading over there now. I told her to take the day off. She was home when I left this morning. Hopefully she's still there sleeping in."

"Okay, man. Let me know if there's something I can do."

"Thanks, Luke."

Jake slapped the cell phone shut and shoved it back into his pocket. He closed his eyes and swore. Why now? Why when he was so close to making Ellie happy again did Ray have to wreck everything?

Even if Ellie hadn't seen the show, how the hell could he possibly keep her from finding out? They lived in small town,

Texas, for God's sake. It was the small town motto. *Know thy neighbor as thy self.*

He got behind the wheel of his truck and drove as fast as he could to Ellie's. Halfway there, he spotted Wes Hoffman's squad car. Wes flashed his lights at him as he tore by, and Jake flipped him the bird. Luckily it wasn't a different cop or he'd have been pulled over.

His cell phone rang a few seconds later. He dug it out of his pocket keeping one hand on the wheel and glanced at the LCD screen. Wes.

"Yeah," Jake said as he put the phone to his ear.

"Where you going in such a hurry?" Wes asked. "Be damned glad I met my quota of tickets this month or I'd write your ass up."

Usually Jake would have grinned and given him hell right back, but he wasn't in the mood.

"It's Ellie," he said. "I don't have time to get into it. If you want the story, holler at Luke."

There was a short pause. "Is there anything I can do?"

"No, but I appreciate it. I'll talk at you later."

Jake hung up and tossed the phone aside. He knew Wes felt a lot of responsibility for what had gone on with Ellie, but it was hardly Wes's fault. It was the dumbass cop on duty the night Ellie had asked for help. Jeremy and Wes both had been torn up when they found out that Ellie had gone to the police and basically been ignored.

It wasn't long after that the cop who had handled Ellie's complaint had left. Jake was certain Wes and Jeremy had a lot to do with that.

A few minutes later, he pulled into Ellie's driveway only to see her car gone. He frowned. They'd made plans to have lunch together. Maybe she was out on a quick errand. He hoped like hell she hadn't seen the story.

He got out and walked in to see if she'd left him a note. He didn't find one on the coffee table or the kitchen table. When he stuck his head in the bedroom, he knew without a doubt she'd seen the show. Shards of glass littered the floor and the TV screen was completely busted out.

He swore viciously even as fear clutched at his chest. Where had she gone? Why hadn't she called him? He could only imagine how upset she was.

A dull ache invaded his temples. Did she not trust him enough to run *to* him? Or was she too busy running *away*?

He hurried back out to his truck and climbed in. He picked up his phone and punched in Luke's number.

"Ellie saw it. No doubt in my mind," he said when Luke picked up.

He quickly explained the scene in her bedroom and that her car was gone.

Luke swore. "I haven't seen her, but I'll be on the lookout."

"If you see her, make her stay put. Then call me."

"I will. Want me to call Jeremy and Wes and have them keep an eye out as well?"

"I just spoke to Wes so I'll call him. You call Jeremy."

They rang off and Jake immediately placed a call to Wes.

"Did you get the story from Luke?" Jake asked as his way of greeting when Wes answered.

"Yeah, man, that sucks."

"Ellie saw it. And she's upset. I don't know where she's gone, but I'm looking now. Do me a favor. If you see her, make sure she stays put until I get there."

"Will do," Wes said. "I can have the other on-duty guys keep an eye out as well. If she's out driving around, someone will see her."

Jake thanked him and hung up. He backed out of Ellie's driveway and put his brain to work figuring out where the hell she would have gone.

Chapter Nine

It was the last place Jake had thought to look, but in retrospect, he supposed it made the most sense. It was where it had all started.

He stared up into the bleachers of the high school football stadium to where Ellie sat staring out over the field. Where she'd watched him and Ray play as teenagers.

She hadn't seen him yet. Her attention was focused on some distant object, or maybe she wasn't seeing anything at all.

He started up the steps. When he got to the bleacher she was sitting on, he sat down beside her. He reached over to take her hand but didn't speak. He wasn't sure what to say anyway.

Tiny quakes emanated from her. Her hand trembled in his. A ragged sigh tore from her lips. It was a sound that ripped his heart right open. He knew she was battling to keep it together.

"Why?" she whispered. "*Why?*"

She broke off and turned her head away from him. But not before he saw her tears.

"I've never understood why," she said brokenly. "I was faithful. I loved him. I supported him. Why did he despise me so much? Why now, when he's been out of my life for two years, does he feel the need to destroy me?"

Jake wrapped his arm around her, pulling her close to him. He cupped her cheek in his hand and bent to kiss the top of her head.

"He's a bastard, Ellie. You're better than him. You've always been better, and he knows that. It eats at him. The only way he can justify the things he's done is by tearing you down."

Her body shook with her muffled sobs. Jake held on to her, not knowing what he could say or do to ease her pain. This helplessness scared him. He could feel her slipping away, back to the shell of a woman who'd barely existed after the divorce. He wouldn't lose her to that woman.

Ellie buried her head in Jake's chest, trying to absorb his strength and warmth. Maybe if she infused herself with enough of his steel, she wouldn't hurt so bad.

"What am I going to do, Jake?"

He stroked his hand through her hair, gently sorting through the strands with his fingers.

"You're going to hold your head high. That's what you're going to do."

"Everyone in the world thinks I'm the reason for our divorce now," she said bitterly. "They think I slept around on the Golden Boy and broke his heart."

Jake pulled her away and cupped her chin in his hand. Then he bent to kiss her lips. She closed her eyes as yet more tears escaped.

"It doesn't matter what they think." He continued to rub his thumb over her cheekbone.

"The divorce was humiliating enough," she whispered. "And now this. At least before all they had was conjecture. Now, they have Mr. Perfect, Mr. All-American, crying into a camera saying how horrible his wife was. If they didn't hate me before, they'll hate me now."

"Is it important that they love you, Ellie?"

She flinched. "No. It's not important. The only person I want to love me..." She broke off in horror at what she'd nearly admitted.

"Is who?" he prompted.

She shook her head, refusing to answer his question.

"Maybe I'm not that person, Ellie, but *I* love you. I've always loved you."

Her gaze flew back to his face. Her eyes widened at his statement. "*Always?*"

"Always," he said softly.

She opened her mouth then ran her tongue over her suddenly dry lips. "I don't understand."

To her surprise, his eyes cast downward in an expression of guilt and a little sorrow.

"What is it, Jake?"

Her heart beat in a rapid staccato. She was still reeling from his declaration of love, but he'd always had feelings for her?

"I fell in love with you when you and Ray were seeing each other. After you got married, I distanced myself as much as possible because it was painful to see you with him. I wanted you, and I was as jealous as hell. If I hadn't been such a dumbass, I would have seen what was going on in your marriage. I could have saved you."

She sucked in her breath. "Oh, Jake." She reached out to touch his face. Tears clouded her vision. "It wasn't your fault."

He captured her hand in his and turned his lips into her palm. "It doesn't matter now," he said in a hoarse voice. "What matters now is whether or not you love me."

She leaned forward and pressed her lips to his. Their breaths caught and hitched. They both shook with suppressed emotion.

"I do love you, Jake. So much. I'm scared out of my mind to say it. I'm scared of what it will mean. But I do love you."

He cradled her face in his hands. "Ellie, you don't have to be afraid anymore. However we need to take this, no matter how slow, I'll be here."

She smiled and pressed her forehead to his. "I need you, Jake." She shivered as she became more aware of the crisp air.

"Let's go home," he said. "My house. I'll cook us some lunch. Build a fire. I know how much you like that."

Tears shimmered in her vision. He was so determined to take care of her. And she wanted to let him, but she was so afraid to relax her guard. Even though she trusted Jake implicitly.

She wasn't a moron. She knew that every man wasn't out

to hurt her. Jake in no way could be compared to Ray, but so much damage had been done to her confidence, to her ability to believe in her choices. No matter that she knew Jake would never hurt her, she still fought a choking panic when she imagined a relationship with him.

Jake eased her upward, wrapping a strong arm around her as he guided her down the steps.

"We'll get through this, Ellie. Promise me you won't let this asshole ruin what we have."

She leaned into him. "I don't know that I've ever told you, Jake, but thank you."

He stopped as they reached the bottom and looked curiously at her.

"For what?"

"For saving me that night," she said quietly.

He pulled her into his arms and squeezed so tight she gasped for air. He tensed as though he'd say something, but no words ever came. He shook slightly against her, and then he relaxed his hold.

"Let's go home," he said.

Later, after Jake cooked lunch, he built a fire in the fireplace, and now he and Ellie lay on the couch watching the flames.

She was draped across Jake's body, and he rubbed one hand absently up and down her back. There was so much she wanted to say, but she didn't want to get into it right now. She was mentally exhausted after her emotional outburst before, and she didn't want to do anything to ruin the intimate moment they were enjoying.

More than anything she wanted Jake to take her to bed and make her forget. When he held her, nothing else mattered. And he loved her.

Her chest swelled, and she physically ached with the

emotion his admission had wrung from her. What would happen now? Was she strong enough to hold her head high in the face of what she knew was coming?

She hadn't been out since Ray's interview. She hadn't yet been to work, fielded phone calls from people she'd known all her life. She hadn't gone to eat in the local café where Ray's picture hung, where the locals liked to brag on the hometown boy.

When she did venture out, she knew she would be greeted differently, if at all. And it bothered her more than she liked to admit. She was only human, and the idea of being a pariah in the town she'd grown up in hurt.

"Why don't you take the rest of the week off?" Jake murmured close to her ear.

She sighed. "I can't, Jake. No matter how long I put it off, I'm going to have to eventually face people. I'd love nothing better than to hide, but I can't allow myself to do it."

He squeezed her in a hug. "At least take tomorrow. I have to run to the jobsite, but what do you say we do something fun. Maybe go to Houston to do some Christmas shopping."

She smiled. He went to such great lengths to protect her. "What's with you and shopping lately? The only kind of shopping I've ever known you to like is grocery shopping and only because it involves food."

He tweaked her ass with his fingers. "I'm trying to be sensitive. Isn't that what you women want? A man who'll go shopping with them, listen intently to their every complaint and be all sympathetic?"

She laughed. "You're starting to sound like a pussy, Jake."

He twisted his hand in her hair and gave it a yank. "Smart-mouthed heifer. So are you saying you don't want to go shopping with me?"

"No, not at all. We can go. I need to clean up the mess in my bedroom. I can do that while you're at the jobsite. You going to buy me lunch in Houston?"

"No," he said. "I thought I'd let you starve."

"Now who's the smartass?"

"I'll take you anywhere you want to go."

"Galleria and The Cheesecake Factory?" she asked hopefully.

He sighed. "As long as you don't plan to make my ass go ice skating, I'll take you to the Galleria."

She grinned and leaned up to kiss him. "I have one more request."

He gave another exaggerated sigh. "And that is?"

She stared intently at him. "Take me to bed and make love to me."

His green eyes glittered. "I thought you'd never ask."

Chapter Ten

Ellie swept the last of the glass up from the floor into the dustbin then dumped it into the nearby trashcan. With a rueful smile, she examined the broken TV for any more loose pieces of glass before returning the broom to the kitchen.

Though she wasn't prone to fits of rage, that one had felt good. She'd been much too quiet and withdrawn until then. Maybe she should cut loose more often and allow the bottled emotions to burst out.

Jake would be here soon, and she still had to finish doing her hair and brush her teeth. The afternoon away with him was a source of relief. She was being a coward, locked away ever since Ray's interview more than twenty-four hours ago, but she wasn't ready to face the open speculation of the small-town populace.

As she ran the brush through her hair for the last time, the doorbell rang. She smiled at her reflection in the mirror, amused by the pink that had rushed to her cheeks.

She hurried to the door, stopping only to collect her purse. She opened the door, a welcoming smile on her face.

"Are you ready to—"

The smile died as quickly as the words broke off. Her purse hit the floor beside her. A bolt of terror blew through her body with the speed of a bullet. Ray Hatcher stood on her doorstep, a bleak expression on his face.

"Ellie, I need to talk to you," he said.

His voice shook her from the paralysis that had taken over

her. She rammed the door shut, fumbling for the lock she couldn't make work.

"Ellie! I need to talk to you," he said louder. His voice carried through the door, and she backed away from it.

She stumbled over the rug and went sprawling onto the floor. Nausea welled in her stomach, and her pulse pounded in her head.

The door opened, and she screamed in fear. She rolled to her feet and snatched the phone from the kitchen bar. The bathroom. If she could make it to the bathroom...she could lock the door and call 911.

She ran into the bathroom and slammed the door behind her. She made sure it was locked then retreated to the most distant point from the door. The shower stall.

She curled into a protective ball as her shaking fingers punched in the phone number.

"Ellie?" Ray's voice sounded closer. He was just outside the bathroom door. "Ellie, there's something I need to say."

Oh, God.

"911, what's your emergency?" The dispatcher's voice came over the line.

"This is Ellie Matthews," she blurted. "My husband is here. *He's not supposed to be here.* He's trying to hurt me." The hysteria made her voice rise another octave. "Don't let him hurt me again!"

The dispatcher's voice faded into the background as Ray's voice got louder. The phone slipped from bloodless fingers as she heard the dispatcher assure her the police were on their way.

"Ellie, please listen to me."

Ray's voice had a pleading quality to it. She buried her head in her arms and rocked back and forth, praying the police would make it in time.

There was a long silence on the other side of the door. She was frozen, her skin so cold, every muscle in her body tensed in the most awful of fears. Memories of the last time she'd tasted such fear seared a path through her mind like the sharpest blade.

"Ellie, I just wanted to say I'm sorry."

Ray jiggled on the doorknob, and a fresh wave of terror assaulted her all over again. Her mouth opened to scream, but no sound came out. She wrapped her arms protectively around herself and curled into the tightest ball she could manage.

"When I saw the playback of that interview...when I heard the things I said...Ellie, I'm sorry."

She heard a scuffle. Police officers identifying themselves. Bumps then a crash. The door jiggled again.

"Ellie, open the door. You're safe now."

She continued to rock. Sobs wracked her body. Sobs she hadn't known were coming from her. She buried her face further into her arms.

A few seconds later, the door flew open. The shower stall door opened, and a hand gripped her shoulder.

"Ellie, it's me, Wes Hoffman. We've got Ray in custody. He can't hurt you, honey."

His soothing voice slid over her, but she was locked in her fear. She couldn't make herself relax.

His hand smoothed over her hair before he carefully pulled her into his arms. "We won't let you down again, Ellie," he said quietly. "We won't let him hurt you."

Another man spoke a short distance away. The sound was muffled to Ellie's ears.

"Jeremy, get him the hell out of here before Jake shows up or Jake'll kill him," Wes directed.

Wes's hand tightened around her. "Ellie, honey, let me get you out of here. You're safe now."

She tensed. She was slow to process what went on around her. Was Ray still out there? She began to shake uncontrollably as what had happened started to sink in. Ray. On her doorstep. Oh God.

She heard the thump of heavy footsteps and then Jake burst into the bathroom. She felt him as much as she heard him.

"Oh God, Ellie!"

Wes pulled away from her and suddenly she was in Jake's arms. She threw herself into his embrace and held on tight. Hot tears coursed down her cheeks, wetting his shirt.

He stood up, picking her up with him. She clung to him, hoarse sobs ripping from her throat.

Jake carried her into the living room and sat down on the couch, her body cradled against his chest.

"Ellie, sweetheart, did he hurt you?"

She shook her head against his chest. Her hands crept around his neck, and she tried to control her trembling.

He caressed her hair over and over, and he smoothed kisses across her brow.

"You're all right now, Ellie. The bastard can't hurt you. I've got you, sweetheart. I won't let anyone hurt you again."

She finally relaxed against him, her eyes closing in relief. She lay limply in his arms, so worn out, so emotionally drained, she couldn't have moved if she wanted.

"Jake, I'll need a statement from her so we can hold the bastard," Wes said.

"Not now," Jake said harshly. "Can't you see she's scared out of her mind?"

She raised her head, surprised at how weak she felt. "No," she said softly. "I'll answer his questions."

"Are you sure?" Jake asked. His eyes held such tenderness, such *love*. Her chest tightened, and tears welled in her eyes once more.

She nodded and turned to Wes who sat across the living room in the armchair.

"Did he threaten you? Did he hurt you in any way?" Wes asked.

Jake tensed against her.

"No. He kept saying he was sorry," she mumbled. "I thought it was Jake at the door. I opened it and Ray was there. I lost it. It's just that..."

"You don't have to defend your reaction," Jake said gruffly.

"Not after what he's done to you."

"I grabbed the phone and hid in the bathroom," she continued. "He came to the bathroom door, but you got here before anything happened."

Wes nodded. Then he sighed and ran an aggravated hand through his hair. He looked apologetically at her and Jake.

"Best we can do is bust him on violating a restraining order. He'll be out before the paperwork is dry."

Ellie stiffened and turned her face back into Jake's chest.

"Just make damn sure he stays the hell away from her," Jake growled. "Tell him to go back to New York where he belongs and to leave her the hell alone. Because if I ever see him back here, I'll kill the son of a bitch."

"We'll find out what he was up to and make damn sure he doesn't pull a stunt like this again," Wes assured them.

"Thank you," Ellie said in a low voice. "Thank you for getting here so fast."

Wes stood. "It won't happen to you again, Ellie. Not on my watch. I'll have a squad car come by here regularly to check in on you."

"She won't be here," Jake said bluntly. "I'm taking her home with me."

Wes nodded. "Take care, Ellie." He turned and walked to the door.

Ellie let out an exhausted sigh as the door closed behind Wes. Jake's arms tightened around her.

"Let's get you some clothes and whatever else you need. You're going to stay with me for a while."

She nodded. As he started to pull away from her, she wrapped her arms around him and held him tightly against her.

"Thank you, Jake. Thank you for coming for me."

He kissed her temple and stroked her hair. "There should never be a doubt, Ellie. I'll always come for you. Now let's get you out of here. You're about to fall over."

Chapter Eleven

Ellie slept most of the afternoon. Jake had tucked her into his bed then climbed in beside her, covering every inch of her body with his. She knew it was his way of reassuring her, and she was glad for it. She had fallen asleep with her face snuggled against his shoulder.

The sun was setting when she awoke. She blinked a few times, trying to make sense of the events of the day. Had Ray really shown up on her door after all this time? Just a day after publicly accusing her of infidelity?

The phone rang, jarring her from her dream-like state. Beside her Jake cursed and rolled slightly so he could yank up the phone.

"Hello?"

There was a long pause as she listened intently.

"Fuck, no. I don't want her any more upset than she already is. Is he leaving, at least?"

Another long pause.

"Good. Maybe he'll stay away for good now."

Jake hung up and tossed the phone away from the bed.

"Jake?"

He turned back to her, curling his arms around her. "Sorry to wake you, sweetheart."

"I was already awake. What was that about?"

He stiffened. "It's nothing for you to worry about."

"Tell me."

He sighed. "Apparently Ray isn't leaving quietly. He's holding a press conference from the airport. He's flying out to Houston and then back to New York in an hour."

A tingle of dread snaked up her spine. "And when is the press conference?"

"In five minutes."

She paused for a long time, uncertainty rocketing through her veins. Finally, she took a deep breath. "Turn on the TV, Jake."

"Ellie, no," he said vehemently. "He's not worth it."

She slid a hand up his chest and touched his cheek. "You're here, Jake. Nothing can hurt me. I believe that. If he's going to cause more trouble, we need to be prepared. We need to know what he's saying if we're going to deal with it."

He blew out his breath in a long whoosh. "Are you sure?"

"As long as you're here with me, yeah, I'm sure."

He reached over to the nightstand and picked up the remote. He turned on the TV then flipped through the channels until he reached the local affiliate.

She sucked in her breath when she saw Ray standing in front of a crowd of reporters. He looked tired and haggard, a far cry from the smooth, polished man she'd seen on television just the day before. He resembled someone with the weight of the world on his shoulders.

Her brow crinkled in consternation as the cameras zoomed in closer and he began to speak. Jake's arms tightened around her in support.

"A few hours ago, I was arrested outside the home of my ex-wife Ellie Matthews."

A flash of something like regret glimmered in his eyes.

"I didn't go there to cause trouble," Ray continued. "I went there to apologize. I handled it all wrong. I shouldn't have just shown up like I did. I ended up scaring her, which was not my intention. Though, she has every right to fear me."

Ellie's mouth opened in shock. She remembered him saying over and over how sorry he was, but all she'd focused on was the fact that the monster who'd hurt her so many times was in striking distance again.

"You see, I lied in my interview with Marty Stevens yesterday. Ellie wasn't the problem in our marriage. I was. It took me watching the playback of that interview to see just how far I had sunk. You'll never know how hard it hit me to see the man I had become."

Her hand flew to her mouth, and she began to shake in Jake's arms.

Ray paused and looked down, no longer staring straight into the cameras. When he raised his head again, his eyes were moist with a sheen of tears.

"I-I abused my wife during our three-year marriage." He broke off again and ran a hand through his hair. "I took a beautiful, trusting woman, and I hurt her in unimaginable ways. I can't live with that knowledge any longer. I can no longer live a lie. She is innocent of the things I've accused her of. I am the monster here. I know she will never forgive me. What I did was unforgivable. I can only pray she finds happiness and peace and that maybe one day I can forgive *myself*."

As he paused again, the reporters, who had stood in stunned silence, surged forward, shouting a multitude of questions. Ray held his hand up, and they fell silent.

"I've spoken to my coach and to the team owner. I'll fulfill the terms of my contract, but I'm seeking out counseling. At the end of the two years, I'm retiring from the NFL."

He leaned forward, staring earnestly into the cameras. "I am truly sorry for all the pain I've caused you, Ellie." Tears fell freely down his face now. "I will never forgive myself for betraying your love and trust in me."

He turned into the shelter of his bodyguards and hustled away from the cameras toward the waiting prop jet in the background.

"Holy fuck," Jake muttered as he flipped the TV off.

Ellie sat there, her eyes wide with shock. She felt like a solid block of ice, no feeling except the cold.

Jake put his hand on her arm, his touch enquiring. "Ellie?

Sweetheart, talk to me. Are you all right?"

Her breath escaped in a stuttering hiccup, her body shaking with the effort it took. Jake took her gently in his arms, tenderly sliding his hands over her.

To say she was stunned was an understatement. She should be thrilled, though how could someone be thrilled when all the dirty secrets from her marriage had been spilled for the world to witness?

Shouldn't she feel vindicated? Exonerated? In a fit of conscience, Ray had admitted to the horrors he'd put her through.

Instead of feeling relieved, she wanted to crawl under a rock and die.

Jake rocked her back and forth. He kissed her on top of the head and murmured sweet words into her ear. She flinched away from him, suddenly feeling unworthy of his undying support.

"Ellie, don't," he protested. "Don't push me away. Not now. Not when you need me more than ever."

She couldn't meet his gaze.

"What is it?" he asked. "Ellie, this is good. Now the world will see him for the bastard he is. He'll never fool anyone again."

She raised her gaze to his. He recoiled for a brief moment. Was what he'd seen in her eyes so horrible?

"I thought people believing lies was the worst thing," she whispered. "I thought nothing could be worse than them believing I was the problem, that I had been unfaithful, a slut, a tramp. But I was wrong. Them knowing the *truth* is much, much worse."

"Ellie, no..."

She hugged her arms around herself, determined not to shed any more tears. Not over Ray. He wasn't worth it. Not even his sincere apology had changed the hatred that burned so deeply within her. In a situation like this, she was supposed to be the bigger person and offer her forgiveness, but it wasn't going to happen. She would never forgive him for nearly destroying her.

Jake sat next to her, bristling with all sorts of disagreement. He was preparing to launch into a whole host of reasons why he was right and she was wrong, and she was just too emotionally exhausted to listen.

"Not now, Jake," she said tiredly. "Please. I just need..." Hell, she didn't know what she needed. She closed her eyes. "I just need some time to think. Or not think. I just want to close my eyes for a while."

Jake leaned in and pressed a kiss to her forehead. His face was creased in concern. She knew he was worried, but she didn't have the fortitude to offer him any reassurances. Not when she couldn't even offer them to herself.

"Rest, sweetheart. This will be over soon. I promise."

Chapter Twelve

Ellie quietly disentangled herself from Jake's arms and eased out of the bed. It was still dark outside. The sun wouldn't rise for another half hour.

She'd lain awake most of the night, her mind in turmoil. Ray's announcement had shaken her badly. Brought years of shame rushing to the forefront. Suddenly her private life had been thrust into the national spotlight. But more importantly, it would be all over the small town she'd grown up in like wildfire.

All that bunk about facing the music and not hiding flew out of her mind as soon as Ray had opened his mouth and spilled their dirty secrets.

She couldn't live this way. Couldn't continue in a place where every time she looked in someone's eyes she saw pity or disapproval shining in the depths.

On silent feet, she went into the living room. She wasn't just going to walk out on Jake without a word. She wasn't a petulant child throwing a tantrum, and God knew, she didn't want to worry him.

She scribbled a note and left it in a spot she knew he'd find. She told the truth. Simply that she needed some time away. Alone. To think. To come to terms with the fact that once again, Ray had upended her life.

As she walked toward the door, she was overcome by sadness. She glanced back toward the bedroom where Jake lay sleeping. She missed him already, but she also knew she couldn't stay. Humiliation curled in her stomach, unsettling her, making a mess of her emotions.

She turned around and walked out the door.

Ellie parked her car outside the Forsythe and Turner construction office, grateful that Jake's truck wasn't there. She'd spent the last several hours making some hard choices. The very fact that she'd already encountered a number of people only too willing to either offer sympathies or their ill will for wrecking an NFL quarterback's career was enough to tell her she couldn't stay here.

She walked into her office and sat down to type up her resignation letter. It was the least they deserved. It seemed rather silly to make it official when she had no intention of sticking around to serve a notice. But it made her feel better to leave it less personal. If she didn't write it, she'd be stuck trying to explain why she was leaving. Far better to simply hand in a letter and leave.

After getting together the few things she wanted to take with her, she went back out to her car and headed for where she knew Luke to be. He had a meeting at one of the jobsites he managed, and he'd be there until noon. Since he and Jake split sites, Jake would be elsewhere.

Ten minutes later, she got out, pulling her jacket tighter around her to shield her from the cold. She'd barely taken two steps when Luke hurried her way, a concerned expression marring his face.

"Ellie, what are you doing here? Are you all right?" he asked as he walked up.

She swallowed nervously. Then she thrust the letter at him. "I came to give you this. And to thank you."

He looked down at the letter and slowly took it from her. "I don't like your tone, Ellie. It sounds too much like goodbye."

She shrugged, the nervous flutterings in her stomach kicking into overdrive as he opened the letter.

He swore softly under his breath then crumpled the paper in his hand.

"I won't accept this, Ellie."

She twisted her lips into a grimace. "You don't have a choice, Luke. It's what I have to do."

"No, it's what you *think* you have to do. Damn it, don't do this. Don't let that bastard win."

"I need to go now," she said softly.

He reached out a hand to stop her. "Wait. Just for a minute. Please."

"Why?" she asked in puzzlement.

He relaxed and looked at a point beyond her shoulder. She turned to see Jake tearing up the drive of the construction site.

She rounded on Luke. "You called him."

"As soon as I saw you drive up," he admitted. "He's worried sick about you, Ellie. You owe it to him to give this to him face-to-face. Not hide behind me."

Her gaze dropped in guilty admission. Luke leaned over and pulled her into a hug.

"I want you to be happy."

He gave her another squeeze then turned and walked away as Jake approached.

She watched as Jake closed the distance between them. Worry darkened his face. He looked as if he hadn't gotten any more sleep than she had the night before.

"Ellie, you had me worried," he chastised. "Don't ever do that again."

He pulled her roughly into his arms and held onto her for a long moment.

"What are you doing out here?" he asked as he drew away.

"I came to give Luke my resignation," she said quietly.

"What?"

She didn't respond.

"What the fuck is going on, Ellie?"

He prodded her chin up with his fingers when she wouldn't meet his gaze.

"I need to get away for a while," she whispered. "I can't stay here. Not now."

"So you're running," he said flatly.

She winced. "Maybe I am, Jake, but it's something I have to do. I can't stay here. It's already started. The pity, the judgment, the anger that I fucked up Ray Hatcher's career. I actually had someone stop me and say that if I had been more of a woman, maybe Ray and I wouldn't have had problems. Can you believe that?"

"Yes," he said calmly. "People say and do stupid shit all the time. That doesn't mean you let them run your life."

"I can't stay, Jake." She barely managed to say it without her voice cracking. "You're right in one aspect. I haven't really dealt with what happened. I just existed from one day to the next, ignoring the fallout, wishing it would just go away. And it *hurts*."

He slid a hand up her arm then over her shoulder to her neck. "I know you hurt, Ellie. God knows I'd do anything to make the pain stop. But this isn't going to help. You're running from me, and *that* hurts *me*."

She looked helplessly up at him.

"I'm torn," he admitted. "Half of me wants to make you stay. To drag you home with me and never let you go. The other half wants to let you go because I'd never do anything to hold you back."

She leaned into his arms and rested her forehead on his chest. "I love you, Jake. Really, I do."

"I know you do," he said quietly. "And I wish it was enough that I loved you."

He cupped her shoulders in his hands and held her away from him. "Just know something, Ellie. Wherever it is you end up, whenever you get tired of running, know that I'll be here waiting for you to come home."

Chapter Thirteen

Jake sat alone in his living room, staring at the brightly lit Christmas tree. Christmas Eve. How many Christmases had he sat here staring at his tree wishing for the same thing?

This year, he thought he'd finally gotten what he wanted. Ellie. In his arms, his bed, but more importantly, as a permanent part of his life.

His gaze fell to the lone Christmas present under the tree. An engagement ring he'd bought for Ellie a few days ago. Ironically enough, the day before she'd left town.

Three days. Three days of self-recrimination. Of loneliness and a sense of loss he could never hope to recover from.

In that time he'd argued with himself countless times. He shouldn't have let her go, let her walk away. But what choice had he had? He loved her too damn much to ever stand in her way.

He closed his eyes and brought his hands up to his face. How on earth could he face this Christmas without her? Knowing that he'd view every future Christmas as a reminder of all he'd lost.

Grief, raw and aching, razored through his system. He'd never loved another woman, and he knew without a doubt he wouldn't again. Not like Ellie.

The doorbell rang, wrenching him from his torment. He didn't want company. Especially not if it was Luke or the others coming over to spread their obnoxious Christmas cheer.

He sat there for a moment willing the intruder to go away.

He had no desire for anyone to see him in this state. Big Jake Turner, former NFL star, reduced to a quivering mass of agony.

When the doorbell rang again, he swore and shoved himself up from the couch. He stalked over to the door, in a hurry to get rid of whoever it was. Only when he opened the door and saw who was standing on the doorstep, he forgot all about making her leave. Forgot everything but the fact that Ellie stood there staring nervously up at him.

She shivered, and he hastily pulled her inside.

"You're going to freeze to death," he said as he pushed her toward the fireplace.

It was a lame greeting, but he couldn't think of one single thing to say to her. He was excited and scared out of his mind all at the same time. Had she come back? Or was she simply back to collect her things and clear out her house? He couldn't stand another goodbye. Not when it would tear his guts right out to watch her walk away again.

He wanted to touch her, taste her, take her to bed and make love to her until she never wanted to leave.

"How have you been?" he asked.

She bit her bottom lip and looked at him with wide blue eyes. Eyes that reflected clear uncertainty. Was she worried he'd kick her out?

She pulled a small gift-wrapped box from her pocket and held it out to him. Her hands trembled, making the ribbon on the present wiggle about.

"What's this?" he asked dumbly as he took the box.

"Open it."

He untied the ribbon and tore off the paper. It dropped to the floor as he fumbled with the box. When he opened it, he saw a single piece of paper inside.

Slowly, he drew it out and unfolded it. In her neat handwriting she'd written: *There isn't a box big enough to hold my love for you. But it will always belong to you. As I will.*

He folded the paper reverently, afraid to believe the implications of what he'd read. He searched her face for some sign of what was going through her beautiful head.

"Do you mean it, Ellie?"

She looked at him, so much love reflected in her clear blue eyes. Tears filled them, threatening to spill over her lids.

"Do you still want me, Jake?" she whispered.

Ellie watched as a multitude of emotions crossed his face. Then he grabbed her with both hands and yanked her into his arms. He crushed her to him, holding her tightly.

"God, Ellie, of course I still want you. I've always wanted you. Where have you been, sweetheart? Promise me you'll never leave like that again."

She pulled away and smiled up at him. "I know I've been an idiot, Jake, and I'm sorry. But I had to get away and clear my head. I was so mired in humiliation and shame that I couldn't see what was important. And what was important, the only thing that mattered in the end, was that you loved me."

"I do love you," he growled. "So damn much."

She sucked in her breath and knew she had to say everything, get it out so she could put it behind her. "For so long, I lived with such shame. I blamed myself for the things Ray did. Even though I knew he was a bastard and nothing I could have done would have changed that, I still couldn't look logically at it. All I knew was I felt dirty, and I never wanted anyone to know my secrets. It was bad enough you'd seen me at my worst moment, but I couldn't bear for the rest of the world to know."

"Oh, sweetheart," Jake said in a voice that sounded like his heart was breaking.

"I never wanted anyone to know what really happened," she admitted. "If Ray hadn't gone public, I would have gone to my grave with those secrets. It's probably wrong of me, but I couldn't wipe away the shame I felt. I couldn't bear the thought of having to face people who knew the truth. Didn't want to see the pity or the scorn. So I ran, thinking if I could go away someplace where nobody knew me, I wouldn't be so humiliated, I wouldn't feel so hurt. I was wrong. It was all still there, only now I was faced with losing the one person in my life who loved me even knowing of all those terrible things."

"What changed your mind?" he prompted.

She chanced a look back into his eyes. "You did," she said softly. "I don't want to live without you, Jake. And I can stand anything as long as you're mine. I've been a terrible coward, but not any longer. I won't let my pride ruin the best chance I'll ever have at love."

He cupped her face in his hand and tenderly pressed his lips to hers. Warmth spread through her frozen heart. She began to rapidly thaw from the days of isolation and pain. She moaned a desperate, needy sound as she twined her arms around his neck and returned his kiss for all she was worth.

His other hand dug into her hair, and his body moved urgently against hers. "I've missed you so much," he said hoarsely. "If you ever try to leave me again, Ellie, I won't be so understanding. I'll drag your ass back home where you belong and I'll tie you to my bed for a week."

She smiled as their foreheads touched. "In that case, I might stage a runaway."

He smacked her on the ass, but his face had dissolved into an expression of relief. Suddenly his eyes gleamed, and he smiled broadly.

"Wait here. I have something for you."

She watched as he hurried over to the tree and bent to retrieve the single present lying underneath. He returned to where she was standing and held out the gift.

"I bought this for you before you left. I wasn't sure I'd have a chance to give it to you, but I kept it in case."

The paper crinkled under her fingers as she lifted the edge and tore. Inside the square box was a jeweler's box. Her hand shook as she pulled it out. She glanced up at Jake then back down at the small box.

"Go on," he said huskily.

She pried the lid open to see a diamond solitaire glitter back at her. "Oh..."

Her gaze shot back up to Jake's face.

"Will you marry me, Ellie?" he asked in a gruff voice. "God knows I've waited long enough for you. Will you put me out of my misery and promise to take care of me until I'm old and gray and incontinent?"

She laughed and threw her arms around his neck, the box still gripped in one hand. "That was the worst proposal I've ever heard!"

He pulled her from his neck and looked at her with such serious eyes that her heart leapt and stuttered.

"I love you. I've loved you for a long time. I don't want to ever lose you again, Ellie. Not even for a day. I want you to marry me so we can grow old together and have our children drive us insane. I can't imagine my life any other way."

Tears shimmered in her vision. "Yes, I'll marry you, Jake. I can't imagine being crazy with anyone else."

The Christmas tree twinkled in their periphery.

"I'll even let you keep your damn colored lights," she said.

He threw back his head and laughed. "Do I get the flashing kind to go outside?"

"Don't push your luck," she grumbled. "We'll let the kids vote on whether or not we turn our house into a neon sign."

"Now that is an idea I can deal with," Jake said. "What do you say we start on the tiebreaking vote right now?"

Overheard

Chapter One

The sun shone high overheard. The sky blazed brilliant blue, and not a single cloud marred the canvas. Sixty-five degrees on the first of February. It was what Gracie Evans loved most about living in South Texas. By the middle of the week, another cold front was poised to move through, dropping temps into the forties. Oh, the horror.

Gracie stretched in her lawn chair and watched lazily as Jeremy Miller tended the barbeque while his wife, Gracie's best friend Michelle, hovered nearby.

"Come on, Gracie, get up and play," Wes Hoffman hollered from the yard.

She glanced over to see him and Luke Forsythe tossing a football back and forth. Boneheads. She was more than comfortable right where she was. After a long week at work and not sleeping worth a damn last night, sitting up to eat was about as energetic as she planned to get.

Luke flopped onto the chair next to her. "What's up, Gracie? You're not usually such a stick-in-the-mud."

She shot him a dirty look. "Busy week at work. I'm just tired."

Of course the worst part of the week had been last night. Her date with her current boyfriend had ended with the usual boring obligatory sex, and quite frankly, she was tired of being disappointed in that area. She'd stayed up most of the night mustering the courage to call him this morning and break things off.

He hadn't taken it well.

"Earth to Gracie."

She blinked and looked back at Luke. "Sorry," she mumbled. "Lot on my mind."

Luke gave her a curious stare but seemed to sense she wasn't in the mood to talk. He got up and ambled over to Jeremy. Wes joined them on the patio, a beer in hand.

Gracie let her gaze flit appreciatively over the men. Not bad, considering they were her best friends and all. She wouldn't mind finding someone like Luke or Wes. Problem was she usually ended up with the frogs. Ugh.

Michelle eased into the chair next to Gracie, and Gracie looked over with a smile. "How you feeling, girlfriend?"

Michelle returned her smile. "Good. Tired but good."

Gracie eyed Michelle's cute pregnancy pooch with a little jealousy. Jeremy was over the moon in love with his wife, and Gracie wondered what it felt like to have that sort of devotion. From what Michelle said, Jeremy was also dynamite in bed. Really, what more could you ask for in a man? Undying love and the know-how in the sack.

Gracie shook her head. She was really going to have to up her standards when it came to boyfriends. Boyfriend. Maybe that was her problem. She didn't need a boy. She wanted a man. Someone who could take her fantasies and make them reality.

"You sure are quiet today, Gracie."

Gracie grimaced. "Sorry. I broke up with Keith this morning."

Michelle jerked around in the lawn chair and all but pounced on Gracie. "Gracie, you didn't!"

"Shhh," Gracie hissed. She glanced up to see if the guys had heard. They already gave her a hard time about the men she chose to go out with. They'd be gleeful that her current relationship hadn't worked out. The *I told you so*s were already ringing in her ears.

"What happened?" Michelle whispered.

"I'll talk to you about it later."

Michelle huffed but didn't protest further.

The two women lounged in the chairs while the men puttered around the grill. Gracie savored these times with the people she considered her best friends.

They got together pretty much every weekend. During hunting season, they spent weekends at the camp and hunted the mornings and evenings. When the weather was warm, they spent all their time at the beach, fishing and soaking up the sun. Gracie loved their group. She felt free to be herself.

Jeremy and Michelle had been married a year and they hosted most of the get-togethers. Jeremy and Wes were both local cops, while Luke was a building contractor.

Wes was handsome in a carefree *I don't give a shit* kind of way. He had blondish brown hair, and in the summer, it was liberally streaked with lighter shades. His sense of humor was what Gracie loved the most about him, that and he didn't tend to get his underwear in a bunch at the least provocation. A more laid-back guy you wouldn't find.

Luke, yeah, he was attractive. Blue eyes, light brown hair and abs you could bounce a nickel off. But he was also a pain in the ass. A mouth-wateringly gorgeous pain in the ass, but an irritant nonetheless. His and Gracie's relationship was a study in competition. Neither could stand to lose, and neither would ever back down from a dare.

Every year the outhunt and outfish contest usually boiled down to Luke and Gracie. Last year, Gracie had crowed when she'd bagged the biggest buck any of the group had ever killed. Luke had sworn to one-up her the following season.

But still, she wouldn't trade him for anything. The group worked well together. They were extremely loyal, which was why she didn't want the guys to know she'd broken up with Keith. They'd make a huge deal out of it, and she simply wanted to forget the whole thing.

A shadow fell over her chair, and she looked up to see Wes standing over her with a beer in hand. He pressed the cold bottle to her arm, and she yelped.

He laughed. "Thought you might want something to drink,

Gracie."

"Gee, thanks."

He handed the beer to her and ambled off again.

"Lug nut," she grumbled.

Michelle laughed. "You know you love him. He's cute when he's not being a pain in the ass."

Gracie nodded. "Yep, the two days of the year he's not a royal pain, he is downright cute."

"I heard that!" Wes called from the grill.

"You were supposed to," Gracie returned sweetly.

"I'm about ready to dish it up," Jeremy said. "Michelle, if you want to set the table, I'll have it up in about fifteen minutes."

"I'll help." Gracie heaved herself out of her chair.

Luke turned and watched Gracie follow Michelle into the house. Her auburn curls jiggled down her back as she walked. He'd always loved her hair. It fit her carefree personality perfectly—only she didn't seem so carefree today. He wondered what was bothering her. It wasn't like her to be quiet and withdrawn. And he didn't buy that line about a busy week at work. Gracie could do her job in her sleep.

Jeremy rammed a tray into his gut. "Do me a favor and take this in to Michelle. Tell her the rest will be a few minutes."

"Sure."

Luke walked toward the sliding door of the patio and eased inside. He strode through the living room and toward the kitchen. When he reached the doorway, Gracie's voice stopped him.

"I called him this morning and broke up with him."

Luke backed away and stood to the side. She'd broken up with Keith? Somehow that didn't surprise him. The guy was a complete pussy. No way he could keep pace with someone of Gracie's caliber.

He strained to hear the rest of the conversation.

"You called him the morning after you had sex and dumped him?" Michelle asked in disbelief.

"Yeah," Gracie replied.

Whoa. Harsh. Luke couldn't wait to hear why.

"Good God, girl. That must have been crushing to his ego," Michelle continued.

Luke nodded his agreement.

He heard Gracie sigh. "I don't care, Michelle. I'm tired of hooking up with guys who suck in bed. And I don't mean my tits either."

Michelle dissolved into laughter, and Luke's eyebrows shot up.

"Was he that bad?"

"He wasn't good," Gracie muttered. She sighed again. "Damn it, Chelle. I want something…"

Luke nearly hurt himself trying to press his ear closer to the doorway. What did Gracie want? This had to be good.

"I want someone who lights my fires. Who makes me think of nothing but taking every stitch of clothing off him and licking him from head to toe."

Luke shifted, an uncomfortable surge of heat racing to his crotch. Damn if the woman wasn't direct. He liked that in a girl.

"That's the problem with you, Gracie. You always settle for men who can't stand up to you," Michelle interjected.

Luke nodded in agreement. Michelle was right on there.

Another sigh from Gracie. "I want someone who can make my fantasies come alive. Is that too much to ask? A guy who can be adventurous in bed and not come across like a freaking fruit loop?"

Fantasies? Luke shifted again and rubbed his palm across his shirt. Gracie had fantasies? Who knew?

"What kind of adventures are we talking about here?" Michelle asked in a cautious voice.

Yeah, what kind of fantasies? Damn it, he only had a few minutes before Jeremy was going to come busting in with the rest of the food. If that happened, he'd never find out what made Gracie tick.

There was a long, silent pause.

"Nothing illegal," Gracie cracked. "At least I don't think they are."

"Quit joking and spill it," Michelle said. "The guys will be in soon."

"Oh, I fantasize about bondage, a little spanking, maybe a whip or two. The idea of being tied up gets me hotter than I'd like to admit," Gracie said ruefully. "But..."

But what? Luke wanted to yell.

"More than anything I'd love to experience a ménage."

"Gracie!" Michelle exclaimed. "Really?"

"Yeah," Gracie said in a low voice. "Two sexy men, all their attention on me, pleasuring me? I think about it a lot. I just don't know how to make it happen."

"Holy shit," Michelle whispered loudly. "Have you considered taking out an adult ad or something?"

"Yeah, I have," Gracie replied. "But it scares me. Who knows what kind of freaks are out there?"

Adult ad? Luke wanted to march in and throttle her. He would have, but he was still thrown for a loop by what she'd admitted. Gracie, *his* Gracie, had triple X fantasies?

"Face it, Chelle. I'm not sure there's a man out there who can satisfy my needs in bed. Maybe I'm expecting too much. I just know I'm not settling for less ever again. I'm done with the Keiths of this world. If I can't find someone, I'll stick to my toys and self-gratification."

Not sure there's a man out there who could satisfy her, huh. Luke's mind whirled with all he'd overheard. So she wanted a threesome. It was obvious Luke had spent far too much time looking at Gracie as a best buddy and a hunting/fishing partner. It certainly wasn't every day he found a woman who wanted all the things that had gotten him tossed out of so many women's beds.

Ménage. She wanted a ménage. He couldn't wait to talk to Wes. He had a feeling his buddy would be very interested in what their good pal Gracie wanted out of her sex life.

Man enough? She didn't realize it yet, but she'd thrown down the challenge. And damn if he wasn't going to answer it.

Chapter Two

Gracie dug into her food, sighing with pleasure as the tender meat hit her tongue.

"Good?" Jeremy asked.

"Run away with me," Gracie declared. "What does Chelle have that I don't? We can live on your barbeque and be beach bums."

Jeremy grinned and started to reply.

Gracie held up a hand. "No, don't answer that. I'm not up for a list of the ways I don't measure up."

Wes and Jeremy looked curiously at her while Luke made it a point to stare down at his plate. Gracie cringed. Instead of coming out jokingly as she'd intended, the statement sounded sad and resigned.

She glanced over at Michelle and made an *oops* face the others couldn't see. Then she focused back on her food, cutting another bite of the brisket.

Her breakup with Keith bothered her more than she wanted to admit. Not only had the sex been a disaster, but his reaction to the surprise she'd planned still made her cringe in embarrassment. He'd made her feel like a freak. Not what a woman wanted when she was trying to be wild and sexy.

Weren't men supposed to enjoy that sort of thing? Didn't they all complain because women weren't adventurous enough in bed? Ha! She'd yet to find a man who liked sex with the frequency and imagination she did.

Maybe she *was* a freak.

She cleared her throat and turned to Luke. "How's Ellie doing? I haven't seen her much since the wedding. Jake seems awfully protective of her."

"He has a reason to be. But she's doing good. They seem happy."

"Isn't she going to counseling?" Michelle asked.

Luke nodded. "Yeah, that whole thing with Ray really fucked her up."

"Stupid son of a bitch," Wes muttered. "I don't trust that little breakdown he had on public television. Seems too calculating to me."

Jeremy raised his brow. "You think he'll try something?"

"Not unless he has a death wish," Luke muttered. "Jake will kill him if he comes near Ellie again."

"And I won't exactly be knocking myself out to stop him," Wes said.

Gracie shook her head. "Ellie's a sweet girl. I hate that she's been through so much. But Jake's good for her."

"He'd be good for me too," Michelle broke in, a devilish glint to her eye.

"Hey," Jeremy protested as he reached over to tweak Michelle's arm.

Gracie laughed. God, she loved these guys. She could never stay down in the dumps for long around them. "If Chelle doesn't want you, Jeremy, you're welcome at my house."

"Are you propositioning my husband?" Michelle demanded.

Jeremy rubbed a hand over his chin. "I kind of like being fought over."

"Catfights are sexy," Wes said with a snicker.

Gracie rolled her eyes. "Like any girl has a chance with Jeremy. He's so gaga over Michelle, it's nauseating."

"Just like I like him," Michelle said with a smug grin.

Michelle stood to clear the table, and Gracie got up to help. As Michelle began running water in the sink, she looked out the kitchen window and tensed.

"Uh oh, Gracie."

Gracie didn't like the sound of that.

Jeremy evidently didn't either. He went to stand behind his wife so he could see out.

Michelle turned around to Gracie. "Keith just pulled up."

"Oh great." Gracie plunked down the plates she was holding.

"Trouble, Gracie?" Wes asked in a concerned voice.

She flashed him a reassuring smile. "Nothing I can't handle." She walked toward the door, determined to meet Keith outside rather than take the inevitable confrontation inside. "Y'all excuse me for a second. This shouldn't take long."

Luke followed her with his gaze until she left the house with a bang. Wes glanced over at him questioningly, but Luke played dumb. He didn't want to let on that he'd overheard Gracie's conversation with Michelle.

"What's going on with those two?" Jeremy asked Michelle as they continued to stare out the window.

"She broke up with him this morning," Michelle murmured.

Wes got up from the table, carrying the plates Gracie had left. He walked to the sink and set them down before peering out the window himself. Luke was dying to do the same, but he made himself sit and appear only mildly interested.

"Can't say it surprises me," Wes said as he returned to sit at the table. "She needs a man she can't run over so easily."

Luke looked at his friend in surprise. On that point they agreed, though they'd never discussed Gracie's love life before. "He looks angry," Michelle said anxiously.

Both Wes and Luke shot to their feet and walked to the window. They were all understandably wary after all Ellie had endured at her ex-husband's hands. No way would they stand by and let Gracie take the brunt of some punk's anger. Keith did seem pretty pissed, and Gracie took a step backwards as they all watched.

"I'm going out there," Luke muttered. "I want to make sure the dickhead doesn't get carried away."

Michelle's frown deepened as she watched her friend. "Jeremy and Wes are the cops, maybe they should go."

"More reason for me to go," Luke said. "I can get away with decking the asshole better than they can."

He didn't wait for a response. He strode for the door and quietly let himself out.

Neither Gracie nor Keith must have heard him because they never turned around. Luke eased down the steps into the yard. Their heated conversation filled his ears, and he stopped so he could listen from a distance.

"Damn it, Gracie, what was I supposed to do? You acted like some kind of a whore. I wasn't expecting it."

Gracie clenched her fists at her sides.

"Just because I suggested we do something other than the usual suck your dick and missionary, that makes me a whore?" she all but yelled.

"Be quiet, for God's sake!"

"No, Keith, I won't be quiet. It's over. I don't know why you're here, but it sure as hell won't change my mind. I said all I had to say this morning."

"You're dumping me? Shit, Gracie, you're being unreasonable. You should have warned me or something. You had *nipple* rings of all things. Like some kind of cheap tramp. What on earth possessed you? Is that what you made me wait a month without sex for? So you could spring this weird-ass surprise on me? And then you go on about how you want me to take control and for you not to have to decide how we do it all the time. Give a guy a break."

Nipple rings? Oh Jesus. Gracie had nipple rings. This most certainly was a new development. Luke had seen her in a bikini on many occasions, and he damn sure would have noticed nipple rings.

So Gracie was trying to branch out and the pussy boyfriend had thrown a fit. Well, good for her for dumping him. He obviously didn't deserve her.

"That's exactly what I'm doing," Gracie said coldly. "Giving you a break. We're done. *Finito.*"

Anger flashed on Keith's face, and Luke started forward.

"You teasing bitch," Keith snarled.

He made a grab for her arm, but Gracie sidestepped him and rammed her knee into his nuts.

"Cock-sucking bastard!" she hissed as he fell to the ground.

Luke stepped between them and hauled Keith up by his shirt. The man was still pale with pain and clutching his dick.

Luke slammed him against Keith's truck and got in his face. "If I ever see you within ten feet of Gracie again, I'll make what she just did look like a blowjob. You got me?"

Keith grunted and struggled to get loose. "Yeah, I get it. Get your fucking hands off me. You're welcome to the psycho bitch."

Luke decked him. Keith fell to the ground, blood spurting from his nose, and he grabbed his face, howling in pain.

He scrambled to his feet and fumbled to open his truck door. "You son of a bitch! If you broke my nose, I'm pressing charges."

Luke chuckled and jerked his thumb in the direction of the kitchen window. "You do that, pussy boy. But you ought to know two cops are watching from that window over there, and I imagine they'll swear they didn't see any such thing."

Keith threw himself into the truck, swearing and swiping at the blood running down his face. In a few seconds, he spun out of the driveway, spewing a trail of rocks and dirt several feet high.

Luke turned back to Gracie whose eyes were wide with astonishment.

"You okay?" he asked gently.

"Yeah, I'm good." Her eyebrows arched in question. "What the hell was that all about?"

Luke knew why she was confused. He'd never intruded on her business like that. Gracie was more than able to take care of herself. He admired that about her.

He shrugged and put a hand on her shoulder. "Just looked like you could use the help, that's all."

"Yeah, well, thanks," she mumbled as they started back toward the house.

She stopped at the steps and glanced up at him, her bottom lip stuck between her teeth.

"You didn't...you didn't hear our conversation, did you?"

Luke almost smiled. Yeah, he supposed Gracie would about die if she knew he'd overheard that and more. From what he'd gleaned from her conversation with Michelle and then her fight with Keith, it would appear she was spreading her wings a bit and venturing into new territory. Territory he was intimately familiar with.

"Nah, I'd just come out when he made a move toward you," he lied.

Her shoulders slumped in relief. "Well, thanks."

"No problem. What are friends for?"

He threw his arm around her neck, letting his hand dangle over her shoulder, something he'd done a million times before. Only now, he was very aware of the proximity of his hand to her breasts. And those nipple rings he was dying to see.

Chapter Three

"So you going to tell me what the hell went on out there earlier?" Wes asked as he popped open another beer.

Luke flopped onto his couch and took a long swig of his own beer. He and Wes had left Jeremy's earlier and had ended up at Luke's place. Luke knew Wes was curious over his interference, not that Wes would have done things any differently if he'd been outside when Keith made his move at Gracie.

He took another fortifying gulp before he eased the bottle from his lips. "Let's just say it's been an interesting and informative day."

Wes leaned back in the armchair and propped his feet up on Luke's coffee table. "How so?"

Luke shook his head. Where to start? With the easy part, he guessed. "When Keith started ripping on Gracie, and she told him to take a hike. He went after her and Gracie kneed him in the balls."

Wes performed a mock salute with his beer bottle. "Good for her."

"I broke his nose for good measure."

Wes shook his head. "Shit, tell me I'm not going to have to arrest your ass when he presses charges."

"He's a pussy. Besides, I told him you and Jeremy were watching and would swear you didn't see anything."

"Gee, thanks," Wes said dryly. "Just what I need, to be arrested with you."

Luke fiddled with his beer, tapping his finger in restless staccato against the cool glass. He hesitated to tell Wes what he'd overheard. Why, he couldn't say. They'd never exactly been discreet with each other, and he knew Wes would find it as surprising as he had. But something held him back.

"What's eating you?" Wes spoke up, intruding on Luke's thoughts. "You've been acting weird all afternoon. You said the day had been informative. So what's the news?"

Luke sighed and leaned forward to set his beer on the coffee table. "It's about Gracie."

Wes cocked an eyebrow. "What about her? You weren't really surprised she dumped her pussy boyfriend, were you?"

Luke shook his head. "I'm not talking about the wimp, and no, I'm not altogether surprised she dumped him. Even less so after what I heard her talking to Michelle about."

"Ah hell, man, what were you doing eavesdropping on the girls? Gracie will kick your ass if she finds out."

Luke grinned. Yeah, she wouldn't hesitate to lay him out. He got the oddest tingle just thinking about her getting in his face. He shook his head. It was the nipple rings, it had to be. Hell.

He cleared his throat. "She, uh, well, she said some interesting things."

Wes dropped his feet to the floor with a thud. "Now you've got me curious. What the hell did she say?"

"Apparently she dumped the pussy because he sucked in bed."

"Yeah, well, again, that's no surprise. She probably ate him alive."

Luke cocked his head sideways and stared at his friend. "Tell me something, Wes. Have you ever thought about having sex with Gracie?"

Wes choked on his beer and coughed several times in succession. "Sex? With Gracie? Shit man, no, not really. I mean she's hot, don't get me wrong. Seriously hot. But—"

"Seriously hot, huh. So you have thought about it, you lying sack of shit."

"You have eyes, man. The girl is a walking goddess. What guy wouldn't get a hard-on around her?"

"Well, get this." Luke leaned toward Wes. "I overheard her telling Michelle that she was tired of men not satisfying her in bed. That she has fantasies she wants to live out."

Wes sat up straighter. "What kind of fantasies?"

Luke shrugged casually, but his blood raced just thinking about all she'd said. "Bondage, a little spanking...and she wants to take on two guys at the same time."

"Whoa." Wes flopped back in his chair. "She said all that?"

"There's more," Luke continued. "Apparently she wanted pussy boy to do some experimenting in bed and he freaked. He called her a whore."

"That little son of a bitch," Wes growled. "I knew I should have gone outside with you."

"She has nipple rings. Must be recent. Keith didn't receive the news so well judging by his comments."

"Holy fucking shit. Nipple rings?"

"Yeah. Now tell me you aren't picturing Gracie in the buff with nipple rings dangling from those perfect breasts."

"Jesus."

"My thoughts exactly," Luke mumbled.

"She wants two guys? She said that?"

"Oh, hell yeah. She said that and a lot more. She wants a guy who isn't afraid to call the shots. Someone who will tie her up, spank her ass and fuck her brains out."

"Goddamn."

Luke laughed. "Is that all you can say?"

"I'm speechless."

"Glad I'm not the only one fucked up over it."

"Does she know you overheard her?"

"Hell no. She wouldn't speak to me for a year."

Wes fell silent, his eyes thoughtful. Luke knew Wes's brain was spinning a mile a minute. He also knew Wes was rapidly coming to the same conclusion he had.

"Hell, if that's what she wants..."

"Yeah," Luke said. "Tell me you aren't thinking the same thing I am."

Wes grunted. "I'd have to be fucking gay not to react to something like that. I mean, she's hot. I've always thought so."

"Valentine's is just two weeks away. Should be enough time for you to make arrangements to be off work."

Wes's eyes narrowed. "What are you thinking about?"

Luke took in a deep breath then grinned. "Well, we've already established the fact that Gracie is hot. We're both attracted to her. Neither of us has any problem with nipple rings or bondage, and we have considerable experience in the threesome arena. So it seems to me that maybe we should give Gracie a Valentine's Day to remember."

"What if she won't go for it?" Wes asked. "I don't want to piss her off and I sure don't want to mess up my friendship with her. We have too much fun for that shit."

"She'll go for it."

He'd seen the longing in her eyes, the need for something she probably couldn't even explain. He knew it because he'd felt the same thing. He also knew that he was the man who could give it to her.

Wes scrubbed a hand over his closely shaved goatee. "I don't know, man. It's not like we're going to fuck some chick we won't ever see again. This is Gracie we're talking about. What happens when it's over with? I don't want there to be any awkward shit."

"You're overthinking this," Luke said impatiently. "We give Gracie an experience she won't ever forget. We show her things she's been craving. If anything it makes us even closer. I mean there's no way in hell I'd fuck her and just go on like nothing ever happened. We both like her a hell of a lot. More than any other woman apart from Michelle, that's for sure. I don't see the problem here."

A peculiar expression crossed his face. "Just how much do you like her?"

Luke shifted uncomfortably. What the hell kind of question was that? "I-I care about her," he said lamely.

Wes continued to stare at him. "Do you have a thing for her?"

"Shut the fuck up," Luke growled. "Jesus, this is sex. Gracie's our friend. Our very gorgeous, hot friend. You can't tell me you wouldn't like to get next to her."

Wes took a sip of his beer. "No, I can't tell you that. But wanting something or knowing I'd enjoy it is different than actually doing it. Look, I just don't want to fuck things up between us all."

"What if she wanted it?" Luke challenged. "I mean what if she wanted what we could give her? Would you be so reluctant then?"

Wes thought for a minute then shook his head. "Hell no. I just don't want to hurt her. That's all I'm saying."

"Well, shit, Wes. Do you think I'd do anything to hurt her? She's one of my best friends. I want to make it good for her."

"You're serious about this."

"Fuck. No, I've just spent the last ten minutes going on about my plan to seduce Gracie for nothing."

"No need to be sarcastic," Wes said with a chuckle. "Okay, you've convinced me. This is your idea, so you plan it. Tell me when and where to show up. I'll be there. But if she shows any sign of not wanting this, I'm out."

Luke scowled at him. "No shit, dumbass. It's not my plan to rape her for God's sake. But I'm telling you, she wants something. Something she doesn't quite understand but knows she wants. You didn't hear the things she said or the *way* she said them. And I think I can give her what she wants."

Wes studied him with that cop look he was so famous for. "Yeah, maybe you can."

Chapter Four

Gracie twisted restlessly in her chair and flipped another contract in the to-be-signed pile. Mondays were always busy. Tickets to process, contracts to go over. It was dull, tedious work, but it paid the bills, and she could do it with half a brain. Important when the other half was consumed with her nonexistent sex life.

Yesterday's encounter with Keith had only reinforced that she'd made the right decision. She still felt the uncomfortable burn of embarrassment that Luke had stepped in when Keith had gone over the line. She didn't like Luke seeing yet another of her failures.

Her office door swung open, and she looked up to see Luke standing there. She blinked, wondering if she'd conjured him. Then she smiled.

"Hey, what are you doing here?"

He ambled further into her office, his thumbs thrust into his jeans pockets. Jeans that were tightly molded to his muscular legs. His leather jacket hung loosely to his waist, and underneath she could see he wore a simple T-shirt. Obviously a day he wasn't meeting prospective clients.

"Hey, Gracie," he said, returning her smile. "I was in the neighborhood and wondered if you wanted to have lunch with me."

Her smile widened. "Barbeque?"

"As if I'd suggest anything else."

She made a grab for her jacket on the floor at her feet

before standing. "As long as you're buying."

As she rounded the desk, he pressed his hand to the small of her back to usher her out the door. It was an intimate gesture, one that puzzled her. He was usually all about punching her in the arm or pointing out a nonexistent spot on her shirt so she'd look down and he could chuck her nose.

They walked outside, and Gracie shivered slightly. Damn cold front had moved in overnight. The sky was overcast and gray, and a cold drizzle escaped in fine droplets.

She slid into Luke's truck and sank into the heated leather seats with a contented sigh. She'd given him hell when he bought the truck. Top of the line, tricked out, no expense spared. He spent money like it was nothing. But then he did have a lot of it to burn.

"Cold?" Luke started the engine and turned the heat on full blast.

She grumbled under her breath and stuck her hands over the vents. He knew damn well she was freezing her ass off. Anything below fifty degrees and she was breaking out the winter parka.

They drove a few miles to the Barbeque Shack and pulled into the crowded parking lot. Aside from a Mexican restaurant and a hole-in-the-wall burger joint, this was the only place to eat without driving into the neighboring town. Which was fine with Gracie, because if it wasn't grilled and slathered with barbeque sauce, it wasn't worth eating.

Luke walked ahead of her, treating her to a glimpse of those very tight jeans stretched across a very nice ass. His hair was all messed up as usual, but that was Luke. The wind blew at it, ruffling it up and sending it scattering across his head. She nearly reached up to smooth it, but caught herself before she did.

He held the door open for her, and she walked by him, sniffing appreciatively as the mixture of leather and the smell that was Luke sifted through her nostrils.

Minutes later, they were sitting at a table by the window sipping their drinks and waiting for their order to come. Luke leaned back in his chair and gazed lazily at her.

"Tell me something, Gracie. How come you and I haven't ever gone out?"

She nearly choked on her drink. She set it down with a plunk and wheezed as she tried to make the last swallow go down.

"What?"

His eyes narrowed. "You heard me."

"Well hell, Luke, I don't know what to say."

Her mind reeled as she stared at him. What on earth had possessed him?

"We like each other, right?"

"Well, of course," she said crossly. She wasn't sure she liked where this conversation was heading, though. Now was not the time for Luke to get some strange bug up his ass.

She was feeling oddly vulnerable after her latest dead-end relationship. Like she was some freak of nature, destined to never find a guy who got her, much less one who could satisfy her.

"We get along great. We understand each other," Luke continued.

Yeah, right. If he only knew. He understood she was a nice girl who kept picking the wrong guy. He had no idea that underneath all the sweetness was a woman itching to break out. She was tired of being good. The girl next door. She wanted to be bad. And she was damn sure tired of being viewed as little sister, good pal, hunting and fishing partner.

"Is there a point to all this?" she asked.

"Yeah," he said slowly. "There is. I'm trying to figure out why we've never gone out on a date."

She stared at him for a long second, debating whether to even go there. But she wasn't a liar, and she wasn't big on playing games. So she just told the truth.

"Because you never asked," she said softly.

They were interrupted by the waitress bringing their plates. Gracie was grateful for the break because Luke was staring at her like he could crawl right under her skin and see everything she was hiding.

The waitress took her sweet time in leaving, and as she started away, she slid a napkin across the table toward Luke. Gracie didn't give it a single thought until Luke picked it up and glanced over his shoulder, a look of surprise on his face.

"What's wrong?" Gracie asked, finally breaking the silence.

Luke turned back around, shaking his head. "She gave me her phone number. Wrote it on the napkin."

A surge of irritation rippled through her chest. "That's probably one reason we've never gone out," she muttered.

"But you were sitting right there," he said, ignoring her comment. "How the hell did she know we weren't here together, that you aren't my girlfriend or something?"

Gracie burst out laughing. "Luke, are you feeling well today? I swear you aren't yourself. Half the town is used to seeing us together. No one's ever assumed you were interested in me."

"Well, what do they know?" he growled.

He stared across the table at her, his blue eyes sparking with something she wasn't used to seeing. At least not when he was looking at *her*.

"I'm asking now, Gracie."

"You want us to go out? As in a real date? I mean, because we usually hook up on the weekends anyway."

He dropped the napkin and leaned forward impatiently. "I mean you and me on a date. No Jeremy, Michelle or Wes. Friday night."

She blinked in surprise. A peculiar sensation ran circles in her belly. She felt *nervous*. For God's sake. This was Luke.

A real date. She sank back in her chair, still staring at him like he'd lost his mind.

"Well?"

"Uh...okay. I mean if you really want to. Friday night is okay."

He smiled then, relaxing in his seat. His blue eyes held a

warm glow, a *triumphant* warm glow.

"All right, then. I'll pick you up around five. We'll go into Beaumont to eat."

She nodded, suddenly unable to taste the food she'd stuffed into her mouth. A date. With Luke Forsythe. Her best friend Luke Forsythe. Holy hell. Michelle was going to shit a brick when she heard this.

A mental groan echoed in her head. They'd never hear the end of it from Wes and Jeremy.

"He did what?"

Gracie winced as Michelle nearly shrieked her ear off.

"Holy cow, Gracie, you and Luke?"

"Yeah, I know," Gracie mumbled as she put the phone back to her ear. Hopefully Michelle's screamfest was over. "Do me a favor. Don't tell Jeremy about this. Or Wes."

"Well, of course I'm going to tell Jeremy. I tell him everything."

I tell him everything, Gracie silently mimicked. Hell.

"And then Jeremy will tell Wes, because he tells Wes everything. And then Wes will tell everyone because that's what he does," Gracie gritted out.

"Gracie, hon, I hate to tell you this, but within five minutes of you and Luke being seen out on a Friday night when everyone and their mama knows you both always come over here, everyone's going to know anyway."

"Fuck me," Gracie muttered. "I don't know why the hell I agreed to this. He's got to be out of his damn mind."

"Why, because he asked you out? I'd say that's the first smart thing he's done in a long time."

"I just hope it doesn't screw things up for everyone," Gracie hedged. "We've got a good thing. No need for Luke and me to fuck it up."

"Oh, please. We're big kids, Gracie. We can handle a little

tension without freaking out and going our separate ways. Stop searching for reasons not to go out with him and just do it. You've got to admit he is one sexy beast."

"You are so not helping here," Gracie grumbled.

Michelle laughed. "Go. Enjoy yourself. You said yourself, you were tired of being with men who can't satisfy you. I can't imagine Luke disappointing a woman in bed. Not with his considerable equipment."

"Michelle!" Grace's admonishment nearly strangled her. "What the hell do you know about his equipment?"

"Oh, you are one lying bitch if you tell me you weren't staring every bit as hard as I was when the men went skinny dipping two summers ago. That was before Jeremy and I got married, and I was staring every chance I got."

There was a long silence, then Michelle burst into laughter. "You were watching. Admit it, Gracie."

"All right, all right, so I was watching. Hard not to when they were flopping around in the buff."

"Uh huh. Now tell me you didn't get an eyeful of his equipment."

Gracie felt heat rush to her cheeks. She hadn't thought about that time in a long while. But yeah, she remembered. She'd stared in pure feminine appreciation at the hard bodies and the gorgeous cocks. Watched while they got out and as the water ran down their bodies. Oh yeah, she'd looked. And looked. And lamented that she'd never had one that nice.

A ripple of awareness skittered over her body. Her nipples hardened, and the rings twitched in response.

"Yeah, I got an eyeful."

There was a long pause before Michelle said, "This is a good thing, Gracie. Maybe...maybe Luke is exactly what you need."

Gracie licked her lips and felt nervous jitters tickle her stomach. Maybe Michelle was right. After all, no man in her past could ever stack up next to Luke. Luke, well, he was in a class all by himself. "Yeah, maybe," Gracie mumbled. "Look, Chelle, I gotta run. It's getting late, and I've got a ton of shit to do at the office tomorrow."

They rang off, and Gracie sat there for a long time, thinking about her lunch with Luke. She felt edgy, unsatisfied. Horny as hell. Had Luke done that to her? Had the idea of going out with him in the capacity of something other than a buddy got her all hot and bothered?

She felt a date with BOB coming on. And later, as she relaxed after a BOB-induced orgasm, she was irritated to note that the entire time she'd gotten herself off, she'd fantasized about Luke. And his damn equipment.

Chapter Five

Gracie waited nervously for Luke to arrive at her house. She'd dressed meticulously, changing her mind a thousand times, and it pissed her off to no end. She, who never spent more than five minutes on dress, hair and makeup, had taken well over an hour angsting over every aspect.

If that didn't make her pathetic, she didn't know what else would.

She glanced down one more time at the black sweater she'd chosen. And if she'd squeezed herself into a pair of jeans she hadn't been able to wear in several months, it certainly wasn't because she wanted to look hot for Luke. She just didn't want to look like a fat ass.

She blew a curl out of her face for the hundredth time and wished she'd used more hairspray. But then if they went anywhere with candles or little kerosene lamps on the tables, she'd go up in flames with as much shit as she had in her hair.

Finally, she heard Luke's truck and headed for the door. She met him halfway across the lawn.

"I would have come and gotten you, Gracie."

She shrugged. "I'm here."

His gaze traveled slowly over her body until a warm flush suffused her cheeks. "You look nice."

She smiled and willed herself not to shake. "Thanks."

He guided her toward the truck and opened her door for her. He got in on his side and turned up the heat before backing out of her driveway.

She studied him as he maneuvered. He must have gone home and shaved because he usually wore a shadow by now. He wore a short-sleeved polo shirt that stretched tightly across his biceps. He worked out regularly with Wes, Jeremy and Jake, something they'd started a year and a half back, and the results were downright yummy. She couldn't wait for the summer when they'd run around shirtless. She hadn't seen Luke's six-pack since last summer, and it had looked pretty damn good then.

"How does seafood sound?" he asked.

"Sounds great to me."

They lapsed into silence, and Gracie wondered if she was the only one who felt the awkwardness between them. If they were going over to Michelle's, they'd be chatting it up, talking about the work week and the weekend ahead. But they were on a date. And that changed everything.

She let out a small sigh and slouched down in her seat. To her surprise, Luke reached over and slid his hand over hers. He tucked his fingers against her palm and ran his thumb over the back of her hand.

"Relax, Gracie. We can do this."

"But *why* are we doing this?" she blurted out.

It just seemed so stupid to ruin the easygoing rapport between them. She snuck another glance at him to see him smiling. What the hell was so funny?

He left his hand over hers as they drove into town. When they reached the restaurant, he hopped out of the truck and hurried around to open her door. He reached up to help her down, and she landed close to him. Close enough to smell his cologne and to feel his body heat.

He tucked a curl behind her ear, his fingers glancing over her cheek. "You're beautiful."

Before she could respond, he wrapped an arm around her shoulders and guided her toward the entrance. A couple. They were acting just like a couple, and it was weirding her out.

Once inside, Luke ordered fish and she ordered shrimp. They both ordered a beer and sat back to wait on the food.

"So how are we doing so far?" Luke asked as he watched

her across the table.

"I don't know. I feel like this is a test or something, only I don't know the rules or what we're supposed to be doing."

He leaned forward and stared intently at her, his blue eyes glowing in the dim light. "You're a gorgeous woman, Gracie. Why do you find it so hard to believe that I'd want to go out with you?"

Her eyebrows furrowed. "Maybe because we've been friends for years, and you've never even hinted at it before now?"

He shrugged. "I wasn't ready."

"And you are now?"

"Maybe."

He took a long swallow of his beer and arched one brow at her. "If you're so unconvinced, then why did you agree to go out with me? What is it you want from this?"

Busted. He'd turned the tables on her completely. She licked her lips and thought about what to say.

"I don't know," she finally said. "Something about it intrigued me. Maybe a part of me lit up at the idea. I'm confused."

"That's what I love so much about you, Gracie," Luke said.

She laughed. "What, that I'm a confused numbnut?"

"No, that you're honest. You're direct. There's no pretense about you. It's sexy as hell."

She blinked in surprise. She hadn't exactly expected him to say that.

The waitress delivered their food, and Gracie dug in, glad to have a distraction from the current conversation. Luke was attracted to her, and she was damn well attracted to him, but it wasn't as easy as going home and having sex. This was Luke. One of her best friends on earth. His respect meant a lot to her. So did his friendship. She didn't want to do anything to fuck up either one.

If they had sex and things didn't work out, how would it affect them? Could they really pick up and go on like it hadn't happened? Continue to spend as much time together as they did? Go hunting and fishing and hang out at Jeremy and

Michelle's?

"You're putting way too much thought into this," Luke said mildly.

She looked up guiltily to see him watching her. "I'm sorry. I'm doing my best to ruin the evening before it even starts."

"Just relax. We always have a good time together."

She smiled. "Yeah, we do."

"Eat up. We'll take a drive. Go out by the lake and watch the stars."

"That sounds great," she said.

The moon was rising when they pulled up and parked at the overlook.

Luke cut the engine. "Want to get out?"

"And freeze to death?" Gracie asked in mock horror.

"I'll keep you warm."

She stared at him, shivering slightly at his promise. Well, she was no wimp, and she was willing to see where this took them. She opened the door and stepped into the crisp night air.

She breathed in deep and stared out over the water. It was a crystal clear night and the stars shone brightly in the sky.

Luke walked around the front of the truck and leaned against the hood. She moved beside him. Damn it, she was already cold. No way she was going to stand out here for long.

He reached for her and pulled her in front of him. Then he wrapped both arms around her body until her back was firmly melded to his chest. He tucked her head underneath his chin.

"Better?" he asked.

Suddenly there wasn't an inch of her skin that didn't feel like someone had taken a blowtorch to it. She nodded.

"So tell me something about you I don't already know," he said.

She laughed. "But you already know everything about me."

"Not true. I think there's quite a bit I don't know about you," he said softly. "I want to know what makes you tick, Gracie. What your dreams are. Your fantasies."

"My fantasies?" she squeaked.

She closed her eyes. No way was she going there. She'd tried that with Keith and it had led to their immediate breakup.

"Hmmm, I can feel you blushing. You must have some juicy fantasies."

She stiffened in his arms. She didn't want to waste her time or his. No, she didn't really want to go into it, but if he were going to scare off, she'd rather it be now than later. If he couldn't handle hearing about the real Gracie, then he certainly wasn't worth her time.

Luke felt the rioting emotions in her. Knew she was waging a battle with herself over whether to share that part of herself with him. He held his breath, hoping she'd trust him.

She turned in his arms, the light of battle in her eyes. "I'll tell you mine, but you have to tell me yours."

She was testing him. He could tell. She thought he'd tuck tail and run just like her last pussy boyfriend. She was afraid to share that intimate part for fear of rejection, and who could blame her with the way dipshit had responded?

"Oh, I'll tell you mine," he said calmly.

"I like sex," she blurted. "Good sex. Or I should say I'd love good sex."

Luke raised an eyebrow. "Boyfriends not satisfying you in that department?"

She ducked her head. "No," she mumbled.

"Go on," he urged.

She stepped back a bit and took a deep breath. "I want a man who doesn't feel like he has to stop and ask permission every step of the way. I want someone who can take control and make it good for both of us. I want someone who is creative and doesn't have to be coached."

"You don't want someone who has to be told how to satisfy you."

"Exactly! And...and...I want to experiment, do something

121

different, and I'd love to have a partner who could make that happen without making me feel like a freak."

They were getting somewhere now.

"What would you like to do, Gracie?" he prompted.

She wrinkled her nose and grinned. "I have a kinky streak in me a mile wide. I'd love to be tied up, spanked and my brains fucked out. And...I'd really love to have a threesome."

"Another woman?" Luke asked, pretending ignorance.

She shook her head adamantly. "No, me and two men."

"Ahh."

"What's that supposed to mean?" she asked defensively.

He put his hands to her shoulders. "Gracie, it doesn't mean anything. You're not a freak. Lots of women have these fantasies. They're healthy, normal fantasies."

She relaxed a little. "You don't think I'm weird?"

He chuckled. "Yeah, I think you're weird, but not because you have kinky sex fantasies."

She surprised him by throwing her arms around him and hugging tight. He eased his arms around her, returning her embrace. He probably shouldn't push things yet, but he'd been dying to taste her all night.

He tugged gently at her hair until her head fell back. He cupped a hand to her cheek and gently ran his thumb down her jaw. Her lips fell open in silent invitation, and it was all he needed.

His lips found hers, hot, flushed and needy. She tasted sweet, and she felt incredibly soft. He loved that, loved the way she fit so perfectly against him.

Her mouth opened wider, and the tip of her tongue feathered over his. He caught it and sucked it further into his mouth. Their tongues rolled and tangled as the sounds of their breathing echoed into the night.

If they were anywhere but at the lake on a cold night, Luke would lay her down and strip her naked. He'd get between her thighs and slide so deep into her pussy that she wouldn't know where he began and she ended.

With more willpower than he thought he possessed, he pulled away from her.

"Wow," she whispered.

"Yeah, I had a feeling we'd be like an inferno if we ever got together."

She stuck her hands in her pockets and looked away for a minute. Then she glanced back at him, her eyes still echoing her need. He reached out a thumb to glide over her swollen lips. Lips he wanted to devour again.

"Want to go out again tomorrow night?" she asked. "I pick the place this time."

Luke arched a brow in surprise. Was this another test?

"Okay. Sounds good to me. What time should I pick you up and what should I wear?"

"Eight o'clock, and jeans and a T-shirt are fine. Don't overdress. You'll be getting hot."

His body surged to attention at her words. Innocent or not, they were full of innuendo. But she didn't elaborate, so clearly she planned to let him wonder.

Chapter Six

Gracie waited inside the door for Luke to come to the steps. He'd seemed bent on collecting her last night, so tonight she let him.

He mounted the steps and knocked lightly. She opened the door and bit back a smile of satisfaction at his double take.

"You look...fantastic," he murmured.

She reached for her jacket and noted his disappointed grimace when she slid it on. "Ready?" she asked.

She grinned smugly all the way to the truck. The top she'd chosen was more suited for warmer weather. The thin straps looped over her shoulders and the built-in shelf made wearing a bra unnecessary. The material molded and cupped her breasts like a lover. Every curve was outlined in vivid detail. She liked to call it her bitch-in-heat shirt. And where they were headed, she planned to work up a sweat.

"So where we going?" Luke asked when they got into the truck.

"Downtown," she said vaguely.

He looked curiously at her but started the engine and drove out of her driveway. When they got into Beaumont, they got off the freeway and headed downtown.

"Take the next left," she directed.

They turned onto a smaller street, and she pointed toward a stop sign.

"Take a right."

She leaned forward in anticipation as she spotted the club.

"Here, turn into the parking lot."

Luke pulled in and parked then cut the engine. "Rave? We're going to Rave?"

"You don't dance?" she asked innocently.

"I've been known to dance."

"Then let's go."

She slid out of the truck and met Luke around the front. She'd shed her jacket and hopped a bit to keep warm in the cold air.

"Let's get inside before you freeze," Luke muttered.

As soon as they stepped inside, the fast beat of the music swelled and pounded. It vibrated the floor beneath their feet and exploded off the walls. Her pulse quickened as the beat invaded her veins.

"Let's dance," Luke shouted beside her.

He tugged her out toward the crowded dance floor. Couples moved and gyrated in time with the music, their bodies meshed in sensual poses.

Gracie hesitated, unsure of herself for the first time.

Luke leaned in toward her ear. "Pretend for a minute that I'm one of your boyfriends. You've brought me here to dance. Come on, Gracie, what would you do?"

He was taunting her, daring her. And damn it, she never backed down from a dare.

She looped her arms over his shoulders and swung her pelvis into his groin. She moved and swayed, getting into the heady beat. She closed her eyes and threw her head back as she rubbed her breasts across his chest.

After a few moments, she rotated her body, grinding her ass into his hard cock. Oh yeah, she could feel the bulge against her behind. She leaned into him and reached up, twining her arms around his neck.

She writhed against him, bumping and thumping as he moved in sync with her. His hands crept around her, moving slowly, seductively over her belly.

She shivered as a flash of need, centered in her abdomen,

shot out in ten directions. Her pussy tightened, her nipples beaded, and the hunger within her grew.

His hands moved up, inching closer to her breasts. Would he touch her in public? She knew the club goers here were about as uninhibited as they came, but she wasn't sure if Luke would feel comfortable indulging in that sort of activity.

Then he cupped both breasts through the thin material of her shirt, and she gasped at the erotic sensation that bolted through her body. He massaged and plumped them both, lightly caressing the sensitive flesh.

One of his hands dropped, sliding down her body as the other kept kneading her breast. Lower still, his thumb brushed over her belt loop and caught there. His fingers dipped to the juncture of her thighs until he touched her pussy through her jeans.

Her body jerked in reaction, and she moaned softly. He continued to rub up and down, dipping farther between her legs. She ground her ass against his cock, her movements becoming more restless by the minute.

"Undo your jeans for me," he said close to her ear.

"Here?"

"This is your place, Gracie. You wouldn't have brought me here if you didn't want this to happen."

She gulped nervously and reached down with shaky fingers to undo the snap of her jeans. Around them, the dancing continued, and no one seemed to notice or care what she and Luke were doing.

"Arms back up," he ordered.

She complied and wrapped them around his neck until she was once more locked in his embrace.

The hand he had on her breast lowered to the hem of her shirt. He dipped underneath, coming into contact with her bare skin. Then he slid his fingers back up toward her breasts and flicked over her nipple.

The nipple ring dangled, and he plucked gently at it.

"Very nice."

She'd forgotten all about the nipple rings and how he might

react to them, but based on his response, he was far from turned off.

He continued to play with the nipple ring as his other hand delved into her pants. She sucked in her breath as his fingers found her clit and began rubbing in a slow, torturous circle.

"I want you to come for me, Gracie. Right here, right now."

Oh God, if he only knew just how close she already was.

He pulled harder at her nipple ring and bent his head to nibble at her neck. His fingers moved faster over her pussy, separating the folds and flicking at the button between them.

Her breathing sped up. Then just as he sank his teeth into her neck, he pulled sharply at the nipple ring and he pinched her clit.

She exploded against him in a rush of heat. She sagged heavily in his arms, and he caught her against him, holding her tightly. Wave after wave of exquisite pleasure poured over her as the music swelled in the background. Her legs shook, and she went weak all over.

Finally he eased his hand from her pussy. He let his other hand fall from her breast and carefully withdrew it from her shirt. He reached around her with both hands and redid her snap before arranging her shirt for her.

"Maybe we should get a drink now," he suggested.

She nodded numbly and followed him off the dance floor. They took a table far enough from the dancing and music that they might actually be able to hear each other without shouting.

"What the hell was that?" Gracie asked after they placed their drink order.

Luke fixed her with one hell of a sexy stare. "I should be asking you. Didn't you set me up for that?"

She opened her mouth but couldn't think of a single thing to say. "No, I mean yes, but no, I wasn't setting you up. I just wanted to see—"

"If I'd run scared if you took me to a place like this?"

"Yeah," she finished lamely. "Something like that."

"I'm not like your other boyfriends, Gracie."

"No, you're not," she said truthfully. "That was, honest to God, the hottest thing that's ever happened to me in my life."

Luke grinned. "Honest. Yep, that's what I love about you."

"You didn't...you didn't mind the nipple rings?"

He stared strangely at her. "Mind? I was turned on as hell. I can't wait to see them. I bet they're incredibly sexy dangling from your nipples."

She grabbed for the drink being delivered and drank greedily. God, she had to do something to cool off or she was going to go up in flames.

Finally she put it down and stared intently at Luke. "Is that where we're headed, Luke? Are we going to have sex?"

"I could lie and say no, but I won't. That's precisely where we're headed, Gracie."

Delicious tickles licked up her spine. Her insides quivered, and her nipples tightened. For the first time in a long time, she thought about sex and had no idea what to expect.

"Not right away," he continued. "I want to go out with you a few more times. I'm having fun seeing you as more than a buddy. You're a beautiful woman, Gracie, and I'm enjoying you very much."

He leaned in toward her until his mouth was inches from hers. "Would you trust me enough to go somewhere with me for the weekend? For Valentine's Day?"

"Valentine's Day?" she echoed.

"Call it our fantasy weekend," he said. "Make plans to get next Friday off work. I'll pick you up Friday morning, and we'll spend the weekend together. I promise you won't regret it."

She sat back in her chair and stared at him openmouthed. Spend an entire weekend with him. Having sex. A fantasy weekend. Her entire body tingled at the thought.

"Do you trust me?" he asked.

She nodded. "You know I do."

"Then let me plan this. Say you'll go."

She must be out of her mind. No one did this sort of thing after two dates. But this was Luke. Not some schmuck she'd just met.

"Okay. I'll do it."

"Good. That's just next weekend. Not long at all to wait."

"No," she agreed. "So what do we do in the meantime?"

"We get to know each other better," Luke said. "And we dance some more."

He gestured toward the dance floor. "You ready for round two?"

Chapter Seven

"So what is Jeremy doing for you for Valentine's Day?" Gracie asked as she leaned against Michelle's counter. She, Ellie Turner and Michelle were all gathered in the kitchen while the men sat in the living room ready to watch the fight.

Michelle stopped stirring the tea and set the pitcher aside. She smiled ruefully. "Nothing romantic, I imagine. He'll probably finish painting the baby's room and we'll go pick out the crib."

"Sounds exciting," Gracie said dryly. "What about you, Ellie? If I know Jake, he's planned something terrific."

A blush worked its way over the pretty brunette's face. "I don't know exactly," Ellie said. "He told me not to make plans."

Michelle grinned. "Jake does plan the most wonderful surprises."

Gracie nodded. "Lucky bitch. What I wouldn't give for a man to look at me the way Jake looks at you, Ellie." Even as she said it, the memory of the way Luke had stared at her on their date sent a slow burn straight up her spine.

Ellie laughed and blushed again. "I'm not complaining. I'm so lucky to have him."

Michelle reached over and patted her arm. "No, honey, he's lucky to have you."

"No doubt," Gracie agreed. "Who else would put up with all that testosterone?"

"Oh, I don't know, Gracie. You have to admit all that bottled he-man stuff is awfully sexy," Michelle said.

"I swear those pregnancy hormones are raging. You must keep Jeremy awfully busy," Gracie said dryly.

Michelle blushed. She actually blushed. Gracie crowed in delight. "Busted!"

The three women dissolved into laughter.

"What about you, Gracie? Got any plans with Luke?" Michelle asked.

Gracie felt her cheeks heat, but damn it, she was not going to betray herself like the other two women. "Yeah, we're spending the weekend together."

Michelle raised one eyebrow. "The weekend as in you'll have a couple of dates, or the weekend as in spending every minute together?"

"The latter," Gracie replied.

"Wow, you guys move fast. Going anywhere special?"

"I don't know, exactly. He's planning it. I just know it involves sex."

Michelle pinned her with a questioning stare. "You nervous?"

"Of course I am. This isn't just any guy. I don't want to screw things up."

"You'll do fine," Michelle soothed.

"Luke's a great guy," Ellie interjected.

"What are you girls doing in here?" Luke asked as he walked into the kitchen.

"Gossiping, of course," Michelle said.

Luke dropped a kiss on Michelle's cheek. "How are you feeling, sweetheart?"

Michelle smiled at him. "I'm doing good. Baby's growing like a weed."

He turned to Ellie and gave her a quick hug. "What about you? Jake treating you good?"

Ellie's smile lit up her entire face.

"I'll take that as a yes," Luke said.

Then he turned his attention to Gracie.

Gracie felt an odd shiver as Luke reached to pull her into

his arms. He kissed her lightly on the lips before pulling away. "The fight's starting. I wondered if y'all needed help with the snacks."

The girls put it into high gear. Gracie shoved a tray at Luke while Michelle collected the tea pitcher and the bags of chips. Ellie grabbed the glasses of ice and followed everyone else into the living room.

It was a familiar scene—one that brought Gracie comfort. All of them gathered at Jeremy and Michelle's to watch a UFC fight.

"Hey, Gracie, come sit," Wes called. He patted the spot beside him on the couch.

Luke sat down on the floor in front of her and reclined between her legs so his back rested against the couch. Ellie sat nestled in Jake's arms, and Gracie felt a pang of longing at the couple's obvious devotion.

They spent the evening laughing and having a good time. Luke didn't go out of his way to latch onto her in front of the others, a fact she was grateful for.

She was uncomfortable flaunting her budding relationship with Luke. She still felt awkward about it and didn't want to extend that discomfort to the rest of the group. And to everyone else's credit, they'd acted completely normal.

The fight had been over a few minutes when the doorbell rang. Jeremy got up and disappeared to answer it. A few seconds later, he reappeared.

"Gracie, Keith is at the door for you."

Gracie stiffened. Why now of all times? Did he never think to call or at least go by *her* house if he had something he wanted to say? Why he was fond of making a scene in front of her friends, she'd never know.

"Has he been drinking?" Gracie asked.

Jake's eyebrows shot up, and his face darkened.

Jeremy shook his head. "I don't think so, and he'd be a damn fool to show up here if he had." He winked at her. "I gave him my best cop stare and told him he better not start any shit."

Gracie grinned. "Thanks, Jeremy."

Luke put a hand on her shoulder as she got up from the couch. "I'm going out with you."

She hesitated for a moment then nodded. As they left the living room, Luke slid an arm around her waist and squeezed reassuringly.

When she opened the front door, Keith, who was standing on the porch with his back to her, turned around. His lips curled in distaste, and his eyes glinted with a little fear as he spotted Luke.

"What do you want?" Gracie asked.

"I'd hoped we could talk alone," Keith said.

Luke pulled her closer up against him, his hand resting possessively on her hip. "Whatever you have to say to Gracie can be said in front of me. Isn't that right, sweetheart?"

"So you're with him now?"

"It would appear I am," Gracie said calmly.

"Damn it, Gracie. You don't even give a guy a chance," Keith complained. "You can't expect to spring shit on me like you did. I know I reacted badly, but what did you expect?"

Gracie raised her eyebrows. "Expect? I don't guess I expected anything from you at all, Keith. I've said all I intend to say on the matter. We're finished, and I'd really appreciate it if you'd quit coming over to my friends' house."

"So would I," Luke drawled.

Keith ran his hand through his hair and swore again. "All right, Gracie. If that's what you want. Your loss."

He turned and stomped off the front porch toward his truck. He peeled out of the driveway and left in a cloud of dust.

"Dumbass," Gracie muttered.

"What did you ever see in him?" Luke asked as they walked back into the house.

"Don't rub it in."

Luke laughed. "Okay, I'll shut up now."

"Good idea."

Jeremy looked up when she and Luke entered the living

room. "Everything okay, Gracie?"

"Yeah, he's gone," she said.

"Maybe you and I should pay Keith a little visit in the official capacity," Wes said to Jeremy. "We could tell him to leave Gracie the hell alone."

Jake scowled. "Is he bothering her? Do I need to go beat his scrawny ass?"

"I can take care of myself just fine, Jake," Gracie said. "But thanks. You guys are the best."

"Who wants a beer?" Michelle interrupted.

Gracie looked gratefully at her, and Michelle winked back.

"Who wants to watch the fight again?" Jeremy asked as he picked up the remote.

Chapter Eight

Gracie leaned back in Luke's truck seat and tried to settle her nervous stomach. They were headed out of town to a cabin on the lake Luke and Wes shared ownership of.

She'd been out before. They'd gotten together for fishing trips and stayed weekends at the cabin, but she'd never gone with the idea of having sex with Luke.

The week leading up to the weekend had been terrific. She and Luke had spent every day together. The sexual tension between them had grown into an enormous entity, but more than that, their relationship had developed beyond their casual friendship.

And now they were adding sex to the equation. It seemed so important to him that she trust him. She did. She'd always trusted him, and it felt right for them to be together. Somehow she *knew* Luke would satisfy all her needs and desires.

"You're quiet," Luke said beside her. "Having second thoughts?"

"No, not at all."

The heat in his gaze peeled a few layers of her skin off. No, she had many thoughts, but she wasn't regretting her decision to see where the weekend would take them.

He reached over and curled his hand over hers. "I'm glad. I'm really looking forward to this. To us."

She smiled. "Me too."

Thirty minutes later, they pulled up to the cabin nestled on Sam Rayburn Lake, and Luke cut the engine. He turned sideways in his seat and stared intently at her.

"I've planned a lot for us this weekend. If you ever feel uncomfortable with the direction we're going or I'm doing something that you don't want, just say so. I'll stop. Otherwise, I expect you to do exactly as I tell you."

A full body shiver worked its way over Gracie's skin. She nodded, her mouth too dry for her to speak.

He leaned in and kissed her, his lips working hot over hers. When he pulled away, his eyes were half-lidded, and desire burned brightly, making them a darker blue.

"I want you to go inside to the bedroom. Remove your clothes and lie down on the bed. Wait for me. I'll be in with our bags."

She swallowed and nodded again.

He handed her the keys, singling out the one to the cabin.

"Just leave them on the coffee table in the living room. Our weekend starts now."

She got out of the truck and headed for the door. She inserted the key into the lock and went inside. Luke had evidently been here in preparation for their weekend. The cabin was warm, and she could hear the hum of the heater. A fire had been laid in the fireplace, just waiting to be lit.

She set the keys down on the coffee table and started for the bedroom. Once there, she ran her hands up and down the sides of her jeans, trying to work up the courage to do as he'd told her.

Her body tingled from head to toe. Her pussy hummed, warm vibrations swirling between her legs. The anticipation was nearly sending her over the edge.

Knowing she was only stalling, she undid her jeans and peeled them down her legs. She pulled her sweater over her head and tossed it aside. She hesitated for a slight moment before removing her underwear and bra.

Feeling vulnerable standing in the middle of the room naked, she moved to the bed and crawled onto the warm comforter. She turned over waited for Luke.

She heard him moments later and glanced over to see him

standing in the door.

"You look magnificent."

She smiled and watched as he moved closer to the bed. He sat down on the edge and reached his hand out to smooth over the skin of her belly.

His fingers worked their way up until he fiddled with her nipple rings. Fine little goose bumps broke out over her flesh as he tweaked and plucked at her nipples.

"Are you ready for this, Gracie?"

"Yes," she whispered.

"Get up," he directed.

She climbed off and stood beside him. He circled an arm around her waist and pulled her down to his lap. At first she didn't understand how he was positioning her, but he turned her so she lay across his lap, belly down. Oh God. She knew what this was about.

His hand glided over her back and to the curve of her ass. Then without warning, his palm smacked down, sending a current of fire through her body.

He petted her and soothed the area before slapping the other cheek with his open hand.

She twisted restlessly against him, needing something, not quite sure what. The blows stung, but directly on the heels of the impact came such delicious pleasure. She was at a loss as to how to describe it, how to react to the erotic spanking. He was giving her exactly what she'd said she fantasized about.

Three, four more times his hand met with the plump flesh of her behind. She moaned softly and squirmed even more.

Then as suddenly as he'd pulled her down, he stood, picking her up with him.

"Stand right here and don't move."

In a few seconds he returned with a piece of rope. She trembled as he pulled her hands behind her back and coiled the rope around her wrists. When he finished, he pushed her gently toward the bed.

"Lay face down, feet on the floor."

She bent over, placing her cheek against the mattress, and planted her feet on the floor. Her ass was vulnerable and exposed in this position, and it made her even wetter.

She heard him walk away then return. Smooth wood made contact with her behind with a crack that made her jump. She closed her eyes and tensed, waiting for the next blow.

Another followed close behind and then another. Her cheeks were on fire, the tingling nearly painful in its intensity. She needed release, needed to come, but she was helpless to his demands.

"I want to fuck you so bad, right here, right now," Luke said behind her. "Your ass is so red, so sensitive."

She moaned again as the paddle came down across her butt. "Please," she whispered.

She heard the sound of a zipper and knew he had undone his jeans. Then she heard the crinkle of a wrapper and before she could process anything further, his hands gripped her thighs, spreading her, and in one motion he plunged into her pussy.

She cried out at the almost unbearable fullness. He hadn't taken off his jeans, merely unzipped them enough to get his cock free. The denim scratched against the tender skin of her ass. She wasn't going to last long.

He began pumping in and out of her, and she was trapped beneath him, unable to move, only able to accommodate his thrusts. She strained against her bonds, needing to be free but delighting in the sensation of being bound, subject to his mercy.

Her orgasm built and spread, preparing to explode. With each thrust, the pressure in her belly grew until she bucked against him, desperate for release.

He wrapped his big hands around her waist and pulled her back to meet his hips. He leaned into her, pressing her further into the bed, his weight pushing his cock even deeper.

"Luke!" she cried out.

Just as she felt him pick up his pace, her orgasm burst upon her with the speed of an explosion. She tried to scream but no sound came out. She had a mouthful of the bedspread, her teeth dug in with the agony of her release.

Every muscle in her body tensed painfully as Luke rocked her body against the bed. He strained forward, holding himself deep as his hips spasmed.

"God, Gracie," he gasped out as he shuddered again.

She went limp underneath him, and he collapsed over her, his ragged breathing close to her ear. He felt good, his big body covering hers, his cock still wedged deep into her pussy. When he finally moved, she made a sound of protest.

He stepped away for a moment then returned and untied her hands. When she was free, he climbed onto the bed and pulled her into his arms.

She cuddled into his chest and rubbed her cheek against his shirt.

"No fair, you're still dressed."

He laughed. "I won't be for long. That was incredible, Gracie. Thank God I brought so many condoms. I think we're going to need every last one of them."

He wrapped his arms tighter around her and held her close as they rested.

"It was perfect," she whispered. And it had been. It was as if he'd reached into her mind and plucked out every exacting detail of what she wanted from a man.

He bent to kiss her. "I'm glad. But we're only getting started."

Chapter Nine

Gracie lay cuddled in Luke's arms for a long moment. Finally, he eased away from her and stood beside the bed. He began shedding his clothing, and Gracie stared with unabashed admiration.

His body was beautiful. There was no other way to describe it. Tight, well muscled, the dips and contours were meant for exploring. She couldn't wait.

As he pulled his jeans off, his semi-erect cock flashed in her view. She ached to reach out and touch it. She wanted to fondle it and stroke it, watch it spring to life under her attention.

He was built for a woman's pleasure. There wasn't a woman alive who wouldn't want a cock this size and wouldn't die of pleasure in the process.

"Do you like what you see?"

She licked her lips. "I want to taste you."

Luke groaned. "Damn, Gracie, you make me crazy."

He got back onto the bed and settled over her body. He lowered his mouth to hers, nipping and sucking at her bottom lip. His lips traveled down the line of her jaw to her neck and then around to her chest.

"I've been dying to taste your nipples," he said hoarsely as he closed his mouth around one.

She arched into him, moaning at the sweet pleasure that streaked from her breasts to her abdomen.

He caught the ring between his teeth and tugged gently. He

swirled his tongue around the stiff peak before capturing it and nibbling delicately at it.

She worked her hands into his hair and held tightly as he sucked at her nipples. He feasted on the sensitive buds, sucking and biting.

Finally he kissed his way to her belly. He ran his tongue around her navel, leaving a wet trail.

He tugged her legs apart as he moved his body down the bed. Her pussy throbbed in anticipation. He gently parted the slick folds with his fingers then bent his head to lick her clitoris.

Her body jerked in reaction, and she sighed in absolute pleasure. His fingers worked lower, sliding into her opening.

She closed her eyes and surrendered herself completely to what he gave her. Already she could feel her nerve endings tightening, on the rise to something wonderful.

He spread her legs wider and moved off the bed long enough to slip on another condom. Then he slid up her body, settling between her thighs.

He played with her nipple rings as his cock nudged at her pussy entrance. He bent and nipped sharply at the quivering peak just as he thrust into her.

As his hips bucked forward, he gathered her in his arms, holding her tightly. His lips moved hotly over her neck and to her mouth, capturing her in a breathless kiss.

He moved powerfully, stroking to her deepest regions. He felt so big. He stretched her, the friction caused by each thrust making her mindless. She grabbed at his shoulders, sinking her nails deep.

His hands traveled down her body until he grasped her buttocks. He squeezed and kneaded as he cupped her against him. He spread her wider, diving impossibly deep into her. Then he trailed one hand between them, finding her clit and pinching it.

She bolted upward, straining against him as he stroked the quivering flesh. He thrust again and again until she panted beneath him.

Her orgasm built to impossible heights and still she hung there, creeping ever closer but not tumbling over the edge. She clamped her teeth together and squeezed her eyes shut as the pressure became nearly unbearable.

He began rocking faster, his thrusts harder. He set an impossible pace and demanded she keep up.

"Oh God, oh God," she chanted as she felt her body began to splinter apart.

She let out a long wail as he slammed into her again. Around her the room blurred, and she felt a thousand strings break in her pussy.

He moved frantically against her, his orgasm racing over him as she found her own. Sweat dripped from his forehead as he arched forward one last time.

She went limp a second before he collapsed over her. It took all her energy but she wrapped her arms around him and held him close as he fought to catch his breath.

"Are you all right?" he rasped in her ear.

"Mmmm hmmm." It was all she could manage.

He rolled to the side and discarded the condom before rolling back over to pull her against him.

"Rest, sweetheart. I'll get up and fix us something to eat in a little while."

She settled against his chest, feeling ridiculously content. He stroked her hair as her eyes fluttered and closed.

Gracie awoke to find Luke standing next to the bed. He bent and smoothed her hair away with his hands then kissed her.

"Time to eat," he murmured.

She stretched and slid out of bed. Luke caught her in his arms and stroked his hands over her naked skin.

"You better get dressed or I'll never eat," he said.

She grinned and reached for her shirt.

As she followed him into the kitchen, she sniffed appreciatively. Then she saw what he'd cooked.

"Oh my God, you made barbeque chicken!"

He smiled and gestured for her to sit down.

She took her seat, and Luke took the chair across the table from her. She dug in with her fork, uttering a contented sigh when the chicken hit her tongue.

"Are you okay with things so far?" he asked.

She paused, setting her fork down on her plate. "Yeah, and you?"

"I just had the best sex of my life. I'd say that qualifies as okay," he said dryly.

Familiar heat flooded her cheeks.

"If you don't stop looking at me like that, you're not going to be able to finish eating," he warned.

She ducked her head but smiled at the desire in his voice.

When they were done, Gracie started toward the sink to put her plate up, but Luke intercepted her.

"You go wait for me in the bedroom. I want you on your knees on the rug. Naked. Hands behind your back."

She swallowed nervously even as a thrill shot down her spine. She nodded and handed the plate to Luke. Her legs shook as she walked toward the bedroom.

She only paused a moment before shedding her shirt. Then she went to the plush rug that covered the floor in front of the bed and sank to her knees.

Rising up slightly, she put her hands behind her so they were clasped in the small of her back. Streaks of need pulsated and radiated from her pussy into her abdomen as she imagined what Luke would do when he came in.

She didn't have to wait long. He strode into the room naked. He stopped when he saw her, his eyes darkening with approval and lust. His cock sprang to attention, and Gracie enjoyed a moment of triumph that she affected him so.

"Do you have any idea how sexy you are?"

He stopped in front of her and thrust his hand into her

hair. He palmed the back of her head, cradling it as he directed his cock at her mouth.

"Take me deep," he commanded.

She opened her mouth, and he thrust to the back of her throat. He rocked his hips back and forth as she swallowed and sucked at him. He gripped her head, holding her tightly against him.

He pumped into her mouth for several seconds before finally easing from her lips. Then he took her hands and tugged her upward until she stood in front of him.

He fiddled with her nipple rings, pulling them until her nipples stretched in front of her. "I love these," he said. "They're sexy. Like you."

She twisted, jittery and needy as he plucked at her breasts. She was hot and restless, ready to see what he had in store for her next.

His fingers trailed down her body, over her belly and lower to her pussy. He dipped a finger between her legs, sliding into her wetness. Her knees shook and threatened to buckle.

"Get on the bed," he ordered. "Belly down, legs apart."

She did as he directed, crawling onto the mattress and lying down so that her cheek met with the comforter. She spread her legs and stretched her arms above her head.

He crawled between her legs, pressing his chest against her back. He nudged her thighs farther apart with his knee then positioned his cock at her pussy opening.

He surged forward, pressing her further into the bed. His body covered her and his hips dug into her ass as he plunged deeper.

He reached above her, holding her wrists with his hands. She was unable to move as he thrust between her legs. Finally he let her arms go and dropped his hands down to her ass. He squeezed and massaged, pushing upward to gain better access to her pussy.

Then he began thrusting in earnest, increasing his pace until the force pushed her up the bed. He bent down and nipped sharply at her neck, causing goose bumps to dot her back.

The throbbing between her legs bloomed and spread outward, radiating to every sensitive region of her body. She loved this dominant side of him, loved that he never once stopped to ask her what she wanted or if what he was doing was okay.

She panted as he rocked against her. She was so close and yet she couldn't get there. Her orgasm built and built until it was painful in its intensity.

He grasped her hips with both hands, pushed up so her body angled to give him better entry, and he plunged home. She let out a wail as her orgasm cracked and burst around her. It hurt, it pulsed, it was the most exquisite form of torture she'd ever endured.

And it went on and on.

He collapsed forward, coming to rest at the deepest point in her pussy. His chest pressed into her back, and his body melded to hers. A perfect fit.

She arched her ass into his pelvis, not wanting him to leave her just yet. They both heaved as they tried to catch their breath. Finally, he rolled off her, and she immediately felt cold without him covering her.

She mewled softly in protest, and he gathered her in his arms, once again wrapping his body around hers. He kissed her softly.

"Go to sleep, Gracie. I'll be here. I'm not letting you go."

Chapter Ten

Gracie woke to the sun shining in the bedroom window. The space beside her was empty, and she smelled bacon cooking. She smiled. Luke must be in the kitchen making breakfast.

She stretched and climbed lazily out of bed. Luke's flannel shirt lay in a heap on the floor, and she reached for it. She slipped it on, leaving it unbuttoned down the front. His scent surrounded her, and she wrapped the shirt tighter around her.

She padded barefoot out of the bedroom toward the kitchen, a wicked smile on her face. She'd tease him with a few glimpses of those nipple rings he loved so much. By the time breakfast was done, he'd be a walking hard-on.

She rounded the corner, letting her shirt gape a bit wider and let out a squeak of surprise. She yanked her shirt closed and stared at Wes who was standing in the kitchen leaning against the countertop.

She started to back up but Wes closed the distance between them.

"I-I didn't know you were here," she sputtered.

She gripped her shirt even tighter, sure her face was as red as a stoplight. To her surprise, Luke stood by the stove, his expression one of interest as he watched her.

Wes stopped in front of her and reached down for her hand. He tugged her forward into the kitchen.

"Come on now, Gracie," he drawled. "You've seen me naked. Time for you to return the favor."

She shivered under his intense stare. "Is this a practical joke or something?"

Wes ran his hand up the lapel of her shirt, nudging it aside until her breasts peeked around the edge.

"No joke. We've been friends a long time, Gracie. I don't want to make you uncomfortable, but I don't think you are. I think you're as turned on as I am right now."

She cocked her head in confusion and shot Luke a panicked look.

"Quit dicking with her," Luke said.

"You want a threesome," Wes said. "Luke and I want to give you one."

Her mouth rounded to an O and her eyes widened. Wes's fingers brushed across her nipples, flicking lightly at the rings.

She glanced back over at Luke again to see him staring intently at her.

"If you don't want this, just say so," Luke said quietly. "We don't want to do anything to make you uncomfortable."

"Wow," she whispered. "I mean, I don't know what else to say. You're okay with this?" she asked Luke.

He smiled. "Who do you think invited Wes?"

"Holy shit." She shook her head, unsure of whether or not she was dreaming. A threesome. Not with strangers. With two men she trusted implicitly. Two men who cared for her and would make it good. Not much to think about there.

"What do you say, Gracie?" Wes murmured.

She nodded. "Okay."

Wes nudged her chin up with his knuckle.

"I don't want things to be awkward for us. We've been friends too long for that."

He leaned in and brushed his lips across hers. His goatee rubbed softly on her chin. Bubbles of excitement took flight in her chest. She relaxed against him, and he deepened the kiss.

Her shirt parted as his hands slid underneath the material and cupped her breasts. His thumbs worked over her nipples.

Shedding her inhibitions, she wrapped her arms around

his neck and kissed him back, letting her tongue roam playfully over his.

It was a different experience kissing Wes. He was more gentle than Luke but every bit as sensual. If she gave herself time to analyze the situation, she'd likely retreat in mortification, but it felt right.

Wes wrapped his hands around her waist and hoisted her upward until she sat on the countertop.

"Much better," he murmured.

Her breasts were now level with his mouth, and he took advantage. His tongue rubbed lightly over one nipple. It puckered and her muscles tightened in response.

He cupped her breasts with both hands and held them up for his mouth to devour.

"I never knew you had such a wild side, Gracie. I like it. The rings are hot."

She moaned as he sucked her nipple into his mouth, his tongue toying with the ring.

"She needs to eat," Luke interjected.

Wes slowly drew away, and it was all Gracie could do not to insist she wasn't hungry so they'd take her to bed. Her stomach contradicted her by rumbling.

Wes lifted her down as Luke set a plate on the table for her. She walked unsteadily to her chair and sank down into it. She tugged her shirt tight around her, suddenly giving up the idea of making Luke crazy. He'd completely turned the tables on her.

The two men sat down on either side of her and proceeded to polish off their plates of food. She managed to nibble down a small amount, but her stomach was in full somersault mode, and she didn't do justice to her food.

"If you're done picking at that, I know something we could be doing that's a whole lot more fun," Wes said.

She flushed and pushed her plate away. Wes held out a hand to her and pulled her from her chair. Luke walked toward the bedroom, and Wes swung her into his arms and followed.

Wes deposited her on the bed, her shirt falling open. She quickly tore it off and tossed it off the bed. Wes and Luke stepped back and stripped off their clothing. She watched, not missing a single detail.

Her heart beat a little faster as Wes moved toward the bed. His cock was impressive. A size that would make a woman stand up and pay attention. It brought to mind all sorts of yummy questions. Would it fit? How delicious would it feel to accommodate all of him?

Wes grabbed her ankles and pulled her toward the edge of the bed. Her legs fell open, baring her pussy to him. He made a sound of appreciation as he bent his head.

Just the anticipation of him touching her with his mouth had her ready to burst. When his tongue finally rubbed over her delicate folds, she nearly came on the spot.

"You taste as good as you look, Gracie," he said. "Sweet."

She arched her back and moaned as his tongue delved deeper. The bed dipped and swayed as Luke climbed up beside her. He bent his head to her breasts, and she cried out as both men tormented her with their mouths.

Wes slid a finger into her pussy. "God, you're so tight, Gracie. I don't want to hurt you."

He left her for a brief moment then he found her again, gliding easily inside. He smoothed lubricant into her, easing his fingers around the walls of her pussy.

She heard the crackle of a condom wrapper and the sound of more lubricant being squeezed out. Then the head of his cock butted gently against her entrance.

Luke moved from her breasts to her lips, kissing and sucking at her mouth. His hands feathered over her nipples, tweaking and pinching at the taut peaks.

Wes inched into her, and she gasped at the fullness. He came to rest deeply within her, and she struggled to process the bombardment of sensations.

"Am I hurting you?"

"God no," she managed to get out.

Never before had she felt this way. Wes was seated deep within her pussy while Luke kissed her and toyed with her breasts. It was the most exquisite pleasure, every one of her most sensitive spots being teased and touched.

Wes began to move, gently at first and then with more force as she arched her hips to meet his thrusts. Her tongue tangled with Luke's, and she wrapped her arms around his neck, holding him close.

Wes pulled away from her and ran his hands over her legs. "Turn over on your knees," he said.

She scrambled over, allowing Wes to position her to his liking. Luke sprawled out in front of her, his cock in perfect position for her to bend down and take it in her mouth.

Gentle hands spread her thighs then Wes mounted her, sliding into her from behind. She closed her eyes and moaned. Luke smoothed her hair from her face as she rocked back against Wes. God, it felt good.

She opened her eyes then slowly lowered her mouth, letting her tongue slide over Luke's hard cock. His hand tangled in her hair, and he groaned as her mouth closed around the head.

"Gracie, honey, you drive me crazy," Wes said in an agonized voice. "You're so tight, so beautiful."

"Very beautiful," Luke murmured below her.

Luke stroked her hair, running his fingers through the strands as she sucked his cock.

"We want to take you at the same time, Gracie. Are you up for that?" Luke asked.

She shuddered, her orgasm lurking so close. Just the image of them both buried in her body had her teetering on the edge.

Wes withdrew, and Luke gently pulled her away from his rigid cock. Then Wes moved beside her and lay down on the bed, his legs hanging over the edge and his feet planted on the floor.

He reached for Gracie, his big hands positioning her over his cock. "Ride me, Gracie."

She let out a moan as she slowly lowered her body onto his erection. He slid in, the friction nearly unbearable. God, he was so big, she didn't know how Luke would accomplish the feat of taking her too.

"Just relax, sweetheart," Luke said as he ran his hands over her backside.

She felt the cool shock of the lubricant over the seam of her ass and flinched as Luke slid one finger inside. Wes played with her nipple rings as she held herself still on his cock.

"We're going to take this slow and easy," Luke said. "I won't hurt you, Gracie, I swear it."

"I trust you," she whispered.

He eased more lubricant inside her, stretching her slightly with his fingers. After several minutes of stroking and preparing her, he positioned his dick at her tight opening.

"Breathe deep," Wes said. "Breathe in and relax. That's it, baby."

Wes's fingers found her nipples again, pinching and plucking at them, distracting her from the burning and stretching of her ass.

She gasped as the muscle gave way and Luke penetrated her anus. He stopped and gave her time to adjust before slowly moving forward again. He inched his way into her until finally his hips pressed into the flesh of her buttocks.

Both men were fully sheathed within her body. She began to shake uncontrollably.

"Easy, sweetheart," Luke soothed. "Make it last. Make it good."

She leaned forward in Wes's arms, letting him support her weight as Luke began to move inside her. Soon they found a rhythm, moving in unison. They both pressed forward, filling her, stretching her.

How she managed to accommodate them both, she'd never know, but she'd never enjoyed herself more than at this moment.

"Are you all right?" Wes whispered close to her ear.

"Very all right," she replied. She nipped his lobe, and he groaned in response.

Wes's hands slid down her waist, gripping her hips. Luke's hands grasped her shoulders, and they held her captive to their embrace.

"I can't last any longer," she gasped. She fought against the rising tidal wave, but knew she only had seconds.

"That's good because I can't either," Wes said. "Let yourself go, we've got you."

Luke surged forward, burying himself in her deepest regions. Wes bucked upward until she gasped at the pain of his penetration.

"Oh God!" she cried.

Her body began to spin out of control. Her vision blurred and she writhed, unable to bear the pressure building within her. She erupted with such force that Wes slid out of her.

He grasped her waist with one hand while he used his other hand to position himself between her legs once more.

The two men rocked against her, each straining with their own release.

She screamed. She couldn't help it. She'd never ever had such a powerful orgasm, and it scared and thrilled her all at the same time.

She fell forward onto Wes's chest, and he wrapped his arms around her, holding her and soothing her as she fought to catch her breath.

Luke surged against her ass, pressing her harder onto Wes. He slumped against her for a few seconds before easing out of her and rolling to the side.

She lay panting on Wes. She couldn't move, couldn't speak even if she wanted to. His hands slid gently up and down her back, and he kissed the curve of her neck.

"You are one incredible woman, Gracie."

"That she is," Luke agreed. "I may never walk again after this weekend."

Wes rolled Gracie to the side, still cradled in his arms. He pulled out of her.

"Let me get cleaned up, and I'll be right back."

As Wes got up to discard the condom, Luke tugged her close and tucked her head under his chin.

"Was that good?" he asked.

She stretched and yawned like a contented cat. "I'm not sure I could deal with it if it got any better. Thank you, Luke. I don't even know what to say. That was fantastic. I can't believe you went to so much trouble to make my fantasies real."

"Trouble? More like my pleasure."

Wes climbed on the other side of her and scooted in close. He pressed a kiss to her shoulder and slid his hand down the curve of her waist.

"Rest up, Gracie girl, and we'll do it all over again."

Chapter Eleven

Gracie lay in bed between Luke and Wes and stared up at the ceiling. Her euphoria had yet to dissipate. Her body was still tingly on the heels of the most fantastic sex of her life.

She glanced over at Luke, unable to control the softening in her chest. The past week with him had been unbelievable. He'd taken their conversations and pieced together her fantasies. He'd made them come alive, and he'd done it because he cared for her.

She wasn't sure exactly when she'd fallen in love with him. In retrospect, she couldn't remember a time when she hadn't cared deeply for him. But the past week had brought it together and shoved it to the forefront. She wanted to be with him.

As if feeling her gaze, he turned his head toward her, his blue eyes glowing with contentment. He reached out a hand to cup her cheek.

"I thought I'd light a fire in the fireplace," he said.

She nuzzled her cheek into his palm. "Hmmm, I'd like that."

"Give me five minutes and I'll be back for you."

She watched as he got up and pulled his underwear on. Then he disappeared out of the bedroom.

A warm hand slid over the curve of her hip, over her belly and up to cup one of her breasts. She closed her eyes, enjoying Wes's caress.

He nibbled lightly at the curve of her neck as he fingered her nipples.

"Did I hurt you earlier?" he asked. "I worried I was too big for you."

She smiled and turned over in his arms. "You won't find me complaining about your dick size," she teased. "I thought I'd died and gone to heaven."

He kissed her lightly, and the penis in question stirred to life against her stomach.

"I can't wait to taste it," she said in a sultry voice.

"Shit," Wes muttered. "I can't wait either."

"We have about three minutes before Luke is coming back to get me." She slid her body farther down the bed until her mouth was even with his erection.

This was the first time she'd gotten this close, and her eyes widened in appreciation. The man was stacked. She licked her lips in anticipation, and Wes flinched beside her.

"God, woman, quit teasing me."

She laughed huskily and lapped her tongue over the head. He flinched again and dug his hands into her hair. She slid her mouth over him, sucking him deep.

"Oh yeah, baby, suck it. Just like that. Damn."

She took him as deep as she could, and his breath left him in one long hiss. She pushed him over onto his back and knelt over his hips, shoving her hair out of the way.

She wrapped her fist around the base of his cock and moved her hand up and down with the motion of her mouth.

"Stop," he moaned. "Baby, stop before I come."

He pulled gently at her hair until he was free of her mouth. His chest heaved with exertion, and his eyes glittered brightly as he stared at her.

"Fire's built," Luke said from the doorway.

She turned to see him leaning against the doorframe, watching her and Wes. She uncurled her legs and stood beside the bed. Wes got up as well, and they walked out of the bedroom into the living room.

She curled onto the couch directly in front of the fireplace and sighed in pleasure. To her surprise, Luke sat beside her and pushed her chest down to the cushions. He pulled her arms behind her back and tied them with the same rope he'd used the previous night.

"Totally and completely at our mercy," he murmured.

She closed her eyes and clenched her teeth against the tide of desire rolling over her body.

Luke stood and pulled her up beside him. He guided her around to the side of the couch then bent her, belly down, over the arm of the sofa. Her feet left the floor, and her cheek rested against the soft material of the couch. Her ass was in the air, vulnerable.

She heard the jingle—of a belt? Seconds later, the sting of leather splintered across her buttocks. She gasped and squirmed. She had no idea who was administering the spanking.

Again the slap of the belt, the sound of it striking flesh, the delicious burn across her ass. After the fourth stroke, she panted for breath. After the fifth and six, she was begging. After the seventh, she felt hands smooth over her burning ass. Fingers curled roughly around her thighs and spread them.

A cock nudged then rammed into her. Wes. Oh God. He wasn't as gentle as he'd been earlier. Maybe he knew now she could accommodate his size. He thrust hard, sending her spiraling into a world of unbelievable pleasure and the thrill of erotic pain.

He paused for a moment, so tightly wedged into her that she couldn't move if she wanted. Then he forced himself deeper and she cried out.

He slipped from her body, and Luke slid into her, immediately replacing Wes. He squeezed and kneaded her ass cheeks as he thrust into her again and again. Then he slapped her butt with his hand, and she yelped. The skin, so sensitive from the belt, tingled under his hand. He rode her harder, spurred on by her cries. His hand rained down again and again until she sobbed her release. And still he continued.

Unbelievably, her body reacted to his demands. She felt herself climb toward another orgasm even as tears streaked down her cheeks from the first.

Then Luke stopped. He smacked her ass one more time before pulling out.

"No!" she cried. They couldn't stop now. Not when she was so close again.

She heard a chuckle and wasn't sure who it came from. Then she felt her ass being spread, the cool lubricant soothing over her anus. She trembled from head to toe. Wes stepped between her legs. She recognized his touch. Oh God, surely he wasn't going to take her ass.

"We're going to go nice and slow, Gracie girl," Wes said soothingly. "You're going to take all of me."

She closed her eyes as he positioned his cock and pushed forward. Slowly, the pressure agonizing. Pleasure ripped through her abdomen even as the pinch of pain unsettled her. It was a heady combination.

The couch dipped and Luke picked up her head and slid underneath her. He fisted his cock in his hand and curled his other hand into her hair. He slipped his cock between her lips just as Wes plunged into her ass.

The momentum carried her forward, forcing Luke's dick deep into her mouth. The tightness in her ass was nearly unbearable. Then Wes smacked her cheek with his hand and she bucked against him.

"I'm going to ride you now, Gracie," Wes said as he began moving within her. "I'm going to ride your ass while Luke fucks your pretty mouth."

Gracie closed her eyes, her body tightening and spasming uncontrollably at Wes's erotic language. She was wild with need. She wanted more. She was helpless between them, unable to move. Her body was theirs to do with what they wanted, and she loved it.

They fucked her mouth and her ass, foregoing their earlier gentle style. This was raw sex, hard, sweaty, the kind she'd dreamed about. They were unrelenting as they made demands of her body. They owned her, they used her, and she never wanted it to stop.

She cried out, but Luke thrust deeply into her mouth. She closed her eyes, squeezed them tightly shut as her body splintered and broke apart under their relentless assault.

The wet, sucking sounds of their fucking filled the room. Luke's hand wound tightly in her hair, pulling her head closer to his groin. Then Wes grunted behind her and let out a shout as he came.

"Swallow it, Gracie," Luke murmured. "I want you to swallow it all."

He moaned and jerked against the back of her throat then flooded her mouth with his come. She sucked greedily, wanting to please him in a way she'd never wanted to please a man.

Wes carefully withdrew from her quivering body as Luke finished in her mouth. Wes reached over to untie her hands, and Luke pulled her into his arms.

She lay on his chest, eyes closed, too worn out to form a coherent thought. Luke hugged her closer as he stood, lifting her with him. He carried her into the bathroom and started the shower.

He washed her gently, taking care with the tender parts of her body. When he was finished, he wrapped her in a towel and carried her to bed.

She burrowed into his chest and was vaguely aware of Wes spooning against her back. Gentle hands soothed over her skin, petting and caressing her. She yawned and allowed herself to drift away.

Chapter Twelve

Gracie opened her eyes, a smile on her face. She sighed and snuggled a little deeper into the covers. It was dark outside, so she'd been sleeping for several hours at least. The guys were gone. Probably in the kitchen since they seemed so determined to take care of her this weekend.

She kicked off the covers and flexed her toes. Lord, but she was sore. Deliciously so. Her body felt heavy and languid, the kind of feeling you could only get from deep-seated contentment.

She pulled on her jeans and her sweater, not bothering with a bra. Chances were she wouldn't have her clothes on long enough to worry about it anyway.

She walked out of the bedroom and headed for the kitchen. She could hear the guys talking in low voices and smiled. As she got closer, she stopped in her tracks. She kept out of sight and listened to the conversation unfold in the kitchen.

"I have to admit, when you came up with this idea, I was skeptical," Wes said. "I wondered if you'd really heard Gracie right."

Gracie wrinkled her brow. What on earth was he talking about?

"You don't think that now, though," Luke said with a laugh.

Wes chuckled. "Hell no. It's obvious she really wanted this. It's too bad you didn't overhear her a lot sooner."

"I doubt she and Michelle discuss it that much," Luke said. "Gracie's a private person. If she hadn't just broken up with dipshit, I doubt she would have said anything at all."

"You're probably right. Still, it worked out great. You were able to set up this entire weekend, and I think she really enjoyed it."

Luke laughed again. "See, there are advantages to eavesdropping. Gracie would kill me if she knew I'd listened to her conversation, but it worked out great in the end."

Gracie's mouth fell open and a wave of humiliation rolled over her with the speed of a Mack truck. She could barely process what the conversation meant. She was too busy trying to control the burning in her cheeks.

The whole thing had been an elaborate set-up because Luke had overheard her talking to Michelle about her fantasies?

She didn't even realize she'd stumbled into the kitchen until Wes and Luke looked up at her. Guilt flashed in Luke's eyes, and hurt washed over her again.

"Gracie..." Luke began.

She held a hand up, trying to control the shaking. She'd already made a big enough ass of herself. Oh God, when she remembered all they'd done, she just wanted to bury herself in the ground.

"Is that all this was?" she said in a trembling voice. "Were you two just cashing in on my fantasies? You see a way to have a good time at my expense? You are supposed to be my best *friends.*"

"God, Gracie, no, you can't think that," Wes protested.

They both started toward her, and she shrank back. Her bottom lip trembled, and she bit down, ignoring the pain.

"I thought...I thought this week happened because you cared about me," she said painfully, her gaze focused on Luke. "I feel like such an idiot. Why the games? Why the elaborate charade? Why let me fall in love with you if none of this was real?"

"Gracie, you have to listen to me," Luke said desperately.

She spun away, grabbing the keys from the coffee table.

"Gracie, wait!"

She ignored him and bolted as fast as she could. She

hurled herself into his truck and locked the doors even as she jammed the key in the ignition.

Luke ran out of the house toward the truck, shouting her name. He tried to open the door as she began to back up.

"Damn it, Gracie, don't go!"

She rammed her bare foot on the accelerator and gunned the engine. When she'd backed far enough out of the drive, she threw it into drive and whipped around.

She raced down the highway, her embarrassment so acute she wanted to curl up and die. If you looked up *ass* in the dictionary, there had to be a picture of her.

A tear slid down her cheek and she wiped angrily at it. Could she have misread the situation any more? She'd just made the biggest fool of herself ever. With guys she considered her best friends on earth. Guys she couldn't even face anymore.

The forty-five minute drive back home seemed interminable. She'd been stupid to take Luke's truck. She'd be lucky if he didn't have her arrested. But then she'd done a lot of stupid things in the past week.

She drove up to her house and parked Luke's truck next to her car. She left the keys in it, knowing he'd come by for it. She went inside long enough to get a pair of shoes and her jacket, then she got into her car and took off.

She was being hysterical and unreasonable. She knew that much. She'd carried on like a complete nitwit, but she was so humiliated to learn the real reason why Luke had gotten close to her.

She drove with no real sense of direction until she found a quiet, secluded place to park. She needed to calm down, start acting rationally again. Again. Ha. She hadn't acted rationally in months.

Her first mistake was going out with Keith. She'd only compounded that mistake by allowing herself to fall in love with her best friend. Her third mistake had been thinking he had feelings for her.

She wasn't going to cry. Even though she felt the sting of tears, she was determined not to give in. She'd already made a big enough ninny of herself.

She sat there, staring at the sky, numb. For several hours. Luke would have his truck back by now. He and Wes would be home, probably wondering what the fuck her problem was.

Emitting a weary sigh, she started the engine and drove slowly toward the main road. She instinctively headed for Michelle's. It was late. Or early depending on your point of view, and she hated to disturb her friend's sleep, but she needed a shoulder to cry on in the worst way. This stiff-upper-lip shit was getting old fast.

It was nearly four in the morning when she pulled into Michelle's driveway. She turned off the engine and slowly got out. Before she closed the door, she saw Jeremy hurry down the steps and stride across the lawn toward her.

She trudged toward him, and he held his arms open to her. He caught her in a hug and kissed the top of her head.

"We've been worried sick about you, Gracie. Come on in. I'll make you some hot chocolate."

She smiled gratefully at him. "I'm sorry, Jeremy. I didn't mean to worry y'all. Especially not Michelle."

"Luke and Wes are worried too," Jeremy said quietly. "I need to call and let them know you're okay."

Gracie stiffened.

"Gracie, Luke is frantic. He's worried something happened to you. I'm just going to call and tell him you're all right."

She nodded, guilt creeping over her.

Once inside, Michelle rushed over and hugged her tightly. Then she dragged her over to the couch and made her sit down.

"What on earth happened?" Michelle demanded.

Gracie sighed and closed her eyes for a moment. "I made an ass of myself. That's what happened."

Jeremy returned and pressed a hot cup of chocolate into her hands.

"Thanks," she said.

Jeremy sat down on the other side of Gracie and put a comforting hand on her leg. "Talk to us, Gracie."

She flushed and set her cup down on the coffee table. "Luke overheard our conversation," she said to Michelle. "The one about my fantasies."

"Ohhh," Michelle said, her eyes wide.

"And apparently he wanted to fulfill those fantasies for me. He asked me out and we spent the week together. I thought he was interested in *me*. I confided those fantasies to him, and he arranged this weekend. Wes was a surprise."

She broke off and ducked her head in embarrassment when Michelle's eyes widened further in shock.

"You mean, you and Luke *and* Wes?"

"Yeah," Gracie muttered.

"You're angry with them for not telling you they knew?" Jeremy asked in a confused voice.

Gracie sighed. "I'm not angry with them," she said quietly. "I'm angry with me. And I'm so humiliated I want to just find a hole to crawl in."

"Oh honey," Michelle said. She reached over and squeezed Gracie's hand. "Why on earth should you be embarrassed?"

"I just wish Luke had been upfront. Told me from the beginning that this was about sex. Instead he made me believe...he made me believe he cared about me. He made me fall in love with him," she said miserably. "And all along it was just a game. His heart was in the right place. I know he's never approved of the men I've slept with. He wanted to give me a weekend I'd remember. I understand that."

Michelle wrapped her arms around her. "I let my mouth get ahead of my brain again, and I basically blurted out that I loved him. Just before I ran like a scalded cat. Now I've got them both mad at me because of a huge misunderstanding. One I perpetuated. I guess in a way, I wanted it to be the truth. I wanted Luke to love me."

"Are you so sure he doesn't?" Jeremy asked.

She nodded, tears burning holes in her eyelids. "I overheard him and Wes talking. And Luke's never said anything to make me believe he cares for me beyond friendship. I just got wrapped up in the whole going out thing and confused sex with love. You'd think I was twelve years old or something."

She bowed her head as hot tears splashed onto her arm. "I screwed up."

Jeremy gently nudged her chin up with his knuckle. "Don't blame yourself, honey. There are two grown men who are as big a part in this as you are. I don't know what the hell happened, but I don't think we have the full story here."

Gracie threw herself into Jeremy's arms. "I'm sorry to put you in this position. They're your friends too. I just needed to come by and talk to Michelle."

He hugged her back and stroked her hair soothingly. "You're always welcome here, Gracie. Michelle and I love you. Nothing will change that."

"Of course not," Michelle said firmly.

"I should get home," Gracie said as she pulled away from Jeremy.

"You're not going home in your condition," Jeremy said. "You're exhausted. It's four o'clock in the morning. You can crash on the couch and go home after you've rested."

"I'm too tired to argue," Gracie said.

Michelle stood up. "I'll get you some pillows and a blanket. We'll talk more in the morning when you're feeling better."

"Thanks, Chelle. I don't know what I'd do without you guys."

Michelle hurried to the closet down the hall. She returned a few minutes later with the linens.

Gracie took them gratefully and made a comfortable spot. Jeremy and Michelle said their goodnights and disappeared into their bedroom.

Gracie sank wearily onto the couch and pulled the covers up to her chin. *Dummy, dummy, dummy.* She closed her eyes. She was even too tired to further castigate herself.

Chapter Thirteen

Luke pulled up to Jeremy and Michelle's house and parked beside Gracie's car. The sun was just starting to peek over the horizon when he mounted the steps to the front porch.

Before he could knock, Jeremy opened the door and motioned for him to be quiet. He followed Jeremy inside and saw Gracie sound asleep on the couch.

"She's wiped out," Jeremy whispered. "She was pretty upset when she got here."

Luke raked a hand through his hair and swore under his breath. What a mess. His gaze drifted back to Gracie, drinking in her appearance. He'd been so goddamn worried when she'd torn off in his truck. He and Wes had driven the entire way home afraid they'd find her wrecked on the side of the road.

"I'm going back to bed with my wife," Jeremy said. "I don't know what all is going on between you and Gracie, but I know she's hurting."

"Thanks for calling me," Luke said softly.

"No problem. I know how worried you were about her."

Luke watched as Jeremy left the room and then he went to kneel beside the couch where Gracie lay. His chest tightened when he saw the evidence of her tears. Tenderly, he stroked her hair away from her cheek, then he leaned forward and kissed her lips.

God, he didn't like to see her hurting. He never had. She had a way of twisting him up on the inside like no other woman had ever managed to do.

He hated to wake her up. God knew she could use the sleep. So could he. But they had to talk. He had to make her understand.

"Gracie," he whispered. "Gracie, sweetheart, wake up."

She stirred, twisting her head slightly, a frown marring her face. Then she opened her gorgeous eyes. Hurt filled her gaze, and he felt like someone sucker-punched him.

"What are you doing here?"

He stroked his hand over her face, wanting to touch her, reassure himself that she was really okay.

"We need to talk, Gracie."

She nibbled at her bottom lip then slowly nodded. "I know."

"Will you come with me?" he asked. "I don't want to hash everything out here with Jeremy and Michelle in the next room, and I don't imagine you want to either."

She pushed herself to one elbow and struggled to rise. He curled his hands around her waist and helped her upright.

"Okay," she agreed.

He breathed a sigh of relief. He'd overcome the first obstacle. Getting her to listen. Now he just hoped he'd be successful in all he had to convince her of.

She stood up, a little shaky on her feet, and he reached out to steady her, but she stepped away. He collected her jacket and held it open for her.

She walked ahead of him out the door, and he carefully closed it behind them. He hurried for his truck, knowing she'd be cold.

He started the engine and turned the heat on high before backing out of the driveway. They didn't speak as he drove toward his house. He didn't know whether to be grateful she wasn't yelling at him or worried that she was so quiet.

A few minutes later, he parked in his garage. He reached over and took her hand. "Come in so we can talk?"

Gracie stared at Luke for a long moment. He did look worried about her, and she hated that she'd acted so stupidly. She was still embarrassed as hell, but she'd just made things worse by running.

She finally nodded and opened the truck door to climb out. Luke waited for her in front of the truck and ushered her inside.

He had a gorgeous house. He'd moved into a spec house he'd built when he started developing the neighborhood. She'd always thought it too big for him, but it would be perfect for a family.

She sighed and directed her thoughts away from a family Luke may or may not have in the future.

Luke guided her into the living room and gestured for her to sit down on the couch. She perched on the edge, just wishing they could get the awkwardness over. She needed to beg forgiveness for being such a dipshit, and maybe, just maybe, they could one day go back to being friends again.

He stood a few feet away, his discomfort obvious. Poor guy probably didn't know what the hell to say in the face of her assumptions. He was probably trying to figure out a way to let her down easy.

She sighed again. "Luke, I'm sorry."

He looked startled by her apology. He started to speak, but she held a hand up. "Let me finish, please.

She lowered her hands and sucked in a few steadying breaths.

"I overreacted. I know that. And I made some assumptions I had no business making. It's just that I wish you'd leveled with me from the get-go. Just told me what you'd planned. You didn't have to go through the whole charade of getting close to me. I thought..." She took another deep breath, willing herself not to crack. "I thought you were coming to care for me as more than a friend and that this weekend was a natural progression of that relationship. Silly, I know, but not knowing that you'd overheard my conversation and made plans to surprise me, well, it's the only conclusion I could draw."

He stared at her, mouth open. Then his eyes sparked. He strode over to where she sat on the couch and knelt down in front of her.

"Luke, I—"

"Gracie, shut up," he said fiercely.

She blinked in surprise.

He blew out his breath in an angry puff then he yanked her to him, kissing her roughly, passionately. She had no time to react, and she was too shocked to do so.

He pulled away from her and collected her hands in his. "Gracie, I love you."

Her mouth fell open. "But—"

"Not a word," he said, his eyes still flashing angrily. "I swear I don't know where you get some of those fool-headed notions of yours. I'm so tempted to turn you over my knee and spank your ass."

Her cheeks warmed as she remembered him doing precisely that.

"This week has been the best week of my life, Gracie. And you're the reason for that. Yeah, I overheard your conversation with Michelle. And yeah, it made me see you in a new light. It made me realize how much we had in common and how stupid I was for never seeing it, for never asking you out.

"Yes, I wanted to give you a weekend you'd never forget, but I also want to give you a lifetime of those weekends. You and me, tearing up the sheets, eating each other alive. Gracie, when I'm with you, I swear I don't even think straight. The chemistry between us is off the charts. But more than that, you're my best friend. I love you. I think I've always loved you, and I want to spend my life with you. There's no one I have a better time with. No one who understands me like you do.

"I fucked up. I should have told you I heard you and Michelle talking, but honest to God, it never even occurred to me that things could go so terribly wrong. I planned to spend the weekend making all your fantasies come true and then I was going to get down on my knees and beg you to make *mine* come true by marrying me."

Gracie stared at him in shock.

"You love me?"

"After a speech like that, can you doubt it?"

She laughed and put her hand up to cup his cheek. "Oh, Luke, I was such an idiot. I was so afraid. I'd fallen so hard for you, and in that moment, I was so afraid you didn't feel the same."

He gathered her in his arms and held on tight. "I'm sorry I hurt you, Gracie. I'd never do anything to hurt you on purpose."

She hugged him back as relief and euphoria like she'd never known rolled through her system.

He pulled slightly away and kissed her. He cupped her face in his hands and kissed her so tenderly, with so much love, that it was hard to hold the tears at bay.

"Will you marry me, Gracie?"

"Yes. Yes!"

She threw her arms around him again and peppered his cheek and neck with kisses.

The door leading from the garage to the kitchen slammed, and Luke whirled around. Gracie saw Wes standing in the doorway to the living room, concern etched on his face.

"Gracie, are you all right?"

She glanced at Luke and, at his nod, stood up and walked over to Wes.

"I'm fine, Wes. I'm sorry for blowing up like I did."

"Ah hell, Gracie, no need to apologize."

He walked forward and wrapped his arms around her. He squeezed her tight and stroked a hand through her hair.

"I'm sorry if we hurt you, girl. I'd cut off my right arm before doing anything to hurt you."

He drew away and kissed her warmly on the lips. He let his tongue mingle with hers as his hands stroked up and down her back.

"I hope you don't regret the weekend," he said huskily. "You're one special woman. Luke is a lucky man."

She hugged him again. "He's asked me to marry him."

Wes pulled away from her and grinned. "And you said?"

"Yes, of course."

"Well, hot damn. Congratulations. To both of you."

He put his hand out to Luke then hauled him into a bear hug. "I'm gonna get on out of here and leave you two to sort things out."

He ruffled Gracie's hair. "Love you, girl."

She smiled. "Love you too, Wes. And I don't regret this weekend."

Fire blazed in his eyes. "I'm glad."

He turned and walked back to the garage, leaving Luke and Gracie standing there.

Luke put his arms around her and rested his cheek on top of her head. "Did you mean it? You'll marry me?"

She smiled into his chest. "Just as soon as I can drag you to the altar."

He loosened his hold on her and stuck his hand into his pocket. "I didn't get you flowers for Valentine's Day, but I hope this will make up for it."

He pulled a small ring box from his pants and held it out to her.

She couldn't breathe.

She opened it with shaky hands and saw a diamond ring nestled against black velvet.

"Oh, Luke, it's beautiful!"

He tugged the ring from its perch and slid it onto her finger. "I love you, Gracie."

She admired her ring for a moment, and then stared into his eyes. Brilliant blue eyes that burned with love. Love for her.

"I love you too," she whispered.

Undenied

Chapter One

Wes Hoffman pulled into the parking lot of Zack's Bar and Grill and killed the engine. It was awfully crowded for a Thursday night.

As he walked closer to the door, he could hear raucous laughter from inside. When he actually stepped into the bar, he winced as a set of girly shrieks from hell pierced his eardrums.

He glanced around the room to see a hoard of females clustered in the corner. Ah hell, he'd stumbled into a girls' night out? And not just any girls' night out. These looked to be hellions.

His eyebrows lifted when one of them plunked down her drink and climbed on top of the table amidst hoots and shouts of encouragement from her friends. She proceeded to do a loud rendition of a twangy country song before one of the other girls coaxed her down.

Wes headed for the bar in full retreat mode. Zack slid a cold bottle toward him as he plopped onto a barstool.

"Thanks," he said as he raised the bottle to his lips. Then he nodded in the direction of the chaos. "What the fuck is going on tonight?"

Zack chuckled and flipped his towel over his shoulder. "Bachelorette party."

Wes groaned. "Say no more."

"What brings you out tonight, anyway?" Zack asked as he resumed pouring a round of drinks. "You're usually over at Jeremy's your nights off."

"They've all turned into a bunch of damn pussies," Wes grumbled.

Zack burst out laughing. "I assume you're talking about the female influence on the male members of your circle?"

Wes took a long chug of the beer. "Got it in one. Babies, wives..." He shook his head. "And then I come here expecting a nice quiet drink and find a bunch of screaming women."

Zack laughed again. "You sound down on the fairer sex, my friend."

Wes grinned. "Oh no, I wouldn't badmouth them. I love them far too much for that. I'm just pissed because everyone I know is at home getting laid, and I'm sitting here bitching to you like a goddamn old man."

Zack inclined his head in the direction of the ruckus. "Plenty of women over there."

Wes snorted. "I don't do about-to-become-attached women."

"They aren't all getting married. Just one."

"Which one?" Wes asked as he swiveled on his barstool.

"The blonde sitting by the redhead over in the corner. Ah hell, is that lingerie they're breaking out?"

"Looks like it," Wes said as his gaze swept over the group. He stopped on one and stared for a long moment, studying her profile. There was something about her.

"Who's the brunette on the end?" he asked Zack. "The one wearing the cowboy hat. I swear I've seen her somewhere before."

"Dunno. The bride-to-be said she had a lot of out-of-towners coming in for the wedding."

Wes continued to stare, the niggling growing stronger. Where had he seen her? As he sat watching her, she turned in his direction. Their eyes locked and a burst of recognition hit him directly in the chest.

Her eyes widened in surprise and then she smiled. She rose and began making her way toward him.

Heat rushed up his neck as humiliation set in. *Fuck me. Oh Lord, anyone but Payton Ricci.* He stood, nearly knocking his beer over in his haste to be as far away from there as possible.

"Wes Hoffman?"

Her voice, husky and sweet, only added to his guilt.

And then she launched herself at him. One minute she was standing just a few feet away and the next she was in his arms, legs wrapped around his waist.

"It is you!" she exclaimed.

One hand clapped on top of the straw cowboy hat she wore, and the other curled around his neck, holding on for dear life. Then she yanked off the hat and tossed it onto the bar before she planted her lips on his.

He registered a hot, needy mouth, but his shock and embarrassment were too great for him to do anything but stand there wishing the earth could open up and swallow him.

Finally she pulled away and slid down his body until her feet hit the floor. She cocked her head to the side, her blue eyes sparkling with mischief. "Do you not remember me?"

He cleared his throat. On one hand he wanted to plead ignorance, but then she'd no doubt explain just *how* they knew each other, and he really didn't need the details all over again. On the other hand, he had no desire to hurt her feelings. He'd already done enough damage to her.

"Of course I remember you, Payton." He even managed what he hoped was a sincere smile.

"I can't believe you're still here, I mean living here. I figured you'd have left right after high school. Didn't you have a scholarship to A&M to play ball?"

Her enthusiasm discomfited him. Why was she being so damn nice to him? He eased awkwardly back onto the barstool and motioned for Zack.

Zack walked over, a smirk on his face that Wes wanted to wipe off with a well-placed fist.

"Can I get you a drink?" Wes asked, not really knowing what else to say to a woman he'd never expected to see again.

She bounced onto the stool next to him and flashed her dynamite smile at Zack, who promptly melted into a pile of slush. Damn fool.

"I'll take a water," she said.

She turned back to Wes, a million questions burning in her eyes. "Well? Tell me about you. What are you doing these days?"

His tongue felt thick in his mouth. Like he'd just swallowed a cup of sawdust.

She looked beautiful, but then she'd always been gorgeous. The years had been good to her—how long had it been? Eleven? Twelve years? Good God, it had been twelve years. She'd been sixteen then. Sweet, innocent and so very beautiful.

She hadn't changed much. Not now when he soaked in her appearance up close and personal. She still had a sparkle about her, something that inexplicably drew him to her, just like it had twelve years ago.

"Wes? Are you all right?"

He blinked and opened his mouth to try and say something to smooth over the awkwardness of the situation, but damned if he knew what to say. Sorry? Apologize for hurting her? Apologize for being a clumsy, inexperienced dumbass?

"I'm fine," he mumbled. He looked around...for what, help? He met Zack's gaze, sure panic was etched in his features.

Zack glanced curiously back at him, nodded once in silent understanding then reached for the phone under the counter. A few seconds later, Wes's cell phone rang.

Wes yanked up his phone, knowing when he answered there wouldn't be anyone on the other end, but he gripped the receiver like a lifeline.

"Yeah," he said shortly. He waited an appropriate amount of time before saying, "Okay, I'll be right in."

He closed the phone and donned an expression of regret. "That was the station. I'm a local cop. They need me to come in. I'll, uh, catch you another time."

"Oh," she said. "Well, it was nice to see you again." She flashed a smile that didn't quite reach to her eyes, eyes that reflected suspicion.

"Uh, yeah, you too," Wes hedged. He nodded in Zack's direction. "Thanks, man. I'll see you later."

He turned tail and all but ran the hell out of the bar. When he reached the outside, he sucked in several breaths, trying to rid himself of the embarrassment blazing a torch over his face.

Bless Zack for resorting to the oldest trick in their repertoire. It wasn't something they'd done in a long time, the last when a very drunk, very married woman had come on to Wes. He definitely owed Zack for this one, and he'd be more than happy to pay up.

Payton sighed and turned her attention to Zack. She pinned him with her stare and arched one eyebrow. "Slick move if I do say so myself."

His eyes widened in exaggerated surprise.

She snorted. "Don't play innocent with me. Come on. That has to be one of the lamest tricks ever. You guys were so obvious, a blind man could have ratted you out."

He chuckled but had the grace to look abashed.

"So what's his problem?" she asked as she stared again at the doorway Wes had fled out of. "I mean it wasn't like I threatened to rape him."

Zack shrugged. "Honestly? I have no clue. I've never seen him act like that. I was kinda hoping you could clue me in. How do you two know each other anyway?"

The soft echo of a memory, a much younger, innocent memory whispered across her mind. "I knew him in high school."

"That's all? I was sure by the way he was acting that you were some crazed felon he'd arrested before."

"Yeah, you'd think," she murmured.

"Can I get you something stronger than water?" he offered. "My treat to make up for the dirty trick I pulled."

She smiled. "Thanks, but no. I'm stuck driving all these lunatics home after they've gotten too drunk to remember their names."

He turned to acknowledge another customer who'd walked up to the bar, but then he looked back at her again. "I don't know what was up Wes's ass tonight, but he's really a good guy. Couldn't ask for better."

"I'll remember that," she said dryly.

She swung around on her stool and leaned against the bar, glass of water in hand. She sipped idly as she watched her girlfriends laugh and whoop it up.

Wes Hoffman. After all these years. And lordy but he'd grown up well. As much as he sent her hormones buzzing when she was sixteen, her adult girly parts were all a-tingle from a simple glance.

When she'd driven into town, she'd wondered about him. Wondered if she'd run into him or if he'd long since left the small town they'd grown up in. But here he was, a cop, apparently still quite rooted in the community.

Had she turned out so awful? Had the idea of seeing her again been so horrible that he'd tucked tail and run at first sight? Because that's exactly what he'd done, and the expression on his face when he'd seen her... Well, it couldn't exactly be classified as priceless.

She sniffed in irritation. She might not be a playboy centerfold, but she wasn't paper bag ugly either. And she knew damn well she had a decent body. Never had a man run from her like Wes Hoffman just had.

The more she thought about it, the more pissed she got. Was that any way to react to someone you hadn't seen in twelve years? Would a *Hey, nice to see you* be too much to ask for?

Jerk. Gorgeous, hunky jerk, but a jerk nonetheless. God, she was a sucker for a man with a goatee. It had bristled across her lips when she kissed him. Okay, well maybe she shouldn't have kissed him, but again, she'd never gotten any complaints before.

Face it, Payton, you were way too damned pushy and you scared him away.

She huffed again and let out a long sigh. Oh well, *c'est la vie* and all that jazz. She wasn't going to lose any sleep over it.

"Paaayyton!"

She grinned as the group of rowdy girls yelled at her from across the room. She turned, grabbed her cowboy hat and slapped it back on her head. Hell, she was here to have a good time. Piss on Wes Hoffman.

Chapter Two

"Do I suck in bed?"

Gracie Forsythe choked on her tea and coughed as she set the glass on the kitchen counter.

"What? Wes, are you smoking some funky weed or something?"

Wes sighed. He'd known this wouldn't go over well. Not only was he further humiliated by airing his insecurities, but if Luke came back before he finished the conversation with Gracie, Wes would never live this down.

"Do I suck in bed?" he repeated.

"No. Now do you mind telling me what precipitated that question?"

"Okay, so I don't *suck*, but am I any good?" he asked, ignoring her question.

Gracie cocked her head then circled around the island to stand in front of where he was slouched against the sink. "What's going on with you, Wes? Where on earth would you get the idea that you're a lousy lay?"

He growled in frustration. He didn't have all night to have this conversation with her. Maybe he shouldn't have brought it up. His best friend's wife probably wasn't the best source for boosting his sexual ego even if she was in a position to judge. And well, she was as much his best friend as Luke was.

"Gracie, will you just answer the question instead of peppering me with more?"

Her eyes softened and she leaned back against the island

so they faced each other. "Wes, the night we had our threesome was honestly the best sex I've had in my life. I couldn't have asked for better lovers than you and Luke."

He shifted uncomfortably at her intense perusal.

"So you going to tell me what brought this up or are you going to make me play dirty?"

"Play dirty?" he asked, though he was afraid to find out what she meant. Gracie could be downright evil when provoked.

"Well, I'm pretty sure you don't want Luke to know about this little conversation." She arched one brow. "Otherwise you wouldn't have waited until he left to get more beer. Nor would you have declined to go with him."

"You wouldn't."

She batted her eyelashes innocently. "Wouldn't I? I would in a heartbeat. This has got to be downright juicy, and I'll do what I have to in order to pry the goods out of you."

He snorted in disgust. "Luke so didn't know what he was getting into with you."

Her eyes twinkled and a smile hovered over her full lips. "Oh, I don't think you'll hear him complaining." She crossed her arms over her chest and eyed him. "Okay, so spill it. Did you make it with some chick who thought you were the worst guy she'd ever fucked?"

Despite his discomfort, he couldn't help but laugh at Gracie's bluntness. It was what he liked best about her. And why he'd decided to come to her with his problem. She liked to joke, but he knew when it came down to it, she'd never rat him out. She was too loyal.

"It's kind of a long story," he said with a heavy sigh.

She made a show of checking her watch. "Well, you better abbreviate it. I figure we have ten minutes tops before Luke gets back."

Suddenly he regretted his impulsive decision to talk to Gracie about Payton. It seemed ridiculous and could only add to his embarrassment. Quite frankly, he'd be happy for no one to ever know, and he'd be even happier if Payton hadn't shown up out of the blue after twelve years. Twelve years in which he'd put the past firmly behind him, only to have it pushed back into his face with one chance encounter.

"Wes," Gracie said softly. "Whatever it is that's bothering you, you can tell me. You know that. Hell, you saw me through one of the most awkward moments of my life. I wanted to drop dead of embarrassment when I waltzed into the kitchen at the cabin, half-naked, only to find you standing there looking at me."

He grinned at that memory. "Ahh, my first glimpse of the infamous nipple rings."

Gracie blushed, which only caused him to grin wider. She planted a fist in his gut, and he doubled over laughing.

"Okay, okay." He straightened his body and took a deep breath. "You're going to think this is ridiculous, but I went over to Zack's to get a beer. There was some wild bachelorette party going on. I was checking out the girls, and I saw someone I know. Well, knew anyway. Then she saw me."

"Run screaming in the other direction?" Gracie asked.

"No, that's the thing. She runs over to me and leaps into my arms and plants a huge kiss on me."

Gracie frowned. "Was she butt ugly?"

"No, not at all. She's...well, she's hot. Gorgeous hot. I mean one of those women a man is just drawn to."

"Okay, so what's the problem?"

"I love women. No secret there. And I haven't exactly had the sex life of a monk."

Gracie snorted indelicately.

"Shut up," he growled.

She giggled and gestured for him to carry on.

"By all rights I should have been all sorts of turned-on. I mean I had a handful of luscious woman in my arms. She's kissing me. Her breasts, gorgeous breasts by the way, were all pressed up against me. And..."

"And?" Gracie prompted.

"Nothing. Absolutely nothing. I think I may have lost an inch or two, my dick shriveled so quick. I think it may have gone into permanent hiding."

Gracie pressed her lips tight together and her body shook with silent laughter. "Uhm, Wes, you could stand to lose an inch or two and still be better off than most of the male population."

Heat slid up his neck much like nails on a chalkboard.

"Okay, I'll strive to be more serious. Hard, though, when you give me openings like that," she cracked. "So how, pray tell, did this dick shriveling incident lead you to the conclusion that you must suck in bed?"

"Well, there's more to the story," he said grudgingly.

"Aha, so now we get to the good part."

"Shut up, Gracie."

She held her hands up in surrender. "Continue on."

He raised his fingers to his hair then slid them down the back of his head to his neck. "Do you remember Payton Ricci from high school? She was two years behind us."

Gracie scrunched her face into a thoughtful expression. "Huh uh, doesn't ring a bell."

"Well, I had a major crush on her the summer after my senior year. We, uhm, well we had sex. I was her first." He winced at the memory. "To make a long story short, it was a disaster. I hurt her. To date, it has to go down as one of the most awkward moments of my life."

Gracie's lips formed an O. "And Payton is the chick from the bar tonight?"

He nodded.

"And you can't get past the fact that you once had disastrous sex together?"

"Evidently not," he muttered. "I mean, don't get me wrong. It's not like I've spent the last twelve years agonizing over it, but when I saw her, all I could remember is the look on her face, her crying out and the tears afterward. I felt like complete shit then, and I feel like complete shit now."

A light of understanding blazed in Gracie's eyes. "Wes, was that what all that stuff was about at the cabin? You seemed overly concerned that you'd hurt me."

He didn't say anything, but then he didn't have to.

She pursed her lips and blew out a long breath. "Wow. I don't know what to say. I can understand why you feel bad, but damn, she was a virgin. Despite what a whole host of romance books might tell you—okay, me, since I'm sure you aren't reading them—the first time for a woman is often a combination of messy and uncomfortable. Throw in a more-endowed-than-average guy, and you get even more messy and uncomfortable."

"What was your first time like?" he asked, unable to resist his curiosity. And maybe he needed for her to say it had been as awful as it had to have been for Payton.

She chuckled. "Forgettable. That's the experience in a nutshell. A few kisses, he touched my boobs, got between my legs and ten seconds later it was all over with."

He cringed. "That sounds eerily familiar, but damn it, I'd never seen that much female flesh up close and personal. I'm not even sure I made it all the way in before I went off like a damn machine gun."

Gracie laughed and put her hand on his arm. "Wes, you're being way too hard on yourself. You were eighteen. Most eighteen-year-olds haven't climbed the ranks to considerate-lover status yet. I'd say you more than made up for it in the years since."

"I just wish A. she hadn't popped out of nowhere, and B. she hadn't been so nice or acted like she was so damn glad to see me. I was more than happy to keep that incident out of my mind. No guy likes to have his sexual failures shoved under his nose."

"But she didn't shove it under your nose. You said she acted genuinely glad to see you. Have you thought maybe the experience was far more traumatic for you than it was for her?"

"Gracie, I hurt her. A girl's first time shouldn't be like that. I made her cry, for God's sake."

"All I'm saying is that, in all likelihood, she views that experience much the same as most women do. Not great but not the end of the world."

"Yeah, yeah, I know. I just picture all her girlfriends asking who I am. And then she says, oh that was the dumbass I gave my virginity to, the dumbass who had as much finesse as a toad."

Gracie lost all control and started laughing. "So this boils down to your fragile male ego. You don't want it to get out that you weren't always a god in bed."

"I fail to see what's so damn funny," he muttered.

"Let me be the first to burst your bubble, stud." Her eyes twinkled in devilish merriment, and he knew without a doubt she was having way too much fun at his expense. "A lot of guys suck in bed. They don't think they do. Ask them and they're God's gift to women. Ask women and you get a whole different story. I know. I've been through enough losers. Oh, they all thought they were the world's greatest lover, but for the most part, it was all I could do not to fall asleep during their version of foreplay, which usually consisted of 'suck my dick'."

He gave her a wounded look. Damn heifer wasn't doing anything to reassure him here. "You just said that I didn't suck in bed."

"No, you don't, but it doesn't hurt for you to think you do. No doubt it'll make you more determined to impress your next woman when it comes time to get between the sheets."

"Bitch. You're supposed to tell me what a great lay I am and that what happened twelve years ago was a freak incident."

She raised an eyebrow. "Isn't that what I've spent the last ten minutes telling you?"

He sighed again.

She leaned up and kissed him on the cheek, and for a moment, all he really wanted to do was take *her* to bed. They had great chemistry, and if anyone could reestablish his confidence it was Gracie.

"Give yourself a break, Wes," she murmured as she pulled away. She put a hand to his cheek and rubbed her thumb over his goatee. "Chances are you won't even see her again."

He reached up and put his hand over hers then turned her palm over to kiss the exposed skin. "Thanks, Gracie. You're the best. I mean that."

The door from the garage opened and Luke Forsythe shouldered his way in carrying a case of beer and a bag of ice.

Gracie's face lit up, and Wes let her fingers fall from his.

Luke dropped the ice on the floor and heaved the beer onto the island. He bent over to kiss Gracie then glanced up at Wes. "Am I interrupting an intimate moment here?" he asked with barely suppressed amusement.

"Not unless you guys are surprising me with another threesome," Gracie said cheekily as she winked at Wes.

Wes laughed and shook his head. God, he loved this woman. He could never ask for better friends than her and Luke. Whatever his reservations had been in the beginning about a threesome causing awkwardness in the relationship, they were gone now. Nothing had changed between them, and if anything, they were closer.

"I was just giving Wes some chick advice," she said. "Butthead needed it."

Luke shook his head. "Not even going to ask." He nodded at Wes as Gracie snuggled into his side. "Well? We gonna stand around the kitchen all night having chick talk or are we going to drink some beer and watch the fight?"

Chapter Three

Payton wrapped her fingers around the steering wheel and sat staring at Wes Hoffman's house. Why in the world she was sitting here in his driveway the day after he'd given her the most blatant brush-off was beyond her. Maybe she was a masochist. Or maybe she just wanted to know what the hell had inspired such a frantic retreat.

She certainly hadn't come to town looking for him, but now that she'd seen him again, her curiosity was eating her alive.

He'd fascinated her as a teenager, but the adult version, the gorgeous man he'd grown up to be, well, he was downright mouthwatering.

She searched her memory, remembering the day they'd driven out to the lake, picnic basket in the back of the truck. They'd spread out a blanket by the water and spent a lazy afternoon gazing up at the clouds.

When evening fell, they'd moved awkwardly closer. He'd kissed her, lightly, searching, sweetly as only a first lover can do.

She emitted a small sigh as the corners of her lips surged upward. It had been a perfect day. Not unlike today. Beautiful, sunny. Really, even as hot and humid as it got so far south, she wouldn't trade summers here for anything.

Her hands tightened on the steering wheel as she pressed back against the seat. She summoned her courage, taking in a deep, steadying breath.

"Well, you can sit out here all day like a freaking loon, or you can go knock on the door and invite him to lunch."

She took in another deep breath, drew up her shoulders then let them fall before she opened the door and hauled herself out of her car.

He intrigued her. Always had. A soft smile eased her nerves as she headed up the short walkway to the door. No, he wasn't a boy anymore. She'd figured that out about the time she hit him square in the chest last night. The possibilities his more manly physique presented were definitely appealing.

"And maybe it's been too long since you got laid," she muttered. Although it hadn't been that long. Certainly not so long that she ought to be panting after the first available male she came across. No, desperation didn't account for her reaction to Wes Hoffman. She was as attracted to him now as she'd been twelve years ago. In some ways, the attraction was heightened. She'd learned a lot more about sex since she tested the waters at sixteen. She grinned. A whole lot more.

She flipped her hair over her shoulders, smoothed her hands down her jeans and pushed the button for the doorbell. She looked from side to side and tapped her foot on the concrete porch as she waited for him to answer.

Then the door opened and Wes's startled gaze met hers.

She glanced appreciatively over his physique. He wore a pair of shorts, no shirt, and she couldn't quite rip her eyes from his well-muscled chest. Not an inch of spare flesh dotted his abdomen. He worked out, and it was obvious.

"Hi...uh, I wasn't expecting you," he said awkwardly.

She smiled. "I know. Thought I'd drop by and invite you to lunch. Catch up on old times. Stuff like that."

Was that panic in his eyes? Guys only got the deer-in-the-headlights look when they got their hand caught in the cookie jar.

"Are you married?" she demanded.

He actually looked appalled. "Why the hell would you ask that?"

She shrugged. "A reasonable assumption given the fact you act as happy to see me as you would a good case of the clap."

He choked on his laughter and a grin creased his face. "Sorry. I mean, you just caught me off guard. You're the last person I expected to see."

"So you want to grab lunch?" she asked. "I'm free until later this afternoon, then I have rehearsal dinner shit for the wedding."

"Uh—" He broke off and shifted uncomfortably, moving his weight from one foot to another.

He really *was* giving her the brush-off. Heat bloomed across her cheeks, but she bit the inside of her lip to control the tide of embarrassment. Damn, just when she'd convinced herself that there was a perfectly good reason for his flakiness the night before.

"On second thought, I can see you'd rather endure a trip to the dentist," she said dryly. She tucked her hair behind her ears and backed toward the edge of the porch. "It was nice seeing you again."

She turned and navigated the two small steps to the walkway cutting across the yard when his voice stopped her.

"Payton, wait."

She stopped and slowly turned, giving him a long, measuring stare. He stared back at her, his eyes thoughtful, a hint of regret simmering in the depths.

"Give me a minute to get dressed, okay?"

Silence fell between them. She shoved her hands into her jeans pockets and rocked back on her heels. "Okay."

Wes watched her for a long second before he turned and went back to his bedroom. She was here. On his doorstep. Inviting him to lunch. And he was acting like a complete chicken shit.

"Suck it up and take it like a man." *Get this over with. She'll leave town. It's just like Gracie said. I'll probably never see her again.*

He glanced down at his embarrassingly flat shorts. "A lot of help you are," he muttered. "A drop-dead gorgeous woman throws herself at you and all you can do is lay there like a fucking pussy."

God, now he was talking to his dick. What a pansy.

He yanked on a T-shirt then fumbled for his tennis shoes which were shoved under the bed. Turning to go, he thought better of it and hurried to the bathroom. There, he yanked up a toothbrush and did a quicky job of brushing his teeth. Hell, she might try to kiss him again. Oddly enough, that idea wasn't as terrifying as it should be.

As he passed through the living room, he grabbed for the keys on the hook by the door and walked outside. It was hot, but he was already sweating, and he hadn't even gotten close to her yet.

He paused at the porch steps and looked at her. Really looked at her. Without all the discomfort her sudden appearance had caused, without the desire to see her vanish into thin air.

The truth was, she was beautiful. The sweet, young girl he'd known had blossomed into one hell of a gorgeous woman. She seemed confident yet relaxed, and she didn't seem like a bullshitter.

She looked up and met his gaze when he neared her. She didn't immediately smile but then one corner of her mouth lifted and she straightened her stance, one hand on her hip as if she was waiting for him to make the next move. Fair enough—she'd made the first one. And the second.

"Want to go in my truck?" he asked.

"Sure, just let me get my purse."

He waited as she retrieved her bag from her car, then opened the passenger side door of his truck for her. She moved past him in a soft swirl of floral-scented air. She reached for the door handle, and he gently shut the door behind her before walking around to get in on his side.

"So where are we going again?" she asked as he backed out of his driveway.

"This was your idea," he said. "Where are you taking me?"

"What are my choices?"

"Well, you can have a burger, Mexican or barbeque. Unless

you want to drive into Beaumont, in which case, you can pick your poison."

"We can do Mexican," she said.

He drummed his thumbs on the steering wheel as he stopped at the one red light in town. He glanced over to see her staring out her window, her expression one of supreme *I don't give a fuck.*

A few minutes later, they pulled into the parking lot of the restaurant. He got out and waited for her in front of the truck then walked behind her inside where they were seated by the hostess.

A waitress dumped a basket of chips with salsa in front of them and then took their drink order. Wes waited until she'd returned and had taken their food order before relaxing in his chair and glancing up at Payton.

She munched on a chip, glancing curiously around the room. Then her gaze settled back on him, and for once he didn't look away. He stared into her pale blue eyes, eyes that currently sparkled with challenge.

"Why are you so uptight around me?" she asked.

He blinked. Well, she definitely didn't have any inhibitions. "Uh..."

She picked up another chip and dunked it into the salsa. "I can't figure you out," she continued. "I catch you looking at me, and I can see the interest, but then the next second, you're running away so fast, you're tripping over your feet. Am I that unappealing?"

"Good Lord, no," he muttered, still reeling over the direct line she'd taken.

She arched one eyebrow. "Then what is it? Got something against brunettes?"

"Honey, I like all women," he drawled.

She snorted. "That's bullshit. If that were true, you and I would have ended up in bed last night instead of you pulling a lame-ass hat trick to escape."

He coughed as a piece of chip went down the wrong pipe. He wheezed and reached for his water. A mournful sigh escaped him, and he briefly closed his eyes. Surely this was a guy's worst nightmare. A gorgeous, vibrant woman offering herself on a silver platter, and his mind and dick weren't in unison.

"Payton, you're a beautiful woman—"

She held up a hand in annoyance. "Good God, if you're going to give me that brush-off speech, save it, please. I don't need you to patronize me. Contrary to what you may think, you don't hold my ego in your little palm. Yeah, I'm attracted to you, yeah, we have a history, but that doesn't mean you're the only guy in the world I've ever wanted to sleep with."

He scrubbed a hand over his face and groaned. This was such a cluster fuck. "That's just it, Payton. Our history is what's the issue here."

Confusion darted across her face. "What?"

He glanced around at the nearby tables, cringing at the idea that he'd be overheard by someone. Then he looked back at Payton who stared at him with a crinkled brow.

"Can we get out of here? Go somewhere else to have this conversation?"

"Uh, okay, I guess."

He stood abruptly and reached for his wallet. He peeled off a twenty and threw it on the table, not bothering to wait for their food. If he was going to have this come-to-Jesus moment with Payton, he damn sure wasn't going to do it in a place where he could be overheard by people he had to face on a daily basis.

He reached for her hand before he thought better of it. She hesitated a brief moment before sliding her fingers into his palm. They walked out of the restaurant, him tugging her behind him in his haste to get out.

"Where are we going?" she asked as he pulled out of the parking lot.

"Somewhere private," he muttered.

She shrugged and focused her attention out the window as he drove through town and hit the highway north into the country. A few miles out, he turned onto a dirt road leading up to an old logging site.

"This must be pretty serious," she said dryly. "Planning to off me and hide the body?"

He pulled over and cut the engine before turning in his seat to face her. "Very funny. I don't remember you being such a sarcastic wench."

She eyed him angelically, the baby blue eyes a fitting accompaniment to her look of innocence. Though he was fast finding out she wasn't the sweet little sixteen-year-old he'd known.

"So why is our history such a big issue?" she asked.

With her sitting across from him, staring expectantly at him, he suddenly felt like a complete moron. It was obvious that she didn't have the same hang-ups he did.

"Payton, I hurt you. Badly. I was clumsy, inconsiderate and I ruined what should have been a terrific experience for you. It was embarrassing as hell, and it's something I'd just as soon try to forget. When I saw you again, my first instinct was to run as far as I could in the other direction."

"You *did* run in the opposite direction," she pointed out.

He huffed in irritation. Did she take nothing seriously?

She stared at him a long moment, her face scrunching up more with each passing second. "You're serious, aren't you?"

Knowing there was only one way to get his point across with the least amount of chitchat and skirting around the issue, he reached across the seat and grabbed her hand. He guided it between his legs, ignoring her expression of surprise.

"Let me put it into terms you can't possibly misunderstand. You feel that? Nothing. I may as well be a fucking eunuch. You're a gorgeous woman. I should be a walking hard-on around you, instead I'll likely have to shove my finger up my ass to push my dick back out of hiding."

She giggled. First a stifled sound like she was trying valiantly to control her mirth. Then she lost all control and began laughing uncontrollably.

"I'm glad you find this so damn amusing," he said through gritted teeth as he released her hand.

She wiped tears from her eyes then dissolved into laughter

again. Wes heaved a long-suffering sigh and stared out the windshield as Payton attempted to collect herself.

She wheezed a few times then tucked her hair back behind her ear. "Wes, tell me you haven't been worked up all these years over the time we had sex."

He shot her a dirty glance. "Of course I haven't been hung up on it for the last twelve years. It's just that, damn it, Payton, I *hurt* you."

The laughter disappeared and her eyes softened. She reached out to touch his arm. "Wes, it was my first time. Of course it hurt. But that's not what I remember about it."

His eyebrows went up. "It's not? What *do* you remember then?"

Her eyes twinkled merrily, and she smiled that sweet smile that made his gut ache.

"So that's what all that crap was about last night? You were embarrassed because of what happened between us in high school?"

"It wasn't one of my prouder moments," he defended. "I realize it sounds stupid, but it was pretty humiliating." He still cringed when he thought too long about it.

"It's not stupid. I think it's sweet," she said, her smile growing broader.

Sweet? Hell, he'd almost prefer humiliation.

Her face took on a dreamy look, and the smile turned wistful. "What I remember is that we were young. I was nervous and excited all at the same time, and you were so sweet and patient with me."

Patient? Clearly they were remembering separate events. He'd acted with no finesse, and premature ejaculation didn't even begin to cover the description of his performance.

He cleared his throat. "Uhm, Payton, are you sure you're remembering the time you had sex with *me*?"

She laughed. "A girl remembers her first time, and she certainly remembers the guy who was her first."

"I wasn't patient," he said gruffly.

"Yes, you were," she chided. "You were incredibly sweet.

You said all the right things. That I was beautiful. You made sure I was with you every step of the way."

"I did?"

She nodded. "I don't know what kind of messed-up event you remember, but it's obvious our perceptions of it are very different. Was it the best sex I've ever had? No. But it wasn't a disaster. In fact, for it being my first time, I don't think it could have been much better."

He swallowed the knot in his throat and went for the final humiliating factor. "It was my first time too," he said grudgingly.

Her eyes widened in surprise. "Really? I was your first?"

"Yeah."

She smiled. "I think that's—"

"If you say sweet, I swear I'll push you out of the truck," he growled.

A peal of laughter rang out. "Okay, I think it's cool. That better?"

He smiled for the first time. "I guess you think this is completely ridiculous."

She reached over and cupped his cheek in her palm. "I think a lot of things. I think I'm flattered by the fact you were so concerned that you'd hurt me. I think you've turned into a great guy, not surprising since I always thought you were positively dreamy." She winked before continuing on. "But ridiculous? No, I don't think you're ridiculous."

Her eyes narrowed until they became half-lidded. She viewed him under a veil of thick lashes, and her tongue came out to wet her lips. She was going to kiss him again.

Not if you kiss her first.

And why not? So far she'd made all the moves. He wanted to taste her, wanted to remember how good she felt in his arms. And damn it, he wanted some kind of reaction from the lower half of his body.

He eased his head forward, meeting her halfway. She framed his face in her hands and pulled him closer. He slid his fingers up her shoulders, over the curve of her neck until they rested just below her ears. His lips met hers. Cautiously at first.

A soft mingling of flesh. Kiss and retreat. Kiss again. Longer this time. His tongue darted out. He wanted her taste, wanted to remember, wanted to replace the undesirable memories with better ones.

This time, the urgency of youth was absent. Instead, there was a slow, sensual exploration, a gentle seduction. This is what she should have had the first time. Not his clumsy attempts.

That thought sent a jolt of reality over him. With a ragged sigh, he pulled away and leaned back against the headrest of his seat.

"What's wrong?" she asked.

It would seem his humiliation knew no bounds. He gestured downward with a casual flip of his hand. "Nothing. That's what's wrong. My mind says yes. Unfortunately, my mind and my body are on two different wavelengths."

"I guess this is where I get the *it's not you, it's me* speech," she said.

He laughed. He couldn't help it. It was either that or die a slow death from embarrassment. "I think it's definitely safe to say it's not you, Payton. Apparently I have more issues than *Time* magazine. Who knew I was so fucked in the head over something that happened twelve years ago."

She rotated her wrist up to check her watch. "Not that I don't enjoy dampening a man's ardor, but I really need to be getting back. I have the rehearsal supper this evening, and I have to drive back to Beaumont to the hotel to get ready."

He saw through her flippant front. He knew he'd hurt her. Again. Not physically this time. His chest felt heavy with regret.

"Payton?"

She looked up.

"You don't know how much I wish...how much I wish that things were different."

She grinned, though her chin trembled just a bit as she spoke. "So what you're saying is that you wish like hell your cock would cooperate so you could prove to me what a stud you've turned out to be."

"Well, I wouldn't have put it like that exactly," he muttered.

She leaned over and kissed his cheek. "Maybe we're better off just being friends and calling it good."

As he started the engine and drove back down the dirt road, her last words echoed in his ears. Friends. Hell, he was friends with Gracie. He didn't want to be friends with Payton. It didn't feel like enough all of a sudden. He felt an odd sort of ache, deeper than his skin, deep in his chest. Like someone had dropped a bowling ball down his throat. And he was hard-pressed to put his finger on why.

Two days ago, he was just fine. Two days ago, he didn't have a care in the world beyond his job and his friends. But two days ago, Payton hadn't walked back into his life.

Chapter Four

She'd spent the entire afternoon and most of the evening thinking about him. She'd cruised through rehearsal and the dinner afterward on autopilot, smiling when appropriate, performing most of the tasks with half a brain.

Now that the shindig was winding down, Payton mulled her course of action over a glass of wine as she watched Brenda smile up at her husband-to-be as they talked with both sets of parents.

True, probably the smartest idea would be to leave this thing between her and Wes alone, go back home to Houston after the wedding and forget she'd ever seen him again. But that wasn't what she *wanted* to do, and she had this little problem called an impulsive nature. She pretty much tended to do what she wanted, regardless of the fact that she might regret it afterward.

And she wanted Wes Hoffman pretty badly. But *why* did she want him? That was a harder question to answer. Was he a challenge? Maybe, but that still didn't explain the deep-down flutter that started the minute she saw him in the bar.

She drummed her fingers along the side of the crystal goblet and took another sip as she contemplated her options. It wasn't as simple as showing up at his house again and asking him if he was interested in a one-night stand. While he might very well be interested (he was a guy after all), his lack of physical response to her was a rather huge stumbling block.

Yeah, that ruffled her pride, even though she *knew* he found her attractive.

What she needed to do was get around his little psychological roadblock. A teeny-tiny smile attacked her face as an idea formed.

Ambush.

Maybe he expected her to be all sweet and innocent, goodness and light. He *did* still see her as a sixteen-year-old virgin. She nearly snorted wine out her nose at that idea.

Yeah, what she needed was a plan of attack. A way to knock him off his feet and get him to see *her*, not some little girl he felt guilty for hurting.

Or...

Not see her at all.

She looked at her watch and calculated the time she'd need to drive back to her hotel and get ready. An hour, tops. She set her wineglass in the window behind her then dug out her cell phone from her purse. Hopefully his number was listed.

Wes walked through the lobby of Payton's hotel and down the hall toward the room number she'd given him. There were a thousand reasons he shouldn't be here. One, he had to work in the morning, two, he needed to just let sleeping dogs lie and three, what the hell could she want?

He'd gotten a phone call from her—surprising enough to hear her husky voice over the line, but then she'd asked him to come to her hotel. Ten o'clock. She'd been very specific.

He should have declined, just said no. But here he was, standing outside her room like a moron on his first date. Despite his initial desire for her to leave and for him to never see her again, he knew that was his embarrassment and discomfort talking. The truth was, she intrigued him. He was curious, and he knew she was equally intrigued with him.

He knocked sharply and waited. Within a few seconds the door opened, and his eyes widened. Payton was half-hidden by the door, but what he could see was downright jaw-dropping.

One long, slender leg peeked seductively around the door. Dainty lace, hip-hugging panties—could you call something that only covered an inch of flesh actual panties?—twined over her curvy hip.

His gaze followed the bare flesh from the waistband of the panties upward until it met with a matching bra. Pink. Sexy and feminine.

She smiled at him, white, perfectly straight teeth flashing as she opened the door wider. "Come in, please."

He started forward on shaky legs, swallowing convulsively when she turned to walk in front of him. The panties rode high, giving him a tantalizing glimpse of the swell of her ass. Her hips rocked in a gentle motion and he had to catch himself as his head began mimicking those motions.

She stopped at a chair that was situated at the foot of the bed. "Sit," she said as she gestured downward.

Dumbly he eased into the chair and looked up, his gaze riveted to her. "Payton, what's this about?"

She leaned down and put a finger over his lips. "Shhh." Her lips hovered provocatively over the finger pressed against his mouth. "This is my show." She reached over and picked up a long black piece of satin from the bed. It trailed across his legs as she circled behind him.

She placed one hand on his shoulder and looped the sash around the front of his neck. Then she raised it until it brushed across his face. With gentle fingers, she positioned it over his eyes.

As the room went dark, he raised his hand in automatic protest, but again she whispered in his ear. "Shhh. Trust me. You'll like this."

He let his hand fall as she gathered the material tight around his eyes. She tied it in the back, and he sat there, waiting for what she would do next.

He jumped when her lips met the curve of his neck. She kissed a soft line upward. Chill bumps broke out on his arms as her warm breath blew over his skin.

Then she sank her teeth into his earlobe, and he nearly

came off the chair. Her tongue swirled around the tender flesh before she sucked the lobe back between her teeth. With a gentle nip, she moved away again.

A slight movement of air alerted him to the fact she'd walked back around the chair. A faint rustle could be heard and then she placed both hands on his knees, slid them up his legs until she grasped his hips.

She straddled his lap, moving in close until her pussy cradled his groin. A surge of excitement shot through his system. His dick came to life after its long stint of dormancy. Okay, so it had only lain dormant for two days, but to a guy it was a fucking lifetime.

He swelled painfully against his jeans. He heard her light chuckle just as she curled her fingers around his hands and lifted them.

She placed his palms on her legs and kept her fingers wrapped around his wrists. Slowly, seductively, she guided his hands up her body. Over her hips, naked hips. She'd ditched the underwear. Oh hell.

Up her waist, sliding sideways over her taut belly. Finally up her ribcage until his knuckles brushed the undersides of her breasts.

Unwilling to let her control the progress any longer, he cupped her breasts and worked his thumbs over her nipples. Soft, velvety, he loved the texture and weight of her breasts. Definitely a C cup, maybe a smaller D.

She shuddered against his fingers.

"Like that?" he murmured as he continued stroking the tips.

In response, she gripped his hands, holding them tighter over her breasts.

"Touch me," she whispered.

"Show me where."

She wiggled on his lap, moving back. Then she guided his right palm from her breast, down her silken skin, lower until he felt the curls of her pussy. They brushed across his fingers, damper the closer he got to her flesh.

"Oh, you mean here."

"Mmm hmmm."

He coaxed the lips apart and eased one finger over the hot, moist flesh between her legs. She jerked in reaction when he stroked her clit.

"You're wet."

"Because I want you," she whispered. "And I think you want me."

"Oh, yeah, sweetheart. I want you."

She cupped his bulging groin, gently squeezing. She laughed huskily, her mouth close to his ear again. "Yeah, I'd say your earlier problem might be a non-issue now."

"I do love an inventive woman."

"I'm just a woman willing to do whatever it takes to get what she wants."

He turned his head in the direction of her voice, his lips colliding with hers. He kissed her, long, hot and hard. He reached up to cup her face, holding her against him as their tongues explored new territory.

He moved his mouth down her jawline then below to the tender skin of her neck. She moaned softly as he nibbled and sucked his way to her shoulder. Her fingers gripped his shoulders, digging into his skin.

In the darkness the blindfold brought, he found his other senses heightened. Every touch, every taste counted. They were his only means to explore her. He wrapped his arms around her waist and lifted her.

The plump swells of her breasts rubbed over his chin, and he reached out with his tongue to lap at her nipple. He sucked it between his teeth, enjoying her sharp intake of breath.

He alternated licking and nibbling. He wanted to taste every inch.

Suddenly she pulled away, climbing off his lap. When he would have protested, she once again pressed a finger to his lips.

"My show, remember?"

He grinned and nodded.

"Good, then stand up."

He stood like a good boy ever hopeful of receiving his reward.

"Take your shirt off," she murmured.

Impatiently, he yanked at the T-shirt, pulled it over his head and tossed it aside.

"Oh, nice," she purred as she pressed both palms to his skin.

He flinched when she touched her lips to the hollow of his chest. As her tongue melted over him, her hands moved lower, between them, working at the fly of his jeans. He shifted back an inch to give her more room to work.

He was so hard he was going to have a permanent cramp in his cock if she didn't get his jeans off soon.

The grating sound of his zipper echoed in the room, and then she slid her fingers inside his jeans, working past the band of his underwear until she cupped his balls.

With her other hand she worked his jeans over his hips, taking his underwear with them. Cool air rushed over his groin, a direct contrast to the aching heat her caresses wrought.

His jeans fell the rest of the way to the floor and he stepped out of one leg and then the other. She gripped his hips, and he felt her body slide down his as she got on her knees in front of him.

Not seeing was torture. He imagined how she must look, kneeling in front of him, his cock inches from her mouth. She hadn't made a single comment about his size, a fact he found enormously relieving. The last thing he wanted was to ruin the mood.

He reached out, wanting to touch her hair, coax her closer, guide his cock inside her hot, wet mouth. She chuckled and pushed him away.

"Patience. I'm enjoying the view."

Her fingers circled his dick, gliding up and down his rigid length. The other hand closed around his sac, her finger rubbing the seam on the backside.

He rocked forward on his toes as her breath tickled over the head. Again she stayed his motion and continued her exploratory caresses.

He groaned. "You're killing me."

"Oh, no, I haven't gotten to the killing part yet."

Lord, he couldn't wait to die then.

She grasped his dick, working it in an up-and-down motion. Then she slid her delicious mouth over the head, paused and let his cock sink deep. He nearly came all undone.

Her tongue rasped the sensitive vein on the underside of his cock, and she moved back and forth. When he butted against the back of her throat, she swallowed, the action milking his erection. A thousand volts of electricity arced through his body like a streak of white-hot lightning.

As she pulled away, a tiny spurt of fluid spilled on her tongue. She swallowed and lapped at the head as if wanting more. He wanted to give her more.

She braced herself against his thighs and slowly pushed herself up, allowing his cock to slip from her mouth. He stood there, waiting for her next move.

She pulled him forward. Then her hand fell away from his, and he heard the chair being shoved aside. A moment later, she returned and walked him backward until the backs of his legs came into contact with the bed.

"Lie down," she directed.

He sat on the bed then reclined.

"Move farther up."

He complied, scooting until his head was on one of the pillows. He reached down, testing to see if she was close, wanting to touch her.

The bed dipped, and she straddled his waist. She bent down to kiss him then slid her mouth over his cheek to his ear.

"Do you want to taste me as much as I want to taste you?"

"There's not an inch of you I don't want to taste," he said.

He felt her smile against his ear. "I want you to lick my pussy while I suck your cock."

"I love a woman who knows what she wants."

"Oh, I know exactly what I want. I've known since I saw you in that bar. And I intend to have you."

"I never argue with a lady."

"Smart man."

She lifted off of him again. She rotated then straddled his face, lowering her pussy until she was just inches from his mouth. He could smell her, sweet, slightly musky. Sexy as hell.

He cupped her ass, positioning her better so he could begin his exploration. As his tongue flicked out to circle her pussy entrance, her mouth sank over his cock, and he moaned low in his throat.

Her ass quivered against his fingers as he gently worked his mouth over her clit. One thing he had learned since his first encounter with Payton all those years ago was that a woman didn't want to be eaten like a damn potato chip. She wanted to be teased, savored, enjoyed like a fine wine. Sipped at, not gulped.

She writhed against his mouth, squirming as he continued his exploration. Her breath came in gasps around his cock, sending sparks through his groin. He arched into her as she twisted against him.

He took his time, nudging her with his mouth, licking, nipping then soothing the delicate folds. Each time his tongue swept over her clit, it tightened and a tiny spasm quaked through her body.

"Are you close?" he whispered.

She moaned. "Yes, but not yet. Please."

He smiled and lessened the onslaught of his mouth. "I want you to come in my mouth. I want to taste you."

She tore her mouth away from his dick and wrapped her fingers around it, moving up and down in slow, long motions. Her chest heaved against his belly.

He parted the soft folds of her pussy, stroking, feather-light. He wanted to see her splayed out over his chest, her femininity bared for him, but at the same time, having to rely on touch and taste was exciting. New. A little disconcerting but in a titillating way.

Slowly, reverently, he pushed one finger inside her, feeling the way the walls of her vagina gripped him. Sweat beaded his forehead as he imagined what it would feel like for his cock to be surrounded by such sweet heat.

When she began to shudder uncontrollably, he withdrew his finger and gripped her ass again, pulling her down to his mouth once more.

His tongue found her clit, and he gently sucked the taut bud into his mouth. She moaned and rocked back as her mouth paused on his cock. "I'm going to come," she gasped out.

He said nothing but swirled his tongue downward, plunging it into her opening. She tensed over him, and a surge of honey spilled onto his tongue. Her legs shook, her body shook, her fingers tightened around his cock.

She cried out as she undulated her hips in his hands. He held her, coaxing her orgasm with his mouth. Several long seconds later, she slumped against his body, her breath coming in big heaves.

She eased off his body. Again he felt the bed dip as she got up. He heard the crinkle of a wrapper. Soon she returned, climbing onto the bed.

She grasped his cock and slid her mouth over the head, sucking and licking down then back up again. Then she rolled a condom on. He waited, nearly breathless with anticipation.

He flinched as her lips met the sensitive skin just above the base of his dick.

"Ready for a ride, cowboy?"

"Oh hell yeah," he ground out.

Chapter Five

Payton applied lubricant to Wes's latex-sheathed cock, wiped her hand on one of the hotel towels then tossed it aside. Her body was still trembling from her orgasm, but she couldn't wait to have him inside her.

She wanted to rip off the blindfold so she could see his eyes glazed over with passion, see him when he came, but she wasn't about to risk ruining the fantasy aspect of the scene she'd carefully cultivated. The last thing she needed was to have his erection die a slow death if he got a chance to think too much.

No, she wanted him to feel, not think. And if she had her way, he was going to feel the best damn sex of his life.

She straddled him, positioning his cock between her legs. She felt him tense as the head brushed across her entrance. She smiled and eased down, slowly, teasingly.

His hands gripped her hips but she batted them away and continued her slow downward assault.

They both moaned as she engulfed him. Tight, so tight. He filled every inch of her, and still she had more to go. Never had she felt anything quite this good.

She braced herself against his chest as she rocked down on him.

"Payton...I'm not hurting you, am I?"

The concern in his voice made her smile. As she'd done before, she placed a finger over his lips. "The question is, am I going to hurt you?"

His mouth quirked underneath her finger as he grinned.

Maya Banks

"Oh, I hope to hell so. I'm a big boy. Hurt me good."

His hands snuck up her hips again, and this time she allowed it. They glided over her belly and up to her breasts where he found her nipples.

As he squeezed and toyed with the erect nubs, she forewent the slow, measured ride she'd started and began a faster pace. His fingers tightened around her nipples, and he arched his body to meet her movements.

She cried out as he slipped deeper. An ache built within her, blooming, radiating through her senses. She loved his touch, tender, giving pleasure. She even loved his concern over hurting her, however misplaced *that* idea was.

She leaned forward, finding his lips, fusing her mouth to his as he gripped her hips, helping her in her ride. His fingers dug into her ass as he lifted her up and down.

"Are you with me?" he whispered into her mouth. "Because I'm close."

Was she with him? Hell, if he didn't come soon, she was going to leave him behind yet again.

She reached down, slid her fingers between their bodies until they stroked over her clit. She rolled the tight button and closed her eyes as her orgasm built.

"Oh, yeah, I'm with you," she said breathlessly.

He arched his hips and began pumping upward in short, hard thrusts. She pressed harder with her fingers, rotating in a tight circle.

As he hit a spot much deeper than he had before, she exploded. Her sharp cry echoed across the room just a split second before she felt the surge of his release ripple through his body.

Once, twice more he thrust hard into her before holding her tight against him as he trembled and jerked beneath her. She slumped forward.

Slowly, his hands smoothed over her body, moving from her hips up her back in a soothing motion. He rubbed up and down and then in a circular pattern, eliciting a sigh of contentment from her as she lay snuggled on top of him.

She reached up to remove the blindfold, suddenly wanting to see the sleepy contentment in his brown eyes. He blinked as the satin fell away, and what she saw reflected in his dark orbs made her stomach clench.

Nothing lazy or contented about him. He looked hungry, aroused, like he wanted more.

He reached up to cup her face. Then he pulled her down to meet his kiss. Hot. Carnal. Ravenous.

When she finally pulled away to catch her breath, she stared down at him, studying his reaction carefully. "Like what you see?"

His gaze dropped to her body, roaming over her breasts. His hand soon followed, touching, exploring.

"Oh, I like," he said softly.

He pulled her down once again, kissing her more gently this time. With his arms wrapped around her, he rolled them over so he was on top. Then he eased from between her legs.

"Let me get rid of this and I'll be right back," he murmured.

She watched as he got off the bed and slid the condom off. He walked to the trashcan and tossed it in before turning back around.

Her gaze ran appreciatively over his body. His cock, even in a state of semi-arousal was a beautiful thing to behold. She stretched, arching her body invitingly. His eyes gleamed, and he moved to the bed again.

He knelt on the end and crawled back up to straddle her knees. He bent and pressed his lips to her belly. She shivered as his warm tongue swirled around her navel.

When he looked back up at her, the hunger in his eyes had intensified.

"What do you say we start this all over again? This time I want to see every inch of you. I want to see you when I thrust into your pussy. I want to see you when you come."

She opened her arms as he moved up her body. "Mmmm, I like the way you think."

Wes woke with a warm, soft body curled up tight against him. One of Payton's arms was thrown across his chest and her head was tucked underneath his chin.

He felt sated. Heavy with contentment. A killer kind of tired a man got from having knock-your-socks-off sex. Carefully, so as not to wake her up, he raised his right arm and looked at his watch.

Fuck. He had to get up now and get his ass on the road or he wasn't going to make it home in time to change and get to work.

Regretfully, he eased away from Payton and sat on the edge of the bed in the dark as he searched for his clothes and shoes. Finally he got up and turned the light on in the bathroom, leaving the door open an inch so he could see. He returned to the bed and began pulling on his jeans.

"Going so soon?" Payton asked around a lusty-sounding yawn.

He turned back to her and slid his hand over her curvy body. "I have to be at work in an hour."

"Then you better get going."

He leaned over and kissed her on the forehead. "Any chance I'll see you again?" He cursed himself the instant it came out of his mouth. He sounded...needy.

She leaned up on one elbow as he retreated off the bed. The low beam from the bathroom bathed her in just enough light that he could see her soft, tousled body. Her hair streamed over her shoulders, and she clutched the sheet over her breasts.

"The wedding is early, and I could be persuaded to skip the reception if you were interested in meeting me back here around nine."

"I'll be here," he said as he finished pulling on his jeans.

He thought about her the whole day. He operated his entire shift on half a brain. Thank goodness it was like ninety percent of all the other days in small-town Texas. Mostly boring. A few traffic stops and one domestic disturbance call that turned out to be a false alarm.

By the end of the day, he was a walking dick. He was hard-pressed to even remember the episode from twelve years ago, and he felt like a dumbass for all the angst it had caused him. He and Payton may have both been inexperienced virgins then, but she'd freaking rocked his world last night.

Quitting time came none too soon, but then he realized he'd have to face several more hours of twiddling his thumbs before he headed to Beaumont. He also needed to remember his own damn condoms this time. Thank goodness one of them had been prepared because he'd left his brain behind last night when he'd gone to her hotel.

As he was leaving the station, his cell phone rang. He looked down at the LCD and saw Jeremy's name. Ah shit. Saturday night. They always got together at Jeremy's on the weekends.

Well, he could go over for a little while, pass the time until he headed for the hotel. He'd enlist Gracie's help if he had to in order to avoid an interrogation about where he was going.

He flipped open the phone. "Hey, man."

"Hey, you coming over or what? We have beer and a fight ordered."

"Everyone going to be there?" Wes asked.

"Yeah, the whole gang."

"Cool. Let me stop off by the house and I'll be over. Need me to bring anything?"

"Nah, we got it. See you in a few."

Wes closed the phone and turned into his driveway. He'd shower and change so he could leave straight from Jeremy's later on.

Twenty minutes later, he left his house again and drove the two miles to Jeremy's. When he pulled in, he saw Luke's and Jake's trucks already parked in the drive.

He walked in the front door without knocking and immediately heard talking and laughing. He sauntered into the living room to see Jake, Luke and Jeremy sprawled in their seats.

"Hey, what's up?" Luke called.

"Where are the ladies?" Wes asked.

"Kitchen," Jake said, pointing around his beer.

"Ah well, not that I don't like y'all or anything, but I'd much rather go say hi to the women first."

Jeremy chuckled. "Gee, and we wonder why he has them all wrapped around his little finger."

Wes grinned and walked on to the kitchen where he saw the three women standing around the bar chitchatting. He wrapped an arm around Ellie first and kissed her noisily on the lips. "Hey, gorgeous."

"Wes!" Her pretty face lit up even as a hint of a blush colored her cheeks.

He turned to Michelle next and picked her up to kiss her. "How's the munchkin doing?"

"He's fine," she said with a smile. "Sleeping right now."

Finally he turned to Gracie, who winked at him just as he bent down to kiss her.

"You look like a man who got laid last night," she murmured so only he heard.

"And what does a man who got laid look like, smartass?" he asked in her ear as he hugged her.

"That shit-eating grin is a dead giveaway."

He pulled away, and she grinned mischievously at him. "I will find out later. Count on it."

"Find out what?" Michelle demanded.

"Nothing," he muttered, giving Gracie a hard look.

She smiled innocently back at him and mouthed *later.*

Later came much sooner than he expected, but then Gracie was determined if nothing else. She cornered him in the kitchen when he volunteered to make a beer run.

"Okay, so spill it," she said as he rummaged in the fridge

for the beer.

He gathered the cans in his arms, backed out of the fridge and nudged the door closed with his elbow.

"Demanding wench, aren't you?"

She grinned. "I just know a juicy story when I see one."

"I slept with her," he said simply.

"I'm assuming we're talking about the chick you said you couldn't get it up for?"

He laughed. "You're such a bitch."

"And you love me for it."

"True. Very true. Yes, I slept with Payton."

"Oh, do share. I guess your impotence issue didn't last too terribly long."

He winced. "Could you not use that word? It sounds so...*medical*. I don't have impotence."

She shook with laughter, her auburn curls doing a jig on her shoulders. "All right, so your dick suddenly started cooperating with you. That better?"

"Much," he said with a grin. "I wish I could claim the credit, but that goes to Payton."

Gracie raised her eyebrow. "Now I know I have to hear the rest of this."

He quickly outlined the events of the night before. When he glanced over at Gracie, she looked chagrinned.

"What?" he asked.

"Damn, why didn't I ever think about a blindfold? I'm so going to have to steal that idea for Luke."

"Luke having problems getting it up?" Wes smirked.

She flipped him the bird. "Are you suggesting he isn't turned on by me anymore?"

Wes laughed. "Hell no, I know better. That man can't be in the same room with you without getting the shakes."

"So what now?" Gracie said, adopting a more serious expression. "You going to see her again?"

Wes nodded. "Tonight. I sort of need your help escaping without getting the third degree. I'd rather not answer a hundred questions."

She nodded then laughed as Luke bellowed from the living room. "No problem. Better get that beer back into the living room. The natives are getting restless."

They both headed back into the living room to see Thad, Jeremy and Michelle's newborn son being passed around. Ellie sat on Jake's lap holding the baby, and they both were extremely gooey-eyed over the wiggling lump.

Ellie made eye contact with Wes, and he raised an eyebrow at the soft joy on her face. Her eyes twinkled merrily, the look of a woman with a secret she couldn't wait to share. Wes smiled back, satisfied to see her so happy.

He sat next to Gracie and Luke on the couch, popped open a beer then glanced back over at Ellie and Jake. "So, guys, got something you want to share with the rest of us?"

Jake glared suspiciously at him then raised an eyebrow in Ellie's direction. She shrugged then laughed.

"I didn't say a word."

"You don't have to, girlfriend," Gracie piped in. "It's there to see on your face. We're all just wondering how long you're going to leave us in suspense."

Ellie blushed, a rosy, ecstatic glow lighting up her face. Jake smiled back at her with such tenderness it made Wes feel a little gooey himself. In a twisted, marshmallow kind of way.

"We're having a baby," she announced.

The room erupted in a chorus of congratulations, backslapping and hugs. Wes sat back and smiled, enjoying the smiles and laughter of his group of friends. They'd all found happiness and the love of a good woman, or so the country song went. And, well, the love of a good woman was hard to find, so he certainly didn't begrudge them that. Even if they *had* all turned into pussies.

Chapter Six

So she'd skirted out of the wedding a little earlier than she should have so she could go shopping for sexy lingerie. She hadn't planned on hooking up for some wild sex while she was here, so she hadn't packed for the occasion.

Payton stood in the bathroom of her hotel room, fiddling with the tie of her satin flyaway negligee. All ego aside, she knew she looked hot. The tie cinched her breasts and plumped them up to their best advantage, and the flyaway portion bared her belly and the tiny lace underwear that hardly covered her pussy at all.

She grinned at her reflection. No blindfold tonight. He was going to see it all, and she wanted it to be an experience he wouldn't soon forget.

Promptly at nine, a knock sounded at her door, and she went to answer, foregoing the coy hide-and-seek act she'd played the night before.

As soon as she opened the door, he swept in and pulled her into his arms. Their lips met, collided in a fury of heat and passion. He backed her toward the bed while she yanked at his shirt.

She fell backwards onto the mattress, staring as he tore his shirt the rest of the way off. His shoes went flying and hit the opposite wall seconds before his jeans and underwear made fast tracks down his legs.

He had that hard, lean look of a hungry male as he loomed over her, his gaze blazing a trail over her body.

"Just the underwear," he said. "Take the underwear off and leave the rest."

"You do it," she said mischievously.

With a sexy growl, he reached for her hips, snagged his fingers in the strings and ripped downward. The material gave way and he tossed the remnants over his shoulder.

His eyes gleamed, and he gave her a predatory smile as he lowered his body to hers.

"Love the outfit," he murmured.

She sucked in her breath when he touched his lips to the swell of her breasts pushed together by the negligee. He proceeded to nibble at the plump flesh, burrowing his mouth between the mounds.

He delved deeper, his goatee scratching against her skin, sending tiny goose bumps to her nipples until they puckered and formed taut points. As he pulled back, he caught the tie with his teeth and yanked, loosening the top until it fell away from her breasts.

Unwilling to wait for the attention she wanted, she buried her hand in his short-cropped hair, and finding little purchase, she slid her fingers to his ear to pull him toward her nipple.

She felt him smile against her skin before he lazily rolled his tongue over the sensitive bud. She moaned, voicing her approval, encouraging him to continue.

He sucked the nipple farther into his mouth and lightly grazed his teeth over the tip. She arched, feeling the shock all the way down to her pussy.

"I want you now," she said, tugging at his shoulders.

"Do you?" he drawled. "It would seem I have the advantage here."

She framed his face in her hands, forcing him to look directly at her. "If you want to keep that advantage, it would be in your best interest to give me what I want."

Laughter rumbled out of his chest, vibrating against her clit which only served to heighten her need. "I do love a bossy woman."

"I can be very rewarding," she purred, arching her breasts

higher.

"In that case," he said as he backed off the bed, "come down here and show me just how rewarding."

She lifted one brow as she regarded his wide-legged stance, his cock straining upward. He grasped the base, and he worked his hand slowly down then back up again.

She was always up for a little payback.

As he bent to dig in his jeans pocket for a condom, she slid off the bed, gliding to her knees in front of him. As she settled down, she shrugged out of the negligee, letting it fall to the floor. She placed her hands behind his knees, running them up, slowly, until her fingers splayed out over his firm ass.

She rose up on her knees until the head of his cock bobbed just an inch from her mouth. Blowing softly, she watched as he flinched in reaction. She kneaded his behind, moving closer to the cleft. Then she trailed one finger down the seam then back up again. His knees nearly buckled, and she smiled.

"Tease," he muttered. He tossed the condom on the bed then wrapped his fingers in her long hair, gathering it in his palms until his knuckles brushed against her scalp. He tugged on her hair at the same time he rocked toward her.

She let her hands fall from his ass and moved them to his front. She curled her fingers around the base of his cock as he strained forward. She opened her mouth the barest of inches, circling just the head with her lips. Holding him there, she ran her tongue over the small slit then underneath to the taut seam. She traced the edge of the soft skin, enjoying the velvety smoothness.

He bucked against her, trying to seat himself farther into her mouth, but she held him firmly, continuing her slow exploration.

A drop of moisture seeped onto her tongue and she lapped at the slit, spreading the small amount of pre-come over the head.

"Payton, please," he groaned.

She pulled away long enough to look up at him and give him her best satisfied smile. "I do so love to hear a man beg."

Her triumph was short-lived. He used the opportunity to his full advantage. Grasping handfuls of hair, he thrust forward, burying his cock in her open mouth.

She swallowed against the intrusion, closing her eyes as he rocketed over her tongue. He bumped the softness at the back of her throat and stilled, holding her there for a long second. Then he withdrew, letting out his breath in a satisfied hiss.

Her hands came back up, and she wrapped one around his cock and slid the other underneath to his sac, massaging and rubbing as she guided him forward again. Her fingers tightened and she worked back and forth in unison with her mouth.

"Oh God, stop, baby, or I'm gonna come."

She sat back on her heels and watched as he took in several ragged breaths. He reached for her and pulled her up to stand in front of him.

"The condom," he said, pointing at the bed.

She turned and retrieved the little packet.

"Put it on me," he rasped.

She faced him again and tore the wrapper, sliding out the thin latex ring. She moved close, grasping him in one hand and using the other to roll the condom on.

He closed his eyes and swore. "Lubricant. Fuck, I forgot it. Please tell me you still have some."

She grinned and walked over to the desk by the TV and took out the small plastic tube of KY. Then she turned and tossed it to him. "I'm not getting all sticky again."

He caught the tube and hurriedly bent to snag his T-shirt, tucking it underneath his arm. With shaking fingers, he tore the lid off the lubricant and squeezed the clear gel into his hand. Then he smoothed it over his sheathed cock, his movements slow but jerky. He tossed the tube aside then snatched his shirt from underneath his arm and wiped his hand. Throwing that aside, he reached for her, and she went willingly.

To her surprise, he curled his hands around her waist and lifted her up. "Put your legs around my waist," he directed as he wrapped one strong arm around her.

When she'd done so, he reached between them with his free hand and positioned his cock between her legs. He arched his hips into her, sinking deep. Wrapping both arms around her, he held her tight against him.

He grasped her ass, lifted her up and then allowed her to slide down the length of his cock.

She threw back her head and closed her eyes. God, he was so deep, and she felt so vulnerable in this position. But that vulnerability only heightened the sensation of balancing on a razor's edge.

His fingers dug into her ass as he bounced her up and down on his cock. When she opened her eyes to look at him, his head was thrown back in a similar manner as hers had been. Ragged gasps spilled from his mouth, and the muscles in his shoulders bulged and flexed from the strain of holding her.

She gripped his neck harder as he walked forward, his cock buried deep, and the motion of his hips sending it deeper still.

She hit the wall with a thud, and he lowered his head to her neck, sucking and kissing, his breaths coming explosively in her ear.

He rocked her against the wall, plunging deep, holding her captive against the hard surface. The rough texture abraded her back, and while each time he thrust forward she experienced an erotic thrill deep within her core, she was distracted by the awkward position.

"The bed," she managed to gasp out. "The wall is killing me."

His head came up, apology in his eyes. He immediately retreated then held her tightly against him as he maneuvered to the bed.

Gently he eased her down, slipping from her body as she came to rest on the mattress.

"I'm sorry," he whispered as he brushed light kisses across her face.

She said nothing but reached for him, spreading her legs in invitation. He crawled onto the bed and settled between her thighs.

With less urgency than he'd displayed before, he used gentle fingers to part the slick folds. His thumb pressed to her clit and rotated in a circular motion, reigniting the fire in her gut.

His hips shimmied between her legs as he sought to spread her thighs wider. His fingers left her pussy, and he cupped his hands around her ass, sliding them down the backs of her thighs. His cock nudged her entrance and slid forward so he was an inch or so inside her. For a moment, he flexed his hips, making short, shallow thrusts.

"Now who's the tease?" she grumbled.

He moved just a little deeper. "Is this what you want?"

She wrapped her arms around him, sliding her palms down his flanks. Her fingers dug into him, urging him on.

"Please."

"I love a woman who begs."

"Smartass."

He grinned then closed his eyes and drove forward.

She gasped and arched into him, her cry stuck in her throat. His hands slipped from her legs and he dug his forearms into the bed on either side of her to hold his weight off her.

He lowered his head, pressing his forehead to hers as he moved sensuously between her legs, thrusting, retreating, going deep, staying still.

His lips hovered close to her own, and then they lightly pressed to hers, a soft smooching sound escaping as he kissed each tiny part of her lips.

Despite his deliberate, measured movements, she felt her orgasm building, not explosive, instead a slow, warm buildup, a gradual tightening, an exquisite sensation like a cool breeze on a hot summer day. Like letting chocolate melt slowly on your tongue.

She hooked her ankles over his legs and pulled them upward until they lodged just underneath his ass cheeks.

Like tightening a screw, her body coiled tighter and tighter as her pleasure mounted, suddenly making her restless and wild.

"I need..."

Wes stroked her hair away from her cheeks with his thumbs, his elbows still planted in the mattress on either side of her. "What do you need?"

She moaned. "I'm close, so close."

He reached for her arm, letting his fingers glide past her elbow to her wrist and finally grasping her hand. He guided it between their bodies, arching up to give her room.

"Touch yourself," he whispered. "Come for me."

She flexed her middle finger over her clit, found the sweet spot and began rotating in tight, slow circles as he raised himself.

Hands braced near her head, he began driving into her body with hard, long strokes. *Yessss.* Every muscle in her body seized. She closed her eyes, shutting out everything but the pulse centered at her very core.

"Open your eyes," he said. "I want to see you come."

Her eyes fluttered open and met his gaze. He stared down at her, tension etched into his face, his jaw clenched tight.

"Are you close?" she managed to gasp out.

"You first," he said behind gritted teeth.

He rammed his hips forward, and she threw back her head, her fingers strumming her clit as she hovered precariously close to the melting point. Once more, oh God, once more.

He began pumping against her in a frantic pace, and suddenly it felt as though someone had blown her up like a balloon and let go. She flew in a dozen different directions.

Her mouth opened in a soundless scream, and then she found her voice and cried out as the pressure, unbearable, released in a cataclysmic burst.

She spasmed around his cock, felt a sudden rush of wetness, and still her nerves twitched and screamed as the orgasm went on and on.

His lips pressed to her forehead before he plunged deep and stiffened around her, his muscles bulging, his body straining to get as far into her as he could.

"Yes, oh God, yes," he said hoarsely.

He convulsed against her body, thrusting once, twice and finally a third time before he stilled. His legs trembled, his arms shook, his chest heaved as he gasped for breath into her hair.

Slowly, she took her hand away, no longer able to bear to touch her hypersensitive clit. Her arms snuck around him, and he lowered himself carefully to her body as she urged him to do. She held him tight, burrowing her face into his neck.

They trembled against each other in the aftermath. She stroked his back, enjoying the feel of his skin, of the muscles, the dips and ridges of his hard contours.

Finally, he slid from her pussy and rolled to the side of the bed to discard the condom. When he turned back to her, she moved against him.

"Get up for just a minute, baby. Let me pull back the covers."

She stood on shaky legs as he arranged the bedding and then he motioned for her to return. She crawled into bed, cuddling against his warm body as he pulled the blankets over them both.

A sigh welled deep within her chest and whispered across her lips, her body relaxing with the flow of it.

"You sound awfully contented." His chest rumbled as he spoke, vibrating against her ear.

"I am." She smiled, a mischievous streak rising fast. "That was incredible. Just think of what we missed out on all those years ago."

"That was extremely uncharitable of you to bring up," he grumbled.

She chuckled softly against his chest. There was another comfortable silence between them, and then he put a finger under her chin and tilted her head upward so she looked him in the eye.

"I don't even know where you live. If I'll see you again."

She kept her expression even, not wanting to betray any hint of reaction. "Do you want to see me again?"

His brow furrowed a moment, and he seemed to grapple

with his answer. Finally he took a deep breath. "Yeah, I like the idea of seeing you again."

Some of her tension eased, though why it should matter if he wanted to see her again was beyond her. She didn't come to town scoping for a relationship.

"I live in Houston."

His eyes widened in surprise. "That's not far."

"Hour and a half," she replied.

He moved his arm up, propping his elbow on the bed and resting his head in his hand. "How did you end up there? I always wondered why you left. I mean after we... After we had sex, you disappeared."

She laughed. "You make it sound so calculated and sordid. My dad got a job transfer and so we moved to Tennessee. When I was in college, he transferred to Houston. I finished college then moved there to be close to them. He's retired now, and they've moved down to Galveston, but I still see them often."

"So what do you do in Houston?"

"I'm a real estate agent. I actually got a degree in nursing, but after six months of the hospital scene, I realized there was no way I could make a career out of sick, needy people. A friend of mine owned a real estate agency so I got my realtor's license and went to work with her. After a year, I decided to strike out on my own. I started small, but my agency is the fourth largest in Houston now."

His eyebrows rose. "I'm impressed."

He laid his hand over her hip, bunching the sheet between his fingers. "That's a hell of an accomplishment."

She smiled, enjoying his touch. "I think so. Or I like to think so. It took a lot of hard work, but the effort's finally paid off."

She rose up on her elbow as well so she was on eyelevel with him. The sheet fell from her chest, and she reached to pull it back up. His hand stayed her motion. He grazed her nipple with his fingers then cupped the soft mound in his palm.

She tried to speak, cleared her throat and tried again. "What about you? Did you always want to be a cop?"

He continued to stroke her nipples, plucking the tips until they were taut and puckered.

"No. I wanted to play football like Jake Turner and Ray Hatcher. We all got scholarships to A&M but I messed up my shoulder my freshman year. Got a degree in criminal justice instead, and when I graduated I came home, got a job with the city. I've been there ever since."

"Any regrets?" she asked softly as she arched more fully into his touch.

He seemed to consider the question for a minute. "No," he said finally. "I love my job. I'm surrounded by my best friends. It's a good life."

She smiled and rubbed her fingers over his goatee. "You make it sound so simple."

He grinned. "I'm just a country boy at heart. Don't need anything more complicated. Beer, good friends and football. Can't ask for anything better than that."

"You left good sex out of there."

His hand left her breast, and he trailed a finger down the line of her jaw. "Oh yes, definitely good sex." He cocked his head to the side and leaned in to kiss her. "In fact, I need a lot more good sex. A whole lot more."

"Mmmm. That can be arranged," she murmured against his mouth. "I hope you brought more than one condom."

He chuckled. "I damn near bought out the store."

"Ambitious, were we?"

"Just hopeful," he said, lightly kissing her again.

Payton yawned and opened bleary eyes. Wes was wrapped tight around her body and she craned her neck looking for the bedside clock. When she saw the time, she shook Wes's shoulder.

He stirred and snuggled tighter against her. She smiled and nudged him again. "You're going to be late for work if you don't get up," she murmured close to his ear.

His eyes flew open. "What time is it?"

"After six."

"Shit."

He palmed her cheek and kissed her before scooting out of bed. "I've got to get going."

She reclined in the bed, pulling the covers up under her arms.

"When are you going back to Houston?" he asked as he thrust one leg into his jeans.

"I'm leaving around noon," she said softly.

He paused, staring at her for a long second. She couldn't decipher the odd expression on his face, sort of a mixture between confusion and disappointment.

"Is this where you promise to call and we say goodbye?" she cracked.

"Or you could call me."

"Hmm, how about we trade numbers and then it's on both of us."

"Deal."

He strode over to the desk where the phone and a tablet of paper sat. He came back over and shoved the pad and a pen at her.

She took the pen and scribbled her number down and handed both back to him. "That's my cell number. It's the easiest way to reach me."

He tore off the top piece of paper then scrawled his number on the second sheet before offering the paper back to her. He bent and gave her a hard kiss. Then he turned and finished dressing.

When he was done, he gave her one more long reluctant look. Then he went to the door and opened it. He paused and turned back to her. "Payton, I—"

He shook his head and walked out, letting the door close behind him.

Chapter Seven

He was sure she'd call on Monday. When that didn't happen, he convinced himself she was playing it coy and she'd definitely call on Tuesday. Wednesday morning, he irritably decided she was playing it cool but she'd call that night. Of that he was sure.

Thursday night he was genuinely baffled. Wes paced his living room like a caged lion. If she had any intention of them getting together this weekend, she would have called by now. Thursday was the D-day for making weekend plans. How the hell was she supposed to know what his work schedule was?

Or maybe she had no intention of seeing him again. Maybe he'd scratched an itch for her and that was it.

He picked up his phone and called Gracie before he could think better of it. She'd offer some insight into the situation, and then maybe he could figure out where the hell he stood with Payton.

After he explained his annoyance, she had the audacity to laugh in his ear. He held the phone away, counted to ten and waited for her to stop howling.

"Are you finished yet?" he demanded.

She wheezed and coughed. "Sorry, but damn I always knew this was going to be funny when it happened. I just had no idea how hilarious it was going to be."

"What the fuck are you babbling about? When what happened?"

"When the mighty Wes fell hard for a woman," she said

before dissolving into laughter again.

"Damn it, Gracie, you're so not funny, and I swear if Luke is sitting there next to you and you just blabbed that shit where he could hear, I'm going to wring your pretty neck."

She died laughing again, and he seriously contemplated hanging up. And he would have, but she seemed to sense he was not very happy and quickly sobered.

"Okay, so what did you want from me?" she asked.

He sighed and counted to ten again. "I merely want a woman's perspective on why the fuck she hasn't called me."

"Maybe she wants you to make the next move, Wes. A woman will only do so much chasing before she decides it's time to see how much interest is reciprocated."

"So, you're saying she wants me to call her."

"Could be. Or maybe she's just busy. Or, perish the thought, maybe you were just great sex and she doesn't want a relationship."

"Well, fuck, Gracie, I don't want to get married. Who said anything about a relationship?"

She laughed again. "I can hear the panic in your voice. Chill out and call her. You obviously want to see her again, right? Is it going to kill you to make the first move this time?"

"So I should go to her and not make her come to me."

"Well, if I was her, I wouldn't keep chasing after you. I'd bait the trap and wait for you to come to me."

"You women are evil. Evellle."

Gracie snorted. "And you men are just stupid. Get off the phone and call her."

Wes grinned. "I love you, Gracie girl."

She chuckled. "Love you too, knucklehead."

He hung up and stared at his phone gripped tight in his hand. Then he fished his wallet out of his pocket. He pulled out the piece of paper she'd written her cell phone number on and punched it in.

After three rings, her husky voice filtered over the line.

"Hello?"

"Hey Payton, it's Wes."

"Oh, hi, how are you?"

He hated these awkward, stilted conversations. He didn't want to fuck around with pleasantries all goddamn night.

"I want to see you this weekend."

There was a long pause. "I'd love to, but I don't think I can make it over. I have an open house on Sunday."

"Actually I was thinking about coming to Houston." Where the hell had that come from? He was impressed with how smoothly that improvisation had come off. "I'm off Saturday," he continued. "We could have dinner Friday night and spend Saturday together if you're interested."

Another small pause. "I'm interested."

He had to physically restrain himself from pumping his fist and muttering, "Yeah."

"Okay, so I'll call you when I get into Houston Friday evening. I can swing by and get you."

"That sounds great. I'll look forward to seeing you then."

They said their goodbyes and Wes hung up, exhilarated over the idea of seeing her. A perplexed feeling fell over him. His eyebrows knitted together in confusion. Was Gracie right? Was he falling for Payton?

He shook his head. It was just sex. Great sex, mind you, but just sex all the same. It wasn't every day you got to go back and correct past mistakes, and his first encounter with Payton had certainly constituted one of his bigger fuck-ups.

Now he had to find a hotel room in Houston. Oh, and he'd have to get back with Gracie for some advice. He wanted Friday night to be special. A night Payton wouldn't forget. A night like she'd deserved twelve years ago. He wanted to do it right this time.

Wes hit the 610 loop on the tail end of rush-hour traffic and was gratified that the line of cars moved at a steady pace.

Beside him in the cab sat four sacks of shit Gracie had been all too happy to foist on him. Damn woman must have shopped for hours for all of it, but when she'd outlined her idea, he had to admit, it rocked. Well, at least in theory.

He found himself looking forward to seeing Payton again. At first, he'd focused on the promise of great sex, but in reality what had stayed on his mind was the time he'd spent lying in bed, *after* the great sex, Payton curled in his arms, the time they'd spent talking.

The thought made him vaguely uncomfortable. He knew he shouldn't admit to liking cuddle time and pillow talk. For God's sake, that was shit all his married buddies got into.

Yeah, he wanted tonight to be perfect, but it just meant he was a considerate guy. It didn't mean he was going to start wearing a pussy label on his forehead.

As he neared his exit, he popped open his cell phone and dialed Payton's number.

"Hey," he said when she answered the phone. "You ready?"

A sigh echoed over the line. "Yeah, I'll be ready."

"Everything okay?"

"Oh, I'm fine. Just tired. Long day."

His brain went into overdrive. She did sound tired. A thought hit him, and he mentally applauded his genius. "Hey, I have an idea. Can you give me an hour?"

There was a long pause. "Uh, okay. What's up?"

He chuckled at her obvious confusion. "Give me an hour, and I'll come get you. It's a surprise."

He closed the phone and drummed his fingers on the steering wheel as he navigated to the hotel he'd made a reservation at. He'd need to hurry, but he was confident he could pull it off.

The original plan had been for them to eat out, but her fatigue gave him the perfect excuse to implement his mad seduction scheme.

He checked in then lugged the bags to his room. He took a quick inventory then hauled out the huge yellow pages phone book and scanned for potential takeout places. When he found what he wanted, he tore out the page and stuffed it into his pocket for later use.

He turned his attention to the large Jacuzzi tub that stood in the corner of the suite. Rummaging around in one of the bags, he pulled out several candles and began strategically placing them up the steps of the tub and along the ledge.

He continued his decoration and when he'd peppered the entire room with the floral-scented candles, he pulled out the two dozen roses, a mixture of pink and red. He felt a little ridiculous as he arranged each single stem amidst the candles, spreading them out for the maximum effect, but when he pictured Payton's reaction, the awkwardness fled. He wanted to see her smile, wanted to see her smile for *him.*

Next, he hauled the small table from the corner and placed it to the side of the tub and arranged the two chairs to face each other.

He tucked the remaining bag under the desk so it would be in easy reaching distance then stood and rubbed his hands together as he surveyed his handiwork. Now he just needed to light all the candles and hope to hell he didn't burn down the hotel while he went to get Payton.

Lastly, he pulled out a red satin sash, letting it glide over his fingers. Then he shoved it into his pocket and headed out of the room.

When he got back into his truck, he spent a few seconds studying the directions Payton had given him to her apartment. He'd chosen the hotel because of its proximity to where she lived, so it shouldn't take him more than five minutes at most to get there.

Payton checked her appearance in the bathroom mirror for the fourth time since Wes had called and said he'd be there in five minutes. She'd foregone the casual, country bumpkin look and opted instead for a sexier, more sophisticated style.

She'd piled her hair atop her head, allowing a few strands

to fall softly down her neck. Simple diamond studs adorned her ears, and she fidgeted with the back on one of them before smoothing the short silk skirt she'd chosen.

Hose and high heels. What man could resist long legs and killer shoes?

When she heard the knock at her door, she hurried out of the bathroom and down the hall. She opened the door to see Wes standing there looking sexy as sin, clothed in tight, faded blue jeans and a T-shirt that stretched across a very broad, muscled chest.

"Hi," he said softly. "You ready?"

"Let me get my purse," she said as she reached to grab it off the hook.

She turned back to him and walked out, closing the door behind her. No sooner had she done so than he pulled her into his arms, tipping her chin up as his mouth slanted down over hers.

She melted against him, loving his hardness, his strength and just how damn good he felt to hold on to. His tongue ran over the seam of her mouth, and she opened breathlessly for him as he plunged inside.

"Hey yourself," she said huskily as he pulled away.

Dark, hooded eyes stared down at her. He ran a thumb across her lip then let his hand fall to wrap his fingers around her wrist and tug her along behind him as he walked toward his truck.

"So what's the big surprise?" she asked when they'd both gotten in.

He glanced sideways at her and grinned. "Well, now, if I told you then it wouldn't be a surprise."

She smiled and settled back against the seat, briefly closing her eyes.

He reached across the space between them and curled his fingers around hers. His thumb massaged her palm in a soft, circular motion. Comforting, soothing. Her worries seem to melt away. He had that effect on her for some reason.

"Rough day?"

She turned her head to look at him and smiled again. "Not too bad. Just long. I had several showings and had a sale go bust on me. It was a big one, so I was pretty bummed about it. Seller backed out at the last minute."

He raised her hand to his mouth and kissed each fingertip. She shivered at the gentle attention, and she didn't want the moment to end.

"I'm sorry. I hope what I have planned will make up for such a pissy day."

"You keep doing that," she said, nodding her head toward her hand, "and I'll be your slave."

"Mmm, I like the sound of that."

So did she.

They drove the rest of the way in silence, but he never let go of her hand. He held it on his lap, the back of it pressed against his thigh and his fingers resting over her palm.

When he turned off into a hotel parking lot, she looked over in curiosity. He just grinned.

"Trust me," he said. "Stay right there."

He got out and came around to her door and opened it. He reached up to help her down and she met the hard contours of his body as she slid to the pavement. Then he took her hand and headed for the entrance.

Tiny butterflies danced in her stomach as she imagined what he had in store. He punched the button to the elevator, and they waited until finally it dinged and the door opened.

When they were inside, he pressed the button for his floor and waited as the door shut once more. Then he reached into his pocket and pulled out a long piece of red satin.

"Turn around," he murmured.

She hesitated a brief moment before doing his bidding. As she had done to him the weekend before, he slid the satin over her eyes. He tied it in back and then she felt his lips on the bare skin of her neck.

He kissed his way up to the sensitive spot behind her ear, causing a million tiny goose bumps to break out on her flesh. His hands smoothed up her shoulders as he sucked the lobe of her ear into his mouth, his tongue toying with the back of her earring.

She shivered uncontrollably in the dark.

The elevator halted, and he slid an arm around her as she heard the door open.

"Your night awaits you," he murmured as he led her out of the elevator.

Chapter Eight

Wes guided Payton down the hall, his arm wrapped around her shoulders. When they stopped, she heard him insert the room card and then he opened the door.

The cool air blew over her body as he walked her inside. She sniffed as a floral aroma danced across her nose. He left her for a moment, and seconds later, she heard the unmistakable rush of water. A bathtub?

He returned and ran his fingers lightly up her neck then across her jaw, stroking, teasing her with his touch. They lowered to the top button of her blouse, and she felt the slight pull of the material over her breasts as he undid it.

More cool air brushed over her as he worked his way down her shirt. He tugged it free of her skirt then pushed the blouse over her shoulders until it fell to the floor.

Leaving one finger on her bare belly, he walked around behind her, letting his finger run a path around her waist to her spine. A shiver took over her body.

His fingers lowered to the zipper of her skirt. The waist loosened as he pulled the zipper downward, but he didn't let the skirt fall. Instead it slid ever so slowly down her hips as he pulled. Finally it pooled around her ankles, and he took her elbow and helped her step out of it.

He moved around until he faced her again, and she could sense him looking at her.

"You are so damn beautiful," he murmured. "Every man's fantasy. A gorgeous woman standing in front of him in heels and thigh-high hose. And pink lace panties and bra. How you manage to look so delectably feminine and devilishly sexy at the same time is beyond me. I alternate between wanting to make slow, sweet love to you and fucking you hard and hot."

His words sent a sharp bolt of arousal flooding through her body. Her legs shook and the burning between her legs intensified. Her clit swelled and ached, and anticipation fluttered deep in her belly.

He moved closer until his chest pressed against her breasts. Wrapping his arms around her, he walked her backwards until she bumped the bed. Now she knew how he'd felt when she'd done the same to him.

"Lay down," he murmured.

She complied, sinking onto the soft bed. He pressed his mouth to her belly, kissing her once, the brush of his goatee tickling the sensitive skin.

He stepped back and raised one of her legs. His fingers glided down her limb, rolling underneath to brush the backside. When he reached the heel of her shoe, he tugged, pulling it free. The shoe slid off and fell with a clunk to the floor.

He repeated the same, slow tease with the other leg until both shoes had been removed.

Her fingers curled into the bedding as he began removing her hose. Each touch, each whisper across her skin sent a delicious shudder up her body. Then he bent to press his mouth against her leg, following the downward progress of her hose with his lips.

She moaned, surprised at the torturous, needy sound spilling from her throat. Unable to see his movements, not knowing where he'd touch her next, heightened her anticipation to a nearly painful threshold.

He eased one leg down and then lifted her other, giving it identical treatment as he removed the stocking. She was awash in desire, her pulse beating frantically, her blood racing, and he had only just begun.

When his fingers slipped underneath the thin lace of her underwear, she arched into him, aching for him to touch her, wanting his fingers to slide between the wet folds of her pussy.

Instead, he eased the panties down over her hips and kissed the skin just above the nest of curls. She flinched in reaction, gasping at the electric shock.

He worked her underwear down her legs until he tugged it free of her feet.

"Roll over," he commanded.

She rolled to the left, aided by his firm hands. Hands that caressed her back and slid down to cup the globes of her ass.

Her fingers curled tighter into the bedding, and she clenched her teeth, sure she'd go nuts if he didn't stop his sensual assault.

Her bra loosened as he freed the hooks. Then he eased her back over, pulling the bra from her body.

"Beautiful," he breathed.

He left her again, and she heard the water turn off. A gentle splash echoed over the room and a second later, he took her hand and guided her up from the bed.

"Over here," he said, leading her a few steps. Then he reached behind her head and untied the blindfold.

She blinked as the room came into focus. She took in dozens of flickering candles, a huge Jacuzzi filled with sudsy water. And roses. There were roses laid carelessly about the room, intermixed with the candles.

"Your bath," he said with a small smile.

She continued to gape around the room as he pulled her toward the tub. He helped her up the step and didn't release her hand until she eased into the water, sitting down as the suds climbed higher up her body.

"Wes, this is beautiful!"

"Glad you like it."

She watched in fascination as he began undressing, unable to tear her eyes away from his muscled body. His cock was hard. Erect. His desire there for her to see in all its glory.

"Mind if I join you?" he asked.

She scooted forward in the tub, only too willing to share the slice of heaven.

He climbed in and settled behind her, stretching out his legs on either side of her. Then he pulled her back until she was cradled against his chest.

"I don't know what to say," she whispered. "This is all so fantastic."

He kissed the curve of her shoulder, working his way to her neck. He stopped at her ear, nibbling and tasting the small indention behind her lobe.

"The night is only just beginning," he murmured.

They lay that way in the tub, her cradled in his arms, hot water lapping gently over the curves of her breasts. After several languid minutes, he reached for the bottle of body wash lying on the side and squeezed some into his hand.

He pushed her forward just enough that he could wash her back. Alternating firmness and gentleness, he massaged her shoulders.

A sigh of bliss escaped barely parted lips, and she closed her eyes. Then his hands worked around to her front, dipping down to cup her breasts.

Against the small of her back, she could feel his cock, rigid, lying flat against his stomach, pressed to her skin. It burned much hotter than the water.

If she lifted her ass just a teeny bit... It would be so easy to have him pull her down, sinking into her pussy in one easy glide.

She squirmed at the mental image and unconsciously shifted, moving upward, inviting.

Wes chuckled in her ear. "Not yet, sweetheart. Not yet."

She sighed and relaxed again, allowing her body to mold to his once more. Her need was making her edgy, and yet she had no desire for his seduction to be hurried. She felt pulled in a dozen different directions. Her demand for satisfaction weighed heavy against her desire to draw out the evening as long as she could. Fortunately for her, she didn't seem to have a choice in the matter.

A knock at their door startled her, but Wes's hand covered

her shoulder. "You stay right here and enjoy your bath."

He stood, and a rush of water rained down his body. She turned to look at him, unable to resist. Her breath caught in her throat and stuttered out in shaky gasps.

He stepped over the side of the tub, giving her a fantastic view of his cock, still stiff and distended. She reached up to cup his balls, sliding her fingers out and over his erection.

He paused in mid-stride and closed his eyes for the briefest of seconds before gently disentangling himself from her grasp. Grabbing a towel from the rack, he whipped it around his waist, tucking one of the ends in so it would stay.

Then he bent to get his wallet out of his jeans pocket and headed for the door. She craned her head, trying to see around his big body as he opened the door, but whoever was there was firmly hidden from view.

Ah well, it didn't matter. She was enjoying all of Wes's surprises so far. She sank back into the tub, reclining so the water seeped up to her neck.

A few seconds later, Wes shut the door and she looked over to see him carrying several containers of food to the table. He glanced up and met her gaze then smiled.

"Take your time. I'm going to set up our dinner and then I'll get you out of the tub."

Just the way he said "get you out of the tub" sent a hundred different shivers and sparks down her spine and tightened the nerves between her legs until she had to force herself to relax.

She watched him from underneath half-lidded eyes as he prepared the table, still dressed in just a towel. Too bad telekinesis was only something for the movies because she could really use some right now. With one mental push she could tear that towel right off him.

Nude food preparation. Now there was a concept. If they all looked as good as Wes, she could envision a successful catering business centered around that idea.

Wes walked toward the tub, the towel sliding precariously down one hip. Just an inch more. He tugged it back up. Damn.

He reached down, cupping her face. His lips pressed lightly to hers, kissing her with gentle regard. Then he grasped her arms and urged her up.

When she stood, he reached for a large towel and wrapped it around her then helped her over the side of the tub. The simple process of drying her off became deliciously erotic.

He took one end of the cloth and rubbed in small areas, light, teasing, sometimes hovering over particularly sensitive spots. He brushed the tips of her breasts. Her nipples drew tight into hard points, and he dragged the soft towel over them again.

Her limbs felt laden, warm, satisfied. A comfortable lethargy settled over her as he massaged, taking care not to miss a single inch.

When his cloth-covered hand delved gently between her legs, she widened her stance to give him better access. The edge of the towel rasped over her clit, and in response, a spasm worked from her pelvis into her belly.

The towel fell to the floor in a heap, and she sighed in regret that the sensual drying was over.

Wes walked over to the closet and pulled out a bathrobe then returned and held it open for her to stick her arms in the sleeves. When it fell over her shoulders, he gathered the lapels and pulled it closed in front, securing the ties in a double knot.

He kissed her once on the lips. "Let's eat."

Chapter Nine

Payton sat across from Wes at the small table, watching him as he ate. The food was good. Chinese takeout. But she'd be lying if she said she remembered that much about the taste other than the preliminary flavor as it hit her tongue. She was way too absorbed in the moment, in wondering what he planned next.

He watched her too. Chewing slowly, he held his gaze on her, his eyes dark with the promise of what was yet to come.

The towel had loosened before he sat, barely staying up on his hips. She wanted to see him, wanted to see just how far that towel had fallen, but his lower body was hidden by the table.

She bit her cheek to staunch the impish grin that threatened to take over as an idea came to her. With careful nonchalance, she raised her foot, stretching her leg until she brushed against the inside of his thigh.

He flinched as her foot traveled higher, and he leveled a baleful stare at her.

When she reached the hard line of his cock, he grabbed her foot, holding her there.

"How am I supposed to eat with you doing that?"

She grinned innocently.

He continued to hold her foot as he ate. He cupped and massaged the instep, kneading with his fingers.

She all but wilted in her chair. Forgotten was the food (or anything else for that matter). She leaned back and propped her other foot between his legs.

"Like that?" he asked as his hand closed around her other foot.

"I like anything that has to do with your touch," she said softly. "My hands, my feet, my body. I'm like a cat. Pet me and I'll purr."

He set her feet gently back down on the floor then scooted his chair back and stood. The towel fell completely away, and she could see his cock, semi-erect, thick and heavy. He stepped around the table so he was catty-corner to her and held out his hand.

"I plan to do a lot of petting tonight," he said.

She slid her fingers into his and stood. He reached down and untied the belt of her robe. When the ends dangled to the floor, he impatiently shoved it over her shoulders, baring her naked body to his avid gaze.

She stepped forward, closing the short distance between them. His cock brushed against her belly, and she grasped the turgid flesh. Like iron encased in silk. Hard, rigid, strong, the epitome of all a man should be. Yet soft, silken, warm and velvet in her palm.

She cupped his heavy sac, running her fingers up and down the soft underside, feeling the separation of his balls when she pressed inward.

"I think I like being petted too," he said in a strained voice.

She reached up on tiptoe to kiss him. He caught her, cupping the area of her neck underneath her jawline. His fingertips brushed the lobes of her ears as he melded his lips to hers.

His tongue met hers, warm, melting. His thumbs pressed into the hollows of her cheeks then slid to the corners of her mouth. He pulled his head away as she sucked in mouthfuls of air. His hands relaxed and slipped away for a brief moment before he grasped her hips and yanked her against his body.

With slow, deliberate movements, he walked her back toward the bed. Midway, he reached down and swept her up. She hooked her arms around his neck and stared up into his eyes.

Their gazes were still locked as he lowered her to the bed. He came down with her, putting one knee on one side of her hips then finally straddling her body.

"We're going to operate on the honor system tonight," he said.

"Oh? This sounds interesting. Which of us is supposed to have the honor, because I'm really hoping it's not me."

He smacked the side of her behind, sending a delicious, naughty thrill through her groin. "Smartass."

He slid his fingers up her sides, and as they glided over her curves, she shivered and flinched.

"Ticklish?" he asked with a grin.

She gave him a dirty look.

He continued his path up her body until his fingers lodged underneath her arms. He pushed, raising them up and over her head.

"Yes, definitely the honor system. You're going to stay exactly how I put you. No cheating. No touching. This is my show."

An excited flutter chased circles around her stomach and into her throat as he threw her own words back at her.

"I can live with that," she said casually, but her voice shook and betrayed the adrenaline coursing through her veins.

He let her arms go with a stern look to make sure she heeded his directive.

"Touch me," she whispered. She ached for him, wanted him so desperately. He cupped her breasts, plumping and kneading. His thumbs brushed across her nipples, sending currents of fire through her chest. He plucked the points until they were stiff, erect and tingling. Applying firmer pressure, he pinched each peak.

She arched into him, crying out, begging for more, needing more.

His hands slid to her ribcage, and he lowered his head until his lips pressed against the spot between her breasts. Wet, warm, languid, his tongue swept out to taste her. The rough texture of his taste buds rasped across her belly as he moved lower. She spasmed uncontrollably.

He backed down the bed as his tongue swirled lower. It was becoming harder to obey his dictate and keep her arms still. She wanted to touch him, to clutch at his shoulders as he drove her mad with his lips.

He parted her thighs and kissed the inside of her leg tantalizingly close to her throbbing clit. Then he burrowed his fingers into her curls and stroked down the seam of her folds, coaxing them apart until she was bared to his touch and to his gaze.

When he lowered his head, she closed her eyes in anticipation of feeling his tongue on her most sensitive parts. He blew gently over her slit, and her groin muscles clenched in response.

She felt hot, needy, restless, like a snake ready to shed its skin. Her blood danced in her veins to a frantic rhythm in tune with the song he played with her body.

"Please," she whispered. "I want your mouth on me."

His tongue flicked out over her clit, sending a red hot bolt of flame spearing through her abdomen. Her nipples puckered. Her breasts plumped and swelled, aching with need.

His fingers further parted her folds, and he gently sucked the sensitive nub into his mouth, holding it there while he licked it repeatedly with the tip of his tongue.

The constant state of anticipation coupled with her heightened arousal was too much. Her orgasm flashed upon her with the speed of a bullet. One moment she was poised on the precipice of a canyon. The next she was doing a swan dive over the edge, feeling the rush of exhilaration as the world raced by.

Just before she hit the ground, she slowed. The world blurred around her, and she floated like a feather blowing with the wind, drifting down to rest in the arms of her lover.

She opened her eyes to see Wes looking at her. His hands were planted on either side of her shoulders, and he used his knees to nudge her thighs farther apart.

Had she been so insensible? How had he gotten the condom on and positioned himself between her legs so quickly?

He smiled at her obvious confusion then leaned down to kiss her. "Enjoy yourself?" he murmured.

She stretched and reached for him, allowing the deep-seated contentment to invade the rest of her body. "If I enjoyed myself any more, I'm not sure I'd survive."

As she wrapped her arms around him, she realized she wasn't supposed to have moved them. She started to withdraw, but he caught her elbow in his hand and held her there.

"No, I like it when you hold on to me."

She let her fingers wander over the bunched muscles above his shoulder blades then down to the small of his back as he shifted his hips in preparation.

With a gentle nudge, he was inside her. She sucked in her breath at the exquisite fullness. Slowly, patiently, he allowed her to adjust to his size then inched forward, burying himself in her bit by bit.

A line across his forehead attested to what his patience was costing him. His jaw set in a firm position, and he took deep, steadying breaths.

She withdrew one hand from his back and feathered it across his brow, wanting to ease the tension etched there.

"Ride with me," she whispered. "Come with me. Love me."

He groaned and dropped his forehead to hers. The position was tender and intimate and allowed their lips to dance back and forth in playful harmony.

Soft smooching sounds filled the air to mingle with the soft smack of his hips against the backs of her legs. Their lovemaking was unhurried, measured. Instead of feeling like she was racing down the side of a mountain, she felt as though they were lying on a warm beach, the surf lapping gently at their bodies.

Mellow, like jazz on a hot summer night. Soft, like the whisper of a spring breeze at the back of your neck. Aching, like the yearning of young love.

She floated on the waves of something truly wonderful, a feeling of completion like she'd never known lulling her, enveloping her, holding her tight.

Tears pricked the corners of her eyes, and she shut them, holding them back, not understanding their presence. All the longing of youth, of that night when she was sixteen came back on the wings of a bittersweet memory.

It was the same yet different. They were the same people yet older, mature, no longer desperate to grasp the trappings of adulthood. That they could revisit, redo, was a chance most never got.

She opened her eyes again and stroked his cheek. He closed his eyes and nuzzled into her palm, kissing the inside.

Their bodies rocked as he moved between her legs. Her release built not as an unbearable explosion but as a gradual swirl. Like a hand dipped into a pool of water. The ripples started small then grew bigger, rolling across the surface.

Wave after wave of sweet pleasure rolled across her as he gathered her in his arms, murmuring endearments in her ear. His entire body went rigid as he thrust once more then held himself against her as a great shudder worked its way over him.

He eased down on her, his muscles still quivering against her. His warm, comforting weight was the perfect conclusion to their lovemaking. She wrapped her arms around him, hugging him closer. When he tried to pull away, she murmured her protest in his ear.

"Let me clean up," he whispered. "I'll be right back."

She reluctantly let him go, and as soon as he left her, she regretted that loss of intimacy. A few seconds later, he crawled back onto the bed and pulled her into his arms.

She snuggled closer, pillowing her head on his arm. His free hand drifted down her body, stopping to rest on her hip. He stroked her skin for a moment then traced a path back up her side until he reached her shoulder. There, he fingered the strands of her hair, gently pulling them back.

"Get some rest," he said as he pressed a kiss to her hair. "I want us to have fun tomorrow."

She smiled against his chest and sighed in contentment. He reached down to retrieve the covers that lay in disarray. When he'd tucked the comforter snugly around them, he wrapped his arm around her and laid his head on the pillow beside her.

It wouldn't take her long to fall asleep. But as her eyelids fluttered closed, her last conscious thought was that she already dreaded spending the week ahead without him. And they'd only just started the weekend.

Chapter Ten

Wes's heart did a funny little two-step in his chest as he watched Payton throw her head back and smile as a ray of sunshine hit her full in the face.

She reached for his hand, curling her fingers around his like an excited kid and hurried toward the zoo entrance.

"Do you know I've lived here for years and I've never been to the zoo?" she asked after he'd paid their fees.

He grinned. "I've lost count of the times I've been. I'm just a big ole kid at heart."

"Ohhh, I want to get ice cream," she said right before she let go of his hand and strode toward the vendor's hut.

Chuckling, he followed behind her.

She chose chocolate, and he got vanilla. As they started to walk away from the little shop, he reached out and reclaimed her hand, sliding his fingers over her palm and downward until they intertwined with hers.

She looked over at him and smiled then tightened her fingers around his. She licked at her cone, her tongue swirling around the ice-cold treat. It was an exercise in torture because he could too easily imagine that delectable pink tongue circling his cock just like it circled the tip of the ice cream.

He thrust the cone toward his mouth, hoping the cold would put a stop to his hot, lusty thoughts.

"Let's go see the monkeys first," she piped up. "They're always the most entertaining. I'd just as soon skip the reptiles." She gave a delicate shudder.

"Snakes don't do it for you?" he teased.

"The only good snake is a dead snake," she muttered.

He laughed. "Well, on that we agree. I once shot a water moccasin out of the backseat of my patrol car. Got wrote up for destruction of city property."

She gaped at him. "You're kidding!"

He shook his head. "Nope. No idea how it got in there, but I damn near flipped the car when I looked in my rearview mirror and saw it slithering across the backseat."

An all-over shudder wracked her body. "I think I'd need therapy after that."

"Some might argue I needed therapy long before the snake incident," he said with a grin.

She rolled her eyes but laughed and shoved an elbow into his side.

They acted like goofy teenagers out on their first date. They held hands, traded ice cream and laughed at the antics of the zoo animals.

By the time they made their way back out to his truck, they were flushed from the heat, but Payton glowed from head to toe.

"Have a good time?" he asked as he started the engine and turned the air conditioning on full blast.

"The best!"

"Want to go back to the hotel, grab a shower then get something to eat?"

"Mmm, only if I get to choose the place," she said, flashing him a sideways look.

"Bear in mind the fanciest thing I brought was a pair of unfaded jeans and a newer T-shirt," he warned.

"Oh, I think you'll be fine. There's a casual place a few blocks from my apartment. It's small, intimate, a little dark, and they have the best jazz band on the weekends."

Small, dark and intimate sounded real good to him right now. He wanted to be closer to her. Wanted to touch her and enjoy the feel of her in his arms.

He couldn't ever remember enjoying himself as much as he

had this weekend and the last. He was at a loss to explain why, but nothing in his past compared to the reality of Payton.

Being with her made him feel happy. Carefree. In a way no one else made him feel. He was comfortable. At ease. He loved the way she lit up, the way she expressed delight over the smallest things. He found himself wanting to do things to make her smile, because God, she had a gorgeous smile.

He watched her from the corner of his eye as he drove out of the zoo parking lot. Then he eased his hand over to take hers. She turned to him and smiled, and he swore he went positively weak. Their palms brushed and she clutched his fingers with hers.

They made a quick run by Payton's apartment to get a change of clothes for her, and then they headed for the hotel.

There they showered together, and he made love to her against the shower wall, the warm water cascading over their bodies. Afterward, he dried them both off and they dressed for dinner.

It only took a few minutes to drive to the club, and as Payton had warned, it was small, housed in the very end of a tiny strip mall.

They walked into the darkened interior, and Wes gazed appreciatively at the intimate setting. There were about ten wooden tables sporting simple tablecloths and adorned with flickering candles. In front was a diminutive platform that must serve as the stage.

To the right a bar with three stools lined the wall, and a waitress wearing a slinky black dress stood arranging drinks on a tray.

Payton looked down at her watch. "We have about fifteen minutes before the band will start. Time enough to sit down and get our food."

He nodded and let her lead him to the far right of the room. She chose a table that afforded them the most privacy while still giving them the ability to view the stage.

When they sat, another waitress in a similar dress as the other server he'd seen walked up with a broad smile.

"Payton! It's good to see you again," the waitress exclaimed.

Payton glanced up in surprise. "Hey, Laura, how are you?"

"I'm great. Did you go to Brenda's wedding last weekend?"

Payton nodded. "Laura, I want you to meet someone. This is Wes Hoffman. He and I knew each other from high school."

Wes fidgeted in his chair, bothered by the introduction. Why, he wasn't sure, but it made him seem like nothing more than a passing acquaintance, a catch-up session with an old friend.

And maybe that *was* what it was.

"Hi, Wes," Laura said brightly.

He gave her his best killer smile. "Very nice to meet you, Laura."

Her eyes widened appreciatively before she cleared her throat and turned back to Payton. "You guys going to eat?"

Payton nodded.

"What'll you have to drink then?"

"I'll take a glass of the house wine."

Laura turned to Wes. "And you?"

"I'll take whatever beer you have on tap."

"Okay, I'll get your drinks right out," Laura said before she walked off at a brisk pace.

Wes looked at Payton in confusion. "But we didn't order food. Or get a menu even."

She laughed, the rich, husky sound floating over him. "They only serve one thing here. Prime rib, medium rare, with a house salad and baked potato. For dessert they serve pecan pie."

His mouth watered. "They're speaking my language."

"Somehow I imagined you wouldn't object to steak."

"I need the protein," he protested. "You've worn me out. No telling how much muscle I've lost."

Her cheeks went decidedly pink in the soft candlelight, but she only smiled and winked. "There are worse ways to get your exercise."

He burst into laughter. "You got that right."

A minute later, Laura returned with their drinks and a few minutes after that, the band began setting up. By the time they got their food, the first strains of music filled the room.

He stared at Payton as they ate, watched how she focused in on the musicians, how she seemed to enjoy every aspect of the experience. She was obviously a person who derived pleasure from even the simplest things. Their trip to the zoo had delighted her, and she'd spent the entire afternoon with an exuberant smile on her face.

He'd found himself wanting to do more, using any excuse to make her light up.

"Let's dance," she said, her blue eyes glowing in the dim light.

And here again, he wanted to do whatever would put a smile on her lips. He wasn't a dancer by any stretch of the imagination. Two left feet didn't exactly cover his lack of grace. But if she wanted to dance, then he'd dance. He'd use any excuse to get close to her, press her body to his.

Wes stood and held out his hand to her. She took it and stood in front of him. Without a word, he pulled her into his arms right there by the table.

The haunting sounds of the slow melody worked its magic as they melted in to each other. Payton closed her eyes and leaned her cheek against his hard chest as he rested his chin atop her head.

Their own little corner of the universe. No one watched them, not that she cared. They swayed and moved in a tight circle. Had there ever been such a perfect day? Not even last night when he'd gone to such lengths to give her a perfect evening. The sex was good, no, make that fantastic, but it was today that squeezed her heart. Two people laughing and carefree, comfortable with each other. Was this what it felt like to be in love?

Her body went tense for a moment. He sensed the change in her because he pulled away to stare down at her, confusion registering in his expression.

She forced herself to relax and give him a reassuring smile.

But her heart beat with a resounding thud, hammering against the inside of her chest like a prisoner trying to escape.

Love. Did she love him? Could she be in love with someone she'd for all practical purposes met only a little over a week ago?

Or did the feelings they'd once had for each other come into play? She frowned against his chest. No, they didn't count. Yeah, she'd had a major crush on Wes at sixteen, but they'd only gotten together the one weekend when they'd had sex. No boyfriend/girlfriend stuff.

Yes, she'd had tender feelings for him then. But love? What the hell had she known about love then? And she certainly hadn't spent the last twelve years pining for him. Hell, she hadn't even thought about him except when conversations came up about old boyfriends/lovers.

That could only mean that whatever connection they had *now* accounted for the warm, fuzzy feeling inside her.

The song ended, and Wes returned her to her chair just as Laura brought dessert and refilled their drinks. They ate in silence, and she knew she was being unnaturally quiet, but she couldn't wrap her brain around her almost-epiphany. Because really, she wasn't ready to admit to herself that she could very well be in love with him.

"You're quiet," Wes murmured as he pushed aside his saucer.

She smiled, just a little shakily. "Just enjoying the night. The day. The weekend. It's been fantastic."

He leaned forward, taking her hands in his. "It's not over yet. I plan to take you back to the hotel—" he raised her hand to his lips, inserting the tip of her index finger in his mouth, laving his tongue over it, "—and make love to you all night."

She sucked in a mouthful of air and tried to calm her frazzled nerves. Nerves? She wasn't nervous. She was anxious. Anxious to get the hell back to the hotel.

"I thought you needed to leave tonight? Don't you work tomorrow?"

He nodded. "I do. Have to work, that is. But I thought I'd

get up early and drive in tomorrow morning. Which gives us tonight." He paused and gave her a sexy grin. "That is, if you're interested."

She met his gaze head-on. "I'm interested."

"Then what are we waiting for?" he asked as he stood.

What, indeed.

Chapter Eleven

Consumed. There was really no other word for it. His entire thought process was a study in a curvy brunette with blue eyes and a killer smile.

Wes sat at his desk filing his latest report, cursing the fact that it was only Monday. Did it make him a pussy that he was counting the hours until he could see Payton again?

With a disgusted sigh, he acknowledged that it probably did, and furthermore, he could give a flying fuck about that.

He checked his cell phone for the hundredth time, just in case she'd called and it hadn't rang. She probably wouldn't call until after work anyway.

"Hey, man, we're all going to Jake and Ellie's after work," Jeremy said from the door. "You gonna come?"

Wes stared up at his friend lounging against the doorframe. "Yeah, sounds good. I'll be there."

"Good. You haven't been around much lately. We were starting to wonder if you'd found better company."

Wes snorted. He wasn't going to walk into that trap. "I'll be there," he repeated.

"Jake wanted me to ask you to get a case of beer on your way over. The girls are taking care of the food."

"Yeah, sure, no problem. I'll go home and change then head on over."

Jeremy nodded and ducked out. Wes sat there a long time pondering Jeremy's innocent statement about better company. The more he thought on it, the more bothered he was.

o

He hadn't lied when he'd told Payton that he enjoyed a simple life. Beer, good times, a job he loved, a town he loved and good friends. His friends had found happy relationships, but things hadn't changed. They were still hanging out together, living a few miles apart. Payton didn't live here, wasn't a part of his circle. A relationship with her beyond sex would entail change for at least one, if not both of them.

The thought of his life changing made him uneasy. He'd always imagined that when he got ready to settle down, he'd do so with a local girl. Just like Jake, Luke and Jeremy had done. Then life would go on as usual only he wouldn't go home alone anymore.

Payton... Well, she didn't seem like the kind of girl willing to give everything up to move to a podunk town for a guy on a city cop's salary.

Nor are you asking her to, dumbass. Way to get ahead of yourself.

But the fact remained. She had a successful business. One she'd built herself. She'd put a lot of time and sweat into her agency. There was absolutely nothing he could offer her that she didn't already have. There wasn't anything his *town* could offer her. As convinced as he was that he didn't want his life to change, didn't want to leave the niche he'd created, he knew she had to be equally determined not to give up her life either.

It shouldn't bother him, them being at opposite ends. But it left a hollow ache in his chest. A morose feeling he couldn't get rid of no matter how hard he tried to convince himself that he should be looking at this as a temporary relationship. Sex. Good times. A little fun. Nothing more.

He had to get a grip. Being this tied up in knots over a girl... Well, it sucked. It was no way to live.

His cell phone rang, and he yanked it up to stare at the LCD. He was annoyed it wasn't Payton, but even more pissed that he'd reacted like a lovesick moron.

Cool it, dude. Seriously.

"Hey, Gracie," he said as he put the phone to his ear.

"Hey, Wes, how was the weekend? I thought you'd call

today and let me know. Did she like it?"

Apparently he wasn't the only one waiting around on a call then.

"Sorry," he mumbled. "Been busy."

"Uh huh. Jeremy told me just how busy you guys have been today."

He sighed at her disbelieving tone. Busted. Hell. He couldn't help the surge of annoyance. He felt hot and itchy, like anything would set him off.

"She liked it. Weekend was great. Look, can we hash this out later? I'm coming over to Jake's. I assume you and Luke will be there."

He cringed at his snotty tone, but he couldn't call it back now.

Dead silence met his response. Finally she responded in a tight voice. "Uh, okay, sorry to bother you then. Yeah, I'll talk to you later."

The soft click in his ear told him she'd hung up. He closed his phone and dropped it on his desk. Fuck, fuck, fuck. When had he become such an ass? And to Gracie, for God's sake. Gracie who'd done nothing but be the best friend in the entire world to him, not to mention all the time she'd spent shopping for all the candles and shit he'd taken to Houston.

He scrubbed a hand over his face. He was losing it. Absolutely losing his freaking mind.

Payton let herself into her apartment, kicking off her shoes as soon as she was in the door. Her feet ached, her head ached, and she needed a long hot bath.

She tossed aside her briefcase and glanced over at her answering machine. Not that it would be blinking. Everyone called her cell phone if they couldn't get her at home. She didn't even think she'd ever given Wes her home number.

She trudged toward the bedroom, stripping as she went.

Yeah, a hot bath sounded good. She could relax and call Wes while she soaked. Already, she missed him, and they hadn't been apart a whole day yet.

The weekend seemed an eternity away, and she was assuming that he'd want or be able to see her again so soon. The problem was, she had no clear idea of this thing between her and Wes. What had started out as simple sex had quickly become a whole lot more. What, she wasn't sure of yet, but she knew she was in deep trouble where he was concerned.

You love him, idiot. That's the whole lot more you've been yammering about. If it was just sex, you wouldn't be thinking about him every second of the day.

God, she hated when she made sense. Hated it even more when she resorted to snarky internal monologue.

"At least say that shit out loud," she muttered. "Then it has more validity, and maybe I can admit that I'm in way over my head."

She started the bathwater and laid her cell phone on the side of the tub. Then she slipped out of her bra and panties and groped around on the counter for a scrunchie to pull her hair back with.

The sound of the phone startled her, and she whirled around. Her heart sped up, and a knot settled in her stomach. Was it him?

She yanked up the phone, not even bothering with the LCD screen. "Hello?"

"Payton, honey, I'm so glad I caught you." Her mother's shaky voice filled Payton's ears, and her heart plummeted.

"Mom? Is everything okay?"

A low sob echoed across the line. Was her mom *crying*?

"Honey, it's your dad. We think he's had a heart attack. I'm at the hospital here in Galveston."

"Oh my God. Mom, is he...is he alive?"

"I don't know anything yet, Payton. They're still working on him. I just don't know."

Payton struggled to stay calm. She didn't want to freak her mother out more than she was already, but the fact was Payton wanted to cry herself. She wasn't ready to lose her father. Not her daddy.

Tears pricked her eyelids as she took in several steadying breaths. "I'll be down as soon as I can, Mom. If there's any change, call me on my cell. I'm leaving in just a few minutes."

"Okay, honey, and be careful please. Don't kill yourself getting down here."

"I will. I love you, Mom."

"I love you, too, baby," her mother choked out.

Payton hung up, numb. The sound of water filling the bathtub broke through her shocked silence, and she quickly turned off the flow. Not bothering to let the water out, she raced into the bedroom to dress and pack a suitcase. Traffic on I-45 would be a bitch this time of day, but she had to get on the road and to the hospital as quickly as possible.

Wes pulled onto Jake's street, drove down and parked at the curb behind Luke's truck. The truth was, he didn't want to be here. He'd rather go home and go to bed, figure out the muddled mass he called a brain. But he owed Gracie an apology in a big way. Besides, being here beat waiting around for a phone call he may or may not get from Payton.

He got out of the truck and walked around to let the tailgate down. He grasped the case of beer and hauled it out. Then he kicked the tailgate back up with his knee and nudged it closed with his hip.

He headed up the walkway, feeling more dread by the minute. It was some fucked-up, twisted-ass shit when he viewed a night with his friends with the same enthusiasm as a trip to the dentist.

At the door, he propped the beer on his knee and rang the bell. A few seconds later, Ellie opened the door and smiled welcomingly at him.

He followed her inside and to the kitchen to dump the beer. "Where is everyone?" he asked.

"Out back getting the grill started. Jeremy and Michelle haven't made it yet. They called and said Thad wasn't feeling well, so if I had to guess they'll either be late or they won't come."

"How are you feeling?" he asked, as he folded her in his arms for a hug. At least he could try not to ruin his friendship with everyone.

He dropped a kiss on her cheek as he pulled away.

"I'm fine," she said with a sweet smile. "Mornings aren't exactly a walk in the park, but Jake's been taking good care of me."

Wes grinned. "Oh, I bet he is."

She blushed, which only made Wes chuckle. "Go on outside," she said, shoving him out of the kitchen. "I'm going to make some tea and then I'll be out." She stopped at the cooler and picked up several beers then held them out to him. "Take these while you're at it."

He kissed her again on the forehead, took the beer and headed toward the back patio. At the glass door, he paused. Jake stood by the grill and Luke and Gracie stood to the side talking and laughing about God knew what.

He took a deep breath, tucked the beers against his stomach with one arm and opened the French door with his free hand. The others looked up when they heard the door. Wes zoomed in on Gracie, though, and at the hurt in her eyes.

"Hey," Jake said. "Beer guy is here."

Wes grinned and stepped outside, closing the door with his hip. "Glad I'm good for something."

He passed out the beers to Jake and Luke first then turned to Gracie. They stared at each other for a long moment, and he held out a beer. "Peace offering," he said.

Her eyes narrowed and she took the beer. She would have turned away, but Wes caught her arm. He didn't want to do this in front of everyone, but it would only look weird if he dragged her off to privately apologize. Besides, their group had never kept secrets.

"I'm sorry, Gracie girl. I was an ass."

"Yes, you were," she huffed, but her expression softened.

Luke walked over to stand by Gracie and pinned Wes with a questioning stare. "You pissed Gracie off? I didn't think it was possible."

"Still friends?" Wes asked. He ignored Luke's question and held his arms out to Gracie.

She rolled her eyes and walked into his hug. Wes folded his arms around her and enjoyed the feel of something warm and feminine in his arms. Of unconditional friendship. It was a nice feeling.

She kissed him on the cheek. "You're forgiven. Now if you guys will excuse me, I'm going to go see if Ellie needs any help."

The men watched as she walked back into the house, and when she shut the door behind her, Jake and Luke both turned to stare at Wes.

He shoved his hands in his pockets and met their stares head-on.

"What the fuck happened between you and Gracie?" Luke demanded.

Wes raised an eyebrow. It wasn't like Luke to get all pissy and possessive. "I was short with her on the phone. Bit her head off. I was an ass, and she didn't deserve it."

"You haven't been yourself lately," Jake observed. "Something bothering you?"

"Definitely not like you to be a dick to Gracie," Luke added.

Wes rubbed the back of his neck. He hated these conversations, probably because they never had them. Any deep, personal shit usually seemed to revolve around the women, such as when Ellie or Gracie had problems. They never stood around and got all mushy over male shit.

"Things are fine," he muttered. "I just had a bad day and took it out on Gracie. She knows I love her to death."

Jake and Luke didn't press, something Wes was supremely grateful for. He already dreaded the confrontation with Gracie enough, because he knew it was coming. No way she was going to let him get away with blowing her off about how the weekend had gone with Payton. And then he'd have to tell her how fantastic it was, at which point she'd want to know what the fuck his problem was if it was so freaking terrific. Then he'd have to explain his real problem. Gracie wouldn't just laugh. She'd get all smug and say I told you so. No thanks.

The women walked back outside, and Wes watched Jake get all gooey over Ellie. The only difference was this time he could understand that gooey feeling. He rather thought he might be getting the same doe-eyed expression if Payton walked out that same door.

He concentrated on his beer, squeezing the can with his hand. Realistically his relationship, if you could call it that, was already causing problems within his circle of friends. Most were at his instigation, but they were there all the same.

He didn't want this awkward alienation. He wanted the same easygoing camaraderie they'd always shared. Pissing on Gracie was inexcusable, and it sure as hell wouldn't have happened if he had his head on straight where Payton was concerned.

It's just sex. Treat it for what it is.

But that thought was as distasteful as shitting on Gracie.

He took a long chug of the beer and admitted to himself that no amount of salvaging could keep the evening from the toilet. He'd ruined it before it ever began. The sooner he carried his sorry carcass home the better, because he clearly wasn't fit for public consumption.

Chapter Twelve

By the end of the week, Wes was glad he hadn't given in to the urge to call Payton. He was annoyed, peeved and a whole host of other synonyms for pissed. He didn't know if she really wasn't interested in seeing him for anything besides sex, or if she was just enjoying yanking him around by the balls on a very short leash.

Neither option was particularly appealing.

Hell, if he hadn't called her the last week they wouldn't have gotten together the previous weekend, and now, again, she hadn't gotten in touch.

While he could understand her preliminary reluctance to make all the moves, after what he'd pulled out of the bag last weekend, it was definitely her turn. He wasn't about to act like a desperate lapdog, panting after her every move.

Friday nights were always a get-together night, usually at Jeremy's, but tonight everyone was going to congregate at Luke and Gracie's because Thad was sick and both Jeremy and Michelle were wiped out.

Wes was determined to have fun and not let thoughts of Payton interfere in his time with his friends. Beer, good food, a UFC fight and the company of the greatest people on earth should set his spirits to rights.

By the time he got to Luke's house, he felt a great deal better. Jake and Ellie were already there, and Luke was manning the grill. Gracie greeted him with a big hug and a sloppy kiss on the cheek, and he tousled her hair, glad that things were back to normal between them.

She looked as though she wanted to ask him a hundred questions, but she refrained, for which he was grateful. She could be pushy and bossy, two things he loved about her, but she always seemed to know when not to push.

He pressed a kiss to her forehead. "Thank you."

She drew away and cocked an eyebrow. "What for?"

He smiled. "Just thank you."

She shook her head and smiled back. "Want a beer?"

"Am I breathing?"

Her soft melodic laughter rang out. "I'll take that as a yes since I haven't killed you yet."

She tossed him a can and jerked her head in the direction of the back patio. "Go on out. Guys are back there. So is Ellie. Poor girl was as green as the shit growing in my fridge. I sent her out for some fresh air."

Wes chuckled. "Sure you don't need any help?"

"Nah, I'm coming out just as soon as I call the cable company and figure out why the fuck I can't order the pay-per-view fight."

"Ah shit, no fight?"

"Not if I can help it," she muttered.

He smacked her playfully on the ass then headed out to join the others. As he stepped onto the cobblestone patio, he felt lighter. A warm breeze rippled his T-shirt, and across the back lawn, lightning bugs were starting to appear in the dusky twilight.

He inhaled deeply, letting the scent of honeysuckle drift across his nostrils. Man, did he love it here in his small town with his friends, his life and his job. Living in a place like Houston? Definitely not for him.

"Hey, Wes," Ellie said as she walked over.

To his surprise she hugged him, tucking her head underneath his chin and squeezing tight. Any hugging that went on between them was always at his instigation and not without a lot of blushing on her part.

"Hey, what was that for?" he asked as she pulled away.

She smiled sweetly up at him. "You just looked like you needed it."

His heart soared a bit higher. He knew it took a lot for Ellie to instigate any kind of intimacy with anyone except Jake. It made him pull her into his arms and give her another big hug. He dropped a kiss on the top of her head and gently squeezed her.

"Thanks, sweetness. As a matter of fact, I always need a hug from a beautiful woman."

She blushed and ducked her head.

"Get the hell away from him," Jake grumbled. "His charm is highly overrated."

"Says you," Ellie said with a wink in Wes's direction. "You're a man. You wouldn't understand."

"Lord, I hope not," Jake said with a laugh. "The day I start understanding the sex appeal of another man, well, that's the day to put me in a pine box and call it good. I much prefer to concentrate on the sex appeal of a certain sexy little brunette."

Ellie's cheeks turned a darker shade of pink, but her eyes lit up with such joy and happiness that Wes couldn't help but smile. It reminded him too much of the way Payton had looked at him.

Gracie walked back outside with a pile of plates and a handful of utensils. Wes moved to help her, and she happily unloaded them on him.

They worked together to set the patio table and Gracie hurried back in for glasses and the tea pitcher. Five minutes later, they were all kicked back watching the deepening twilight and enjoying amiable conversation.

The sounds of crickets and tree frogs filled the air. In short, it was a perfect evening. The first stars were starting to pop in the sky, and in the distance an almost full moon peeked over the horizon.

Luke dished up the steaks while Gracie poured tea and replenished beer cans. When they all sat, Gracie raised her tea glass.

"To a perfect evening with good friends, those here and

those who couldn't be with us."

"Hear, hear," Luke said as he raised his beer.

Wes raised his beer in salute as Jake and Ellie raised their drinks as well.

This was what he didn't want to change. Ever. The idea positively depressed him. But then so did the idea of not seeing Payton again. She'd blown him off, not the other way around. And he damn sure wasn't going to go chasing after her ass.

His cell phone rang, interrupting a bite of steak on its way to his mouth. With a sigh, he set his fork down. He hoped to hell it wasn't a call in to work.

When he looked at the LCD, his heart stepped up a few beats. Payton. But why call now? Friday night, when they had no hope of weekend plans.

He flipped it open and slapped the phone to his ear. "Hello," he said curtly.

"Wes, hi, it's Payton."

When he didn't respond, she continued on.

"I, uh, thought I'd drive up tomorrow. I'd like to see you if you're free."

"I'm not."

"Oh. I see."

"Sorry, I have to work," he said, mentally cursing himself for A. lying, and B. feeling the need to soften the refusal with an excuse. It should have been enough to just simply refuse.

"Too bad," she said with a sigh. Was that regret he heard in her voice? The thought of that irritated him further. She had all damn week to line out weekend plans with him if she was so damn set on seeing him. "I had some unexpected—"

"Look, this isn't a good time," he cut in before she could continue. It sounded rude, but he damn sure wasn't going to pretend he wasn't annoyed as hell.

"Sorry to have bothered you," she said softly before a click sounded in his ear.

He closed the phone and let it slide down his chest before he shoved it back into his jeans pocket. He avoided the stares of the others and resumed eating.

He heard Gracie curse softly under her breath, but he refused to look up. The steak that had tasted so damn good just moments before now tasted like a giant turd.

They ate in silence. No one seemed willing to break it with conversation. When they'd finished, Gracie got up and began clearing the plates. When Wes stood and offered to help, Ellie stuck a hand out. "We'll get it. You guys enjoy the evening and a beer."

He sank into his chair and leaned back, staring up at the sky. He heard the girls go in and shut the door. Then he mentally counted to three. Sure enough, about the time he said three, Luke cleared his throat.

Wes righted his head and looked over at Luke. "Gracie ratted me out, didn't she."

Luke's body jerked with muffled laughter. "Yeah, she did. I held out on her until she caved."

"Bastard," Wes muttered.

"It doesn't take a fucking genius to see you're miserable," Jake pointed out. "The question is what are you going to do about it?"

Wes sighed. "It's complicated."

Luke arched an eyebrow. "Judging by the brush-off you just gave her, I'd say it's not too complicated now. She'd have to be awfully thick not to get it after that conversation."

Wes closed his eyes. "It's twisted, I know."

"Try me," Jake said dryly. "I know a thing or two about twisted. Twisted described every aspect of my feelings for Ellie until the time we got together. Hell, the woman still manages to tie me in knots."

"That's me," Wes said morosely. "Tied up in one big fucking knot. I don't know my head from my ass anymore."

"So why the brush-off?" Luke asked.

"It sounds stupid. I don't want my life to change. I want to be with her, but I only want it on my terms. And she doesn't seem to have any interest in me beyond a good fuck."

Luke and Jake exchanged amused glances.

"Cut that shit out," Wes growled. "Last thing I need is you two smug bastards gloating."

"Well, to address your first issue, I hate to tell you this but any time you get involved with a woman, your life is going to change. Suck it up and deal with it like a big boy," Jake said with no trace of sympathy in his voice.

"Yeah, but you and Luke didn't have to change your lives. You married women who fit into the life you already had. We all still get together. We still share good times."

Luke burst out laughing, and Jake choked on his beer.

"Jesus are you deluded," Luke said around his wheezes. "Not change? Okay, I think I know where you're headed with this. From what I've been able to learn from Gracie, this chick you're involved with lives in Houston. You want the girl. You like the girl. But you don't want to give up any part of your life here. You want to keep your friends close, carry on like always, only have the woman you want."

Wes nodded. "Basically."

Jake shook his head. "First of all, get the notion that our lives didn't change when we got married right out of that tiny brain of yours. Marriage is all about change. It's about compromise. It's about wanting to make the woman you love happy. Hell, I gave up my damn colored, blinking Christmas lights because Ellie wanted the plain-ass, boring white ones. I'd do anything to make that woman smile. My first priority is her happiness. Don't think I don't love you guys, enjoy the time we spend together, but you and the others? Not my priority. Ellie is. Always will be. She comes first."

Luke nodded in agreement. He met Wes's gaze. "I understand where you're coming from, buddy. I do. But you're going about it all wrong. What's the worst that happens? You move to Houston and only see us every other weekend? We're not going anywhere. We'd visit your ass, you'd come visit ours." He shrugged. "Besides that, Gracie would have a kitten if she didn't see you on a regular basis. Believe me when I say, the girls are way more attached to our get-togethers than we are. They'd work around the obstacles. I'm willing to bet they'd have us getting together regardless of where you ended up."

Wes grinned. "I love those women."

"Not nearly as much as we do," Jake said, cracking a smile. "And it's only because we love them so much that we tolerate your outrageous flirting. I swear if you don't keep your lips off my wife, I'm going to have to rearrange them for you."

Luke snorted then dissolved into laughter. "I'm guessing a threesome with Ellie is out then."

Jake shot him a glare that would have melted lead. "You're a twisted motherfucker. There is no doubt about that. There ain't another man who'll ever touch Ellie."

Wes held his hands up, knowing that if he didn't stop Luke, he'd egg Jake on to infinity.

"So you think I'm being unreasonable," he said, directing the conversation back to his issue.

"Look, I don't know the whole situation. Just the bits and pieces I've gleaned from Gracie. I do know you sounded pissed on the phone a while ago."

"That's putting it lightly," Jake said.

Wes sighed. "I think she's playing a fucking game with me. I don't know for sure. When I'm with her, she acts like I'm the only man in the world but as soon as we part, I don't hear from her. It's like I don't exist. She made all the initial moves. I'll give her that. But I wagged my ass down to Houston last weekend and spent the weekend making her feel like the only woman in the damn world. And I don't hear a word from her all week except for Friday night when it's too late to make any weekend plans."

Jake pinched his lips together in a tight line and shook his head. "Dude, I hate to tell you this, but if you're keeping score, you're doomed to disappointment. Relationships don't work on an equal opportunity basis. They're solely what you make of them. Sometimes it's you going the extra mile. Sometimes it's her. The beauty is in not noticing when who is doing more than the other."

"So you think I'm being an unreasonable dickhead."

Luke snickered. "Uh yeah, basically."

"Great. Just fucking great." Wes closed his eyes and

massaged the bridge of his nose between his fingers. "Honest to God, I don't know what to fucking do. I've only known her for two weeks. Way too fucking soon to feel this kind of angst."

"Do you love her?" Luke asked.

Wes blinked in surprise at the directness of Luke's question.

"Forget how long you've known her. It's a simple question. Do you love her?"

Wes glared over at Luke. "That's not a fucking simple question and you know it."

"Actually it is," Jake said casually. "You have to ask yourself why you're sidestepping the question. If you don't love her, your reaction should be automatic. A simple no. But you haven't denied it. Which tells me you're fighting it tooth and nail but you're already a goner."

"Fuck you," Wes growled.

"I'll take that as a yes," Jake said with a snicker.

"I—yes, I love her. Or at least I think I do. I don't really know. The idea strikes bloody terror in my heart. I don't understand it, but there it is."

"Yeah, well, join the club," Luke said. "We're guys. We're not supposed to understand why we suddenly can't live without a woman. Why the idea of being without her gives us cold sweats."

"Fucking pussy. God. I've turned into you," Wes said mournfully.

Jake chuckled. "The only pussy I see around here is you. I'm man enough to admit my downfall. I have *one*. A petite brunette with blue eyes and the sweetest smile this side of the Mississippi."

"I was an ass," Wes said morosely. "I seem to have developed the habit lately of hurting the women I most love."

"Yeah, well, Gracie has already forgiven your ass. Now you just have to get Payton to."

"I don't suppose you'd loan me your wife for lunch tomorrow?" Wes asked hopefully. "If anyone can kick my ass back on track it's her. I'm sure she can tell me exactly how much groveling it's going to take me to get back into Payton's good graces after tonight."

Luke rolled his eyes. "Yeah, you can have Gracie for lunch. But then, Wes? Get your own damn woman. I'm tired of sharing mine with you."

Wes grinned. "You're just pissed because she loves me."

"I love her, but I never said she had good taste," Luke said sourly.

Chapter Thirteen

Payton rubbed tired eyes as she turned onto 59 out of Beaumont. She hadn't slept much the night before. Hell, she hadn't slept a wink all damn week. But she wanted to see Wes. She needed to see him. After spending the week at the hospital, praying for her dad to recover, she wanted nothing more than the comfort of Wes's arms.

She gripped the steering wheel tighter as traffic zipped by her in the left-hand lane. Monday night had been a sleepless, tense night, holding onto her mother as they waited to hear some word of her dad's condition.

He'd spent Tuesday and Wednesday in critical condition but by Wednesday night had shone signs of improvement after the bypass operation he'd undergone.

Thursday, he'd been awake and alert, much to Payton and her mother's relief. She'd stayed the afternoon with her father, telling him how much she loved him.

Friday, her mother had all but kicked her out of the hospital with strict instructions not to return until the next week. She'd been reluctant to go, but the thought of seeing Wes again after her harrowing week was a strong incentive.

Now she was but a few miles from town. Wes had said he had to work, but she could wait around until he got off. She'd stop to get something to eat and then call him to see when his shift ended.

Remembering the choices he'd offered her before, she mulled over whether she wanted barbeque, Mexican or a burger. None of it sounded good, but she was hungry and needed to eat. Zack's offered a few grill items and it was as good a place as any to sit back and relax.

Decision made, she rolled her shoulders and stretched her neck as she drove into town. A few minutes later, she parked outside Zack's and wearily got out of her car.

She opened the door and headed straight for the bar. She slid onto a barstool and caught the eye of the young bartender. After placing an order for tea and a grilled cheese sandwich, she sat back and looked around the interior.

When she got to the far corner, she froze, blinked and refocused on the table. No, she wasn't mistaken. Wes was sitting with a redhead who was smiling up at him. He clasped her hand across the table, and she laughed at something he said.

Working? The asshole had said he had to work. That was his excuse for not seeing her today. Unbelievable. Why lie? Why not just save them both the trouble and tell her he wasn't interested in seeing her anymore. Or maybe she was just sex on the side while he made time with the auburn floozie.

She seethed while she considered her options. Part of her wanted to disappear out of the bar, go home and wipe Wes Hoffman from her existence. But damn it, she hadn't done anything wrong. She wasn't the one spitting out lies. No way in hell she was slinking off like some shrinking violet. Maybe that was the kind of woman he was attracted to, but fuck that.

She slid off the barstool and stalked over toward the table. Halfway there, the redhead glanced up and blinked. Probably saw the murder in Payton's eyes. The woman nudged Wes's hand and nodded her head in Payton's direction.

By the time Wes looked up, Payton was standing over the table like an avenging angel come to kick some demon ass.

"Payton!" Wes said, his eyes widening.

The redhead's eyes also widened. Then she smiled. "Oh you're Payton. I've been dying to meet you. I'm Gracie Forsythe."

"And I don't care," Payton said through gritted teeth. She summarily dismissed the redhead and turned her ire on Wes. "You cock-sucking bastard. You lied to me. If you would have just told the fucking truth, you would have saved me a trip over here, not to mention the embarrassment I'm about to cause you."

Wes stood, holding his hand out to cup her elbow. She yanked her arm away. "Don't you fucking touch me." She turned to storm off, but he caught her arm.

"Payton, please. Let me explain."

Tears burned her eyelids but she was determined not to cry in front of him. "There's nothing to explain, Wes. You made yourself perfectly clear last night. I was just too thick to get it. But why the lie? Why not just tell me you didn't want to see me? I've been straight with you from the beginning. You owe me the same, damn it."

"Straight?" he echoed. "How can you say you've been straight? I don't have a fucking clue where I stand with you. You haven't once called me. I called the week before. I instigated the weekend in Houston. I thought it was time for you to call me." He shifted his feet and looked uneasily away before continuing, "I didn't want to come across as a desperate loser."

She gaped at him. "You want to know why I didn't call you, Wes? I was at the hospital all fucking week because my dad had a near-fatal heart attack. I didn't have *time* to call you. I was too worried about losing my father. I spent the week worried sick and at the end of it all, I just wanted to see *you*. Be with *you*. No games. No scorecard."

A tear trickled down her cheek, and she swiped angrily at it with her sleeve. "You know what? Fuck you, Wes Hoffman. I don't need your shit."

She stomped across the floor and out of the bar. Wes caught up to her as she wrenched open the door to her car. He grabbed her wrist, preventing her from getting in.

"Payton, no. You can't leave like this. You're too upset to drive. Please, just stay and talk to me."

"Why, so you can feel less like a desperate loser? Drop dead," she said in an acid voice. She slid into her car and slammed the door.

Her hands shook as she jammed her key in the ignition.

Finally, she got the engine started, and she turned her head to look behind her as she backed out of her space. When she got turned around, she spared one last glance at Wes as she peeled out of the parking lot.

Wes watched her go, a relentless ache snaking through his chest. His fingers curled into fists at his sides as he sought to control the shaking.

Everything in the last two weeks came down to this. Payton was walking out of his life, much like she'd walked back in. In a whirlwind. Only he had no desire to see her go.

She was furious, and he deserved every bit of her anger. He closed his eyes, willing the sick feeling in the pit of his stomach to go away.

He didn't want to *lose* her.

"I like her," Gracie announced from behind him.

He turned and looked questioningly at her.

Gracie grinned. "She was ready to kick my ass. She seems a little possessive of you."

"She just told me to fuck off," Wes said grimly.

Gracie shook her head and grasped his arm. She tugged him back into the bar and shoved him onto a barstool.

"I've fucked up, Gracie."

She made a sound of exasperation. "You make it sound like you've already lost her."

"Haven't I? I lied to her. Now she thinks I'm screwing around with you behind her back."

"Men are so stupid when it comes to women, I swear. Do you think that little show was because she wanted nothing to do with you? Hell, she was ready to scratch my eyes out. A woman who doesn't care doesn't go to that kind of trouble, Wes."

"I've got to talk to her."

Gracie nodded. "Yes, you do, but before you do, you need to figure out what it is exactly you're going to say to her once you make her stop to listen."

He opened his mouth to speak but nothing came out. What

did he want to say to Payton?

"You'll only get one chance," Gracie said softly. "Make it count. Don't be afraid to lay it on the line. If you don't, you risk losing the best thing that's ever happened to you."

His hands trembled and the knot in his stomach grew. "How did you get so damn smart?" he muttered.

"I've been in your shoes, honey. Or don't you remember my little hissy fit I threw at the cabin before running off like an idiot? Once I settled down, I knew I only had one chance to make things right with Luke, and it was too important for me to screw up. The idea of being without him..."

Wes saw the flash of pain cross her face as she contemplated her own words.

"And you know you're going to have to explain about us," Gracie added. "All of it. You don't want to chance her finding out from someone else."

He groaned. "I'll be lucky to get her to understand my fucked-up way of saying I've fallen in love with her, but when I tell her you're only my best friend, but that I happened to have sex with you a few months ago... I don't see that going over too well."

"Are you holding her accountable for everyone she's slept with in the past?" Gracie asked as she crossed her arms in front of her.

He gave her a sharp look. "Of course not."

"And she won't either. Or at least she shouldn't. But if she finds out later, she'll wonder *why* you didn't tell her. It'll seem like you have something to hide. Never a good thing."

"You're right." Wes sighed.

"I'm always right," she said cheekily. "Glad I can get someone to admit it. Now. You need to get your ass on the road. Track down your girl. I need to get back to my husband."

Wes leaned down and kissed her hard on the cheek. "Thank you, Gracie. I hope you know how much I love you."

She gave him a fierce hug. "I do. Now go."

Chapter Fourteen

Wes pulled up at Payton's apartment complex and heaved a huge sigh of relief when he saw her car parked in her spot. He'd called her at least a dozen times, but she'd refused to answer. After the third time, his calls went straight to voicemail so he knew she'd turned it off.

He sat for a moment collecting himself, preparing for the biggest fight of his life. Not an argument, but a fight to keep her. To make her understand.

This was important. He hadn't been sure just how important until he'd seen the tears she'd tried so hard to hide. And listened to her tell him to get the hell out of her life.

His heart pounding relentlessly, he got out and walked down the sidewalk to her unit. Once there, he rested one arm on her door for a long moment before finally knocking. He leaned forward, pressing his forehead to his arm while he waited for her to answer.

He knocked harder then stood back, thumbs shoved into his pockets. A lifetime later, the door opened to reveal a very pissed Payton. His chest tightened when he saw the red streaks around her eyes.

"Can I come in?" he asked quietly. "There's a lot I need to say to you."

She hesitated, and her fingers gripped the edge of the door until they were bloodless. Then she shrugged and backed away before turning to walk inside, leaving him to follow.

Once inside, he shut the door behind him. Payton stood

several feet away, arms crossed defensively over her chest. She looked tired. She looked small and vulnerable. His chest ached at the hurt he'd caused her.

He moved closer to her. "First, I'm very sorry about your dad. Is he going to be okay?"

"He's going to live," she said shortly.

He turned away for a moment and paced across the living room, hands behind his back. Then he swiveled again and stared at her.

Payton watched as a multitude of emotions crawled across Wes's face. He looked uncomfortable, like he had a lot to say but no way to say it.

She emitted a tired sigh. She wished he hadn't come all this way just to end things. She'd done a perfectly satisfactory job of that at the bar. If he had anything further to say, he could have left her a voicemail.

"I'm drawn to you, Payton."

She snorted. "You have a damn funny way of showing it."

He continued on as if she hadn't popped off.

"And it scares the hell out of me. I shouldn't need you like this so soon. But when I'm not with you, I'm thinking about you, anxious to see you again. I can't explain this thing between us. God knows I've tried, but I do know I don't want it to end."

Her heart did a funny little flip-flop in her chest.

"It didn't have to end," she said softly. "I didn't want it to end either. There was no reason we couldn't have seen where it could have taken us. I wasn't the one keeping score. I wasn't the one hiding behind some bullshit exterior, afraid that I'd be seen as too desperate or needy."

He crossed the distance between them and took her shoulders in his hands. He stared down at her, his gaze searing holes in her face.

"I lied to you, Payton. Not the best way to start a relationship. And I do want a relationship. With you. I told myself I didn't. The idea scared me shitless because I liked my life just fine before you swept back in and turned my world upside down. I knew that things would change, that I'd have to make concessions, meet you halfway. And the selfish part of me wanted to have my cake and eat it too.

"But I'm here because, Payton, I don't want to be without you. Is it too soon to feel this way? I don't know, but I can't change that fact. I'm as sure of that as anything in my life."

He turned his head away for a moment as if grappling with the emotion she saw so clearly in his eyes just seconds before. When he looked back at her, his eyes were suspiciously wet.

"Payton...I think...I think I might just love you."

She smiled. A watery, pitiful smile that only grew larger with every passing second. "I think I might just love you too, Wes."

He framed her face with shaky hands. She could hear the harsh exhalation of his breath. He closed his eyes, and when he opened them again, there was such love and relief, and a hunger that fed her hopes and dreams.

He kissed her. Lightly, reverently. Then he slowly pulled away to stare down at her. "What do we do now?" he asked hoarsely. "I'm so tied up in knots I can't even see straight. I've never...I've never felt this way about a woman. It's kind of like being drawn on by a suspect and realizing I don't have a weapon."

She laughed, a choked, husky sound. "I scare you that badly?"

"You terrify me," he whispered. "I'm terrified of losing you. I'm terrified of not being with you, of not being able to touch you, to make love to you. In such a short time, you've become so very precious to me. I don't understand it. I don't care."

Tears spilled from her lids and streaked down her cheeks. She went into his arms, wrapping hers around him. She buried her cheek against his chest, feeling the erratic beat of his heart.

"I don't want to be without you either."

He held her, stroking her hair with his hand. He kissed the top of her head.

"I need to explain about Gracie."

She stiffened and pulled away. "Who is she?"

Wes slid his fingers up and down her cheek. "She's my best

friend. One of them. She's married to my other best friend, Luke."

Payton relaxed and smiled, nuzzling her cheek into his hand. "I guess I was rude to her."

He chuckled but then sobered. "There's something more. I wanted you to hear it from me."

She cocked her head and stared inquisitively at the strain on his face. A bead of dread trickled down her spine.

"Damn, this is hard to explain," he muttered. "It's going to sound worse than it is."

She sighed impatiently. "Just say it, Wes. No bullshit. No games. Just be upfront."

"I've slept with Gracie. I had sex with her a few months ago."

Payton blinked in surprise, and her chest tightened at the unexpected shock. "But you said she's married."

"She wasn't then. And it's not because we were together. It's a long story, but Luke and I were fulfilling a fantasy for Gracie. She wanted a threesome."

She took several long, measured breaths as she absorbed his explanation. She had no right to be jealous, but damn it, she was. "That's some friendship you have there," she muttered.

"I just wanted you to know, because if I get my way, you're going to be spending a lot of time around my friends, and we don't have secrets. I didn't want you finding out from anyone but me, and I didn't want you to think I had anything to hide."

She smiled and put her finger to his lips. "Shhh. I'm glad you told me."

"You're not upset?"

"Should I be?" she asked. "If this is going to work between us, we have to trust each other. You told me she's only a friend. I believe you. Just in the future, I'd appreciate you being a little *less* of a good friend."

Wes's shoulders sagged, and he tugged her into his arms. His fingers tangled in her hair as he clutched her tighter to him. "I thought I'd lost you, Payton. You don't want to know what that did to me."

She smiled against his chest and closed her eyes.

"I'm sorry for being such an ass," he continued. "I'm so sorry about your father. I wish you would have called me. I would have come and stayed with you."

She pulled away and gazed up at him, blinking away tears. "You're here now. That's all that counts."

"I'll always be here, Payton. We'll figure out a way."

She smiled. "I know we will. I figure we have a lot to learn. There's still so much I don't know about you, but together... We'll learn together."

Epilogue

"Ellie, come on, you can't decorate the entire house in white lights," Jake grumbled "Let me at least do the mantel in colored lights."

Wes grinned as she ignored Jake's outburst and calmly handed him yet another strand of the boring-ass white lights she loved so much.

She cupped her swollen belly and smiled as she looked down. The baby must have moved again.

"If you're going to get this done before everyone else shows up, you better get a move on," Wes drawled.

Jake flipped him the bird. "I don't see you doing much, Hoffman. Weren't you supposed to come over and *help*?"

"I helped. I told Ellie what lovely taste she had in Christmas decorations. And I helped her decorate the tree."

Jake muttered something unintelligible under his breath. A few seconds later, he climbed down the ladder. "All done."

Ellie smiled up at him, and Wes watched as Jake melted into a puddle of mush.

The doorbell rang, and Ellie turned toward the door.

"I'll get it," Wes said. "You two continue on with whatever it is you were doing."

Wes opened the door, and a rush of unseasonably cold air blew in. Gracie shoved by him and made a beeline for the fireplace. He chuckled as she stuck her hands out, teeth chattering a steady staccato.

Luke walked in at a much slower pace and removed his

coat.

"Merry Christmas, Gracie," Wes called over to her.

"Come over here and I'll hug you," she replied. "But my ass isn't moving from the fire."

He and Luke exchanged amused glances and both moved over to where Gracie stood. Wes held his arms out to her, and she curled herself around him, shaking like a leaf the entire time.

"Damn, girl, it's not that cold out there."

She shot him a dark glance as she moved from his arms to Luke's in her effort to get warm.

Ellie and Jake walked over and exchanged hugs with Gracie. Luke smiled at Ellie. "How's the little one doing?"

Ellie smiled. "Active. Keeps me up a lot at night."

The doorbell rang and Luke turned in the direction of the door. "That'll be Jeremy and Michelle. They were leaving the same time we were."

A few seconds later, Jeremy walked in holding a baby carrier, Michelle right behind him.

Lively chatter ensued as they gathered around the tree to ooh and aah over Ellie's handiwork. Presents were dropped on the floor and shoved underneath.

Amidst all the laughing and good cheer, a soft knock sounded at the door. Wes slipped away and went to open it. His knees went weak when he saw Payton standing there in the doorway.

He hauled her inside, into his arms and kissed her long and hard. "I missed you," he whispered.

She smiled and kissed him again.

"Close the door!" Gracie exclaimed.

Payton laughed and turned to slam the door shut. Wes took her hand, tucked it into his and pulled her into the living room where the others were gathered.

She received hugs from all around before Gracie promptly confiscated her, dragging her over to the fire to chat.

He smiled. He'd gotten better about sharing her with his

friends. Now it gave him a surge of satisfaction to see her accepted by the people so important to him.

Things had been a wee bit awkward between Payton and Gracie the first time they all got together, but Gracie, in her usual straightforward manner, addressed the issue head-on, cleared the air, and the two had been at ease with each other ever since.

After a while, Payton made her way back to him, just as she always did. She slipped her arm around his waist and stood beside him as he talked with Luke and Jeremy. Automatically, his hand came up to stroke her hair, his need to touch her ever-present.

"Let's eat," Ellie said from the doorway of the dining room.

They all filed into the formal dining room, and murmurs of appreciation filled the air as everyone saw how beautifully Ellie had decorated the table.

When they were all seated, Jake cleared his throat and rose from his chair. He reached for the wineglass in front of him. He looked vaguely uncomfortable, but then he gazed down at Ellie, and a soft smile lit up his face. She reached up and squeezed his hand, returning his smile.

Jake kept her hand in his and raised his wineglass with the other.

"This past year has seen a lot of changes. All of which have been good." He glanced down at Ellie again. "The woman I love more than anything put me out of my misery and married me, and now we're anticipating forward to the birth of our first child."

A tear rolled down Ellie's cheek, and she wiped at it self-consciously. As Wes stared around at the others gathered, he saw a mixture of emotions on all their faces.

Did it get any better? His chest was about to expand to bursting. Mushy? Yeah. Did he give a fuck? No.

Jake raised his glass in Luke and Gracie's direction. "And our good friends finally saw the light, decided they couldn't live without each other."

Luke folded his hand over Gracie's on the table and leaned

over to kiss her. She gave him a dazzling smile then raised her glass toward Jake and blew him a kiss.

Jake lowered the glass to his right where Jeremy and Michelle sat with Thad in Michelle's lap. "We got to see the first baby born to our group. A precious little boy sure to grow up with many doting aunts and uncles."

Then he raised his glass higher and stared down the length of the table to where Wes and Payton sat. "And we gained a new friend. Payton, you're a welcome addition to our group. You make that ornery bastard happy, and that's all we can ask."

Payton curled her fingers into his under the table as she smiled broadly back at Jake. She and Wes raised their glasses to Jake.

"May we always be as happy as we are right here, right now," Jake said, encompassing the entire table with a sweep of his glass.

They all raised their glasses in a toast. As silence descended, Wes released his grip on Payton, looked over at her and nodded. She smiled and let him go. He stood, holding his glass with him.

"A word if you don't mind," he said.

All eyes turned in his direction, and Gracie looked like she might burst into tears at any moment. Wes grinned and shook his head. The hormonal lunatic.

He glanced once more at Payton then reached down to pull her up beside him. He wrapped an arm around her shoulders, holding her tightly against him.

"We have something we want to tell you." Wes took a deep breath. "I've asked Payton to marry me."

An outburst of congratulations and whoops made it around the table. Beside him, Payton wrapped an arm around his waist and squeezed reassuringly.

"We're moving to Liberty County. I'm going to be taking a job with the sheriff's department there. Payton will be close enough that she can commute to Houston, and we'll still be within an hour's driving distance of you guys."

Gracie, bless her heart, promptly burst into tears. Luke did his best to console her until she informed him they were happy tears.

The entire group crowded around, hugging, shaking hands, congratulating him and Payton. His fear of leaving everything that was familiar to him slowly dissipated. He still had his friends, people who meant more than anything to him, but better yet, he had *Payton*.

She looked up at him as the others returned to their seats. Her blue eyes shined with such love and understanding. Unable to resist, he lowered his head to kiss her.

"I love you," he whispered.

"I love you too."

"And he calls us pussies," Luke said in disgust.

Payton laughed and pulled away, but Wes kept a firm grip on her hand.

He shot Luke a cocky grin. "If having the love of a good woman makes a man a pussy, then I guess we're all pretty much screwed."

That earned him a smile from every woman seated.

About the Author

To learn more about Maya Banks please visit www.mayabanks.com. Send an email to Maya at maya@mayabanks.com.

One woman's campaign to win the hearts
of the two men she loves.

Brazen
© *2008 Maya Banks*

Jasmine left the Sweetwater Ranch and the Morgan brothers, no longer able to bear the painful dilemma of loving them both. After a year away, in which she gains new perspective, she returns home with one goal. To make Seth and Zane Morgan hers.

Jaz may have left an innocent girl, but she's returned a beautiful, sensual woman. Seth and Zane aren't prepared for the full on assault she launches and each battle an attraction they've fought for years.

She wants them both, but Seth has no intention of sharing his woman. It's up to her to change his mind because she can't and won't choose between two men she loves with equal passion. For her, it's all or nothing.

Warning, this title contains the following: explicit sex, graphic language, ménage a trois, handcuffs, a committed ménage relationship.

Available now in ebook and print from Samhain Publishing.

CPSIA information can be obtained at www.ICGtesting.com
Printed in the USA
BVOW041520280612

293926BV00001B/47/P